DEVIL MUSIC

a novel

MICHAEL PENNING

DEVIL MUSIC

First Edition. May 2025
ISBN: 978-1-7388551-8-6 (Paperback)
ISBN: 978-1-7388551-7-9 (Hardcover)

www.michaelpenning.com

For Jeanine,
who knows how to fight demons.

TRANSCRIPT OF PROCEEDINGS

In the matter of:
Case #9036CR001031
People of Essex County v. T. Chapman

SENTENCING HEARING

Pages: EXTRACT (3-4)
Place: Salem, MA
Date: Oct. 22, 1990

WHEREUPON, the proceedings in the above-entitled matter commenced

BEFORE: THE HONORABLE NOAH L. COBBETT, JUDGE

ROWAN PIERCE

delivered the following victim impact statement in open court:

STATEMENT:

Your honor, thank you for the opportunity to speak today. My name is Rowan Pierce, Lily Pierce's mother. On October 31, 1989, my world was shattered when my beautiful daughter was taken from me in the most horrific way imaginable by the two young men sitting before you today.

Lily was just fourteen years old. She was vibrant, full of life, and had dreams as big as the sky. She loved nature, and painting, and making omelets, and she had a laugh that could light up the darkest room. Lily was my sunshine, and her future was filled with endless possibilities.

But all of that was stolen from her on that dreadful night. These two young men subjected her to unimaginable violence and cruelty, the details of which haunt me every single day. The pain of losing my daughter is a burden that I carry with me every waking moment, and it is a weight that no parent should ever have to bear.

Losing Lily has left a void in my life that can never be filled. My husband is dead and I have no other children. Lily was all I had—she was everything. I can no longer hear her laughter, see her smile, or watch her grow into the amazing woman she was destined to become. Every milestone, every holiday, will forever be a painful reminder that she is not with me. Her room remains untouched, a sanctuary of her memory, but it is a constant, silent reminder of the future we will never have together. Every day, I wake up to an empty house that used to be filled with her laughter. The silence is deafening, and the pain is unbearable. There are no words to describe the sorrow and devastation I feel always.

I miss the simple things the most. Lily coming home from school and telling me about her day, her excitement over a new song by her favorite bands, or just sitting with me while we watched TV. These ordinary moments were precious and irreplaceable, and now they are gone forever. I struggle with the reality that I will never see my daughter graduate, never watch her fall in love, get married, or have children of her own. These are experiences every parent dreams of sharing with their child, and they have been ripped away from me forever.

And now, I want to speak directly to the two monsters who did this—Troy Chapman and Daley Banks. You have destroyed my life, shattered my dreams, and taken the most precious person in my world. You didn't just take her life; you took away my future with her. You acted with such cruelty and malice, and you have shown a level of inhumanity that is beyond comprehension. I hope what you did haunts you every day for the rest of your lives. I hope you feel the same fear, pain, and helplessness that you inflicted on my child. You tortured, raped, and murdered my daughter because you wanted to go to Hell, and I hope with all my heart that you get your wish—if only I could be the one to send you there.

Chapter 1

Rowan Pierce wouldn't let her daughter's killer get off so easily. She would put a bullet in his head the moment he walked free.

Her fingers curled around the cold steel of the pistol in her coat pocket, her knuckles white with tension. Seven years of grief and rage had hollowed her out, leaving only this moment, this chance for retribution. She had never been a violent person, had always abhorred the thought of hurting others. But her world had changed, and she had changed with it.

Rowan's hard green eyes glinted with determination and a hint of fear as they fixed on the yawning prison gateway. Her heart was a thunderstorm, rumbling and crackling with electric energy. The thumping in her ears nearly drowned out the media frenzy that had descended upon the Massachusetts Correctional Institution in Shirley.

The scene was a whirlwind of reporters and onlookers eager to glimpse the boogeyman about to be released. Camera shutters clicked in rapid succession like a swarm of mechanical insects, their erratic flashes igniting a lightning storm. Reporters jostled elbows and shouldered through the crowd, each vying for a vantage point that promised their lens or microphone an advantage over the others.

"Move it!" hissed a cameraman as he muscled past Rowan. She stumbled, her hand tightening around the grip of the Smith & Wesson nestled in her pocket like a viper coiled to strike.

"Excuse me." Her retort was terse, her voice lost to the din of journalists barking questions into the charged air. She pulled her hood lower over her head, twirls of her ginger hair escaping from within as she glanced around. Did anyone recognize her? Seven years ago, the media plastered her face across every TV screen and newspaper in the country. But now, no one seemed to know or care that the mother of the victim was milling among them. She wasn't the reason they had descended on this place.

Daley Banks was.

"Any moment now," someone shouted nearby, sparking a fresh wave of agitation through the crowd.

Rowan's mind was a spinning record of memories and what-ifs, each more haunting than the last. She imagined Lily's face, frozen in terror as Daley and his friend…

No. Focus.

"Any second now," repeated the voice, this time with an edge of urgency. The collective heartbeat of the media mob surged, and Rowan's own heart kept pace.

Justice…

The thought lingered in her consciousness, a mantra that had fueled her through seven years of sleepless nights and hollow days. Rowan had planned this moment since the parole board announced Banks' early release last month, but she had dreamed of it since the day he led the police to Lily's remains seven years ago. Now, she would make at least one of her daughter's murderers suffer for what they had done. The other one—Troy Chapman—was far beyond her reach, locked away in Bridgewater State Hospital.

But this one. Daley Banks…

Rowan's finger caressed the pistol's trigger, imagining the satisfaction of putting a bullet between Banks' eyes. It would be so easy. So right. An eye for an eye, a life for a life. One bullet. That's all it would take. One tiny piece of lead to erase the stain of Daley Banks from the world forever. She could hear the gun whispering in her mind.

Do it. Make him pay for what he did to Lily. For what he took from you…

"Here he comes!" someone shouted. A ripple coursed through the crowd as everyone braced for the emergence of the young man who once personified their darkest fears.

The voice of a nearby reporter in the middle of a live report snagged Rowan's attention. "…Banks' lawyer claims full rehabilitation…"

Rehabilitation? she thought bitterly. *There's no coming back from what he did.*

An electric current charged the November air as the roar of questions launched by the media horde reached a fever-pitch, each reporter clamoring to be the voice that anchored the moment in history.

"Do you think he'll speak to us?" one voice cut sharper than the rest, its owner perched atop a makeshift platform.

"Does he feel any remorse?" another demanded.

Their words faded into the background. The weight of the gun in Rowan's pocket grounded her, anchoring her to the present moment, to the opportunity that lay before her. She swallowed hard against the burgeoning fear that clawed at her insides. It was almost time. The pistol pressed against her hip, a reminder of the line she was about to cross.

Don't be afraid. I'll give you all the strength you need...

The gate groaned, and a hush swept over the crowd as it inched open. It was the pause before the storm, the intake of breath before the scream. And there, framed by the monolithic doorways, was Daley Banks—every parent's nightmare come to life.

He stood at an unassuming height with a wiry build, but there was a quiet intensity in his demeanor. His once-boyish face had hardened over the years, etched with the shadows of prison life and the heavy burden of his past. His eyes were a stormy gray, dulled by the cold lights of the cell block and bearing the haunted look of a man who has seen too much too soon. They flickered with a combination of trepidation and steely defiance as he eyed the crowd clamoring for his attention beyond the prison gates. The secondhand jeans and faded shirt provided by the prison hung from his frame. His dark chestnut hair had grown into unruly waves that just brushed his collar. It hung down over his forehead, partially obscuring his eyes, as if trying to shield him from the gaze of the curious and judgmental. Years of being starved of sunlight had made his skin pale, almost sallow. Tattoos peeked out from his sleeves—amateur inking done by fellow inmates, each marking a moment, a pact, or a protection in a world where vulnerability could mean life or death.

Rowan's heart locked up like rusted gears grinding to a halt. Hatred and revulsion coiled in her gut like venomous snakes. Her eyes bored into Banks, tracing the contours of the face that had haunted her nightmares for seven long years. The face of the murderer who had stolen her daughter's life, snuffing out her light with a brutality that defied comprehension.

The reporters surged forward, a tide of voracious curiosity, but Rowan stood motionless. This was it. The moment of reckoning. Her heart beat like a moth trapped against a glowing lamp.

Time slowed to a crawl, each second an eternity. The crowd's murmurs faded into white noise, drowned out by the roaring in Rowan's ears. Her gaze locked onto the dark maw of the prison entrance, unblinking, unwavering. Waiting. Anticipating.

Sweat beaded on her brow despite the crisp autumn breeze. Her fingers twitched around the pistol's grip. One squeeze, and it would all be over. Lily's soul could rest. The scales of justice would finally balance.

The air was thick with anticipation, and as Rowan watched the prison gates inch ever wider, a surge of adrenaline ignited her veins. It coursed through her body, a fiery current that set her senses on edge. She exhaled slowly, trying to steady the tremors that threatened her courage.

"He deserves this," she murmured to herself. Lily's lively image flashed through her mind, focusing her determination like a honed blade.

But as the seconds ticked by, the chilling whisper of doubt

wove its way back into her thoughts. Fear, insidious and paralyzing, gnawed at the edges of her resolve. Her heart skittered, her courage beginning to fracture like thin ice underfoot.

Can I really do this?

The question was a splinter in her mind, digging deeper with each passing second.

Yes, you can, the pistol whispered. *This is your chance. Pull the trigger and end the nightmare.*

"Forgive me," Rowan breathed as hot tears sprang to her eyes. She wasn't sure for whom the plea was meant—herself, her daughter, or some higher power she no longer believed in.

The gates parted fully, and an almost imperceptible shudder rippled through Banks' lean frame. The air outside tasted different, fresher. He breathed it in deeply, as if trying to cleanse his lungs of the staleness of incarceration. A flicker of relief crossed his face, quickly replaced by apprehension as he registered the sea of cameras and microphones before him.

The world around Rowan faded away, narrowing to a single point of focus—the man who had shattered her life, the monster who had stolen her daughter's future. The pistol grip bit into her palm. A split second of pressure on the trigger, and it would all be over. The pain, the grief, the endless nights spent drowning in the depths of her own despair.

Do it! the gun whispered. *Now's your chance! Shoot him now!*

Daley was just steps away now, close enough that Rowan could see the coldness in his eyes, the utter lack of remorse. Her finger twitched, testing the trigger's resistance. This was her only chance. If she didn't kill him now, he would lose himself in society and fade into obscurity. She would never get another opportunity for justice, and she would have to live knowing he was out there somewhere, living as a free man.

But even as she started to pull the gun from her pocket, Rowan found herself frozen, trapped between the pull of vengeance and the whisper of her conscience.

An echo of Lily's voice sprang into her thoughts, not quaking with terror as it had been at the end, but a ghostly whisper that carried more weight than any bullet could. A night long ago flashed back into Rowan's mind. She saw herself snuggled in bed with her little girl, reading a fairy tale that Lily found frightening.

"Does it have a happy ending?" Lily had asked meekly, looking to her mother for reassurance.

"Yes," Rowan replied with a gentle smile. "The monsters never win."

Rowan's fingers recoiled from the gun as if scorched by the fires of Hell itself. The glint of the cameras became a glaring spotlight on her conscience, illuminating the grim truth that vengeance wouldn't resurrect her little girl, or quiet the sorrow that haunted her soul.

"I'm sorry. I can't…"

A sob clawed its way up her throat, and she bit down hard on the inside of her cheek to stifle it. No, she couldn't do this —not here, not now. She couldn't let herself become the monster.

The prison gate started groaning shut on electric hinges, a steel maw disgorging its most notorious occupant. Daley

Banks emerged into the cold autumn sun, his emotionless face concealing years spent imprisoned behind those imposing walls. His wary eyes swept over the crowd, and for a heart-stopping moment, his gaze seemed to lock with Rowan's.

Now! screamed the pistol. *Do it now!*

But the gun remained hidden, her arm a dead weight at her side.

"God damn you," Rowan hissed toward Banks. The ghost of the gun's touch still lingered on her fingers. She had come so close, had held vengeance within her grasp, only to let it slip away.

The prison gates clanged shut, severing the final physical chain that bound Banks to his past atrocities. He stepped into his newfound freedom with an air of casual dismissal. With a duffel bag of his scant belongings slung over his shoulder, he took his first steps into a world that had moved on without him. He wove his way through the gauntlet of cameras and microphones, a careful deliberation in each step, as if trying to minimize his presence. There was a certain wariness in his posture, a sense of perpetual readiness, as if expecting an attack from the shadows at any moment.

As he climbed into the waiting taxi, Rowan clenched her hands at her sides, nails digging into her palms until they threatened to draw blood. She wanted to scream, to shatter the facade of normalcy that the world so readily embraced, but her voice was trapped beneath layers of despair. The justice she had imagined—the moment of reckoning—crumbled to dust before her eyes.

The taxi door slammed shut, sealing Banks away from the

world. Rowan stood rooted to the spot, the crowd ebbing and flowing around her as the media surged forward; a tide of questions and flashes. Their voices were a distant hum that barely penetrated the fog of her despair. She watched as the taxi pulled away, its taillights receding into the distance until they were nothing more than pinpricks of light.

I had him. He was right there…

Rowan's fingers twitched, muscle memory reaching for the trigger she'd never pulled. In an act as wrenching as tearing roots from parched earth, she turned her back on the spectacle. She felt the crowd close in around her as she moved through them like a ghost, invisible in her suffering. The taste of defeat was bitter on her tongue. She had failed. Failed Lily, failed herself.

The monsters had won.

TRANSCRIPT OF PROCEEDINGS

In the matter of:
Case #9036CR001031
People of Essex County v. T. Chapman

Pages: EXTRACT (5-27)
Place: Salem, MA
Date: Aug. 15, 1990

WHEREUPON, the proceedings in the above-entitled
matter commenced

BEFORE: THE HONORABLE NOAH L. COBBETT,
JUDGE

DALEY BANKS

called as a witness for the Commonwealth of Massachusetts,
having first been duly sworn, was examined by Assistant
District Attorney NELSON CRESS and testifies as follows:

DIRECT EXAMINATION:

MR. CRESS: How old are you, Daley?

WITNESS BANKS: I'm fifteen.

MR. CRESS: How long have you known the defendant, Troy
Chapman?

WITNESS BANKS: Since we were little—since, uh, since grade school.

MR. CRESS: You started a band together in middle school, didn't you?

[witness nods head in affirmative]

MR. CRESS: What was the name of your band?

WITNESS BANKS: Corpsefeast

MR. CRESS: Corpsefeast. What kind of music did you play?

WITNESS BANKS: It's, uh—it was death metal.

MR. CRESS: What is death metal? How would you describe it?

WITNESS BANKS: It's like the most intense, hardcore music. It's all about super heavy, bone-crushing guitar riffs and these blasting drums that feel like a thunderstorm right in your face. The singers, or growlers, have these insanely deep, guttural voices that sound like monsters from a horror movie or pigs squealing.

MR. CRESS: And what about the lyrics?

WITNESS BANKS: They're usually about dark, brutal stuff

—serial killers, necrophilia, satanism, torture.

MR. CRESS: So you could say that it's violent?

WITNESS BANKS: Yeah. Yeah, for sure.

MR. CRESS: And this is what you and the defendant wrote about? What you listened to?

[witness nods head in affirmative]

WITNESS BANKS: All the time. It's all we were into.

MR. CRESS: What about Lily Pierce? Did she listen to that music too?

WITNESS BANKS: Yeah, she was into it. I mean, she didn't look like it. She was pretty clean-cut and wore dresses and, like, looked like, like a normal girl, you know? She played sports and got good grades and was really good at like, painting and stuff. But yeah, she liked our music. Not many girls are like that. I think maybe that's why Troy was obsessed with her.

MR. CRESS: Troy was infatuated with her?

[witness nods head in affirmative]

WITNESS BANKS: Yeah. They were friends at school before Troy got kicked out. They never really stopped talking.

MR. CRESS: Is that why she agreed to meet the two of you on the night of October 31 of last year?

MR. KNOWLES: Objection, your honor. Calls for witness speculation.

THE COURT: Sustained.

MR. CRESS: Withdrawn. Tell us what happened that night, Daley.

WITNESS BANKS: Uh, Troy invited Lily to meet us in the woods and—

MR. CRESS: That's the Lynn Woods Reservation?

WITNESS BANKS: Yeah, the Lynn Woods. It was near her house on Pennybrook. Troy told her we'd hang out and listen to music and smoke weed. Her mom was kinda strict, so he told Lily to say she was watching horror movies at a friend's.

MR. CRESS: Because it was Halloween.

[witness nods head in affirmative]

MR. CRESS: Why did Troy really invite her to the woods that night?

WITNESS BANKS: Because, um, because we—we were

going to kill her.

MR. CRESS: The two of you planned to murder Lily Pierce that night?

[witness nods head in affirmative]

MR. CRESS: Why?

WITNESS BANKS: We—we were going to offer her as a sacrifice to the devil. She was blonde and had blue eyes and she was a virgin, and if we, if we killed her, Satan would give us the power to take our band to the next level.

MR. CRESS: What do you mean, "the next level?"

WITNESS BANKS: To make it big, you know? Get a record deal and tour. We thought a perfect sacrifice like Lily would give us the craziness we needed. We'd be harder, more brutal. Our guitars would be better—faster, heavier.

MR. CRESS: I see. Where did you get that idea from?

WITNESS BANK: From the music we listened to. Haruspex.

MR. CRESS: Haruspex is a band, correct? A death metal band?

WITNESS BANKS: Not really death metal. Uh, more like thrash metal. They're still fast and heavy, but there's more, like, real singing. More melody. Haruspex are like the biggest. We studied their lyrics for, like, deeper meanings, you know? Troy especially.

MR. CRESS: Hmmm. Let's get back to that night, Daley. What time did Lily meet you in the woods?

WITNESS BANKS: Some time after eight. The trick or treaters were all gone.

MR. CRESS: What did you do when she arrived?

WITNESS BANKS: We walked to Dungeon Rock. Troy gave her some weed to smoke—we all smoked.

MR. CRESS: You all smoked marijuana. Is that something you did often?

WITNESS BANK: Me and Troy, yeah, all the time. Weed, acid, meth. It's why Troy got kicked out of school. All we'd do is drugs and listen to heavy metal.

MR. CRESS: What happened when you got to Dungeon Rock?

[witness does not immediately respond]

MR. CRESS: Daley? What happened at Dungeon Rock?

WITNESS BANKS: We hung out there for a bit. It was full

dark by then. After about ten or fifteen minutes, Troy came up behind Lily with a bass string and started to strangle her.

MR. CRESS: A bass guitar string?

WITNESS BANKS: Yeah. It's, uh, it's thicker steel and wouldn't cut into his hand when he pulled it tight. We were going to use it to play music with later, once we'd killed Lily with it.

MR. CRESS: What happened next? Once Troy started strangling Lily with the bass string?

WITNESS BANKS: Troy took out his hunting knife and stabbed her in the stomach. He handed me the knife and I—I stabbed her too. We took turns. Troy let her go and she was screaming and moaning and she hit the ground and she was bleeding all over, but she wouldn't die. She was just laying there, crying for help—crying for her mother. That was the worst part, hearing her begging for her mom like that. We didn't know why she wasn't dying. I mean, she was bleeding so much. That was when—when Troy stomped on her neck. She went quiet then. He had the knife and he—he started carving.

MR. CRESS: Carving Lily's flesh?

[witness nods head in affirmative]

WITNESS BANKS: He was carving symbols, you know?

Satanic things. Pentagrams and some other things we saw on Haruspex albums.

MR. CRESS: What did the two of you do next?

WITNESS BANKS: We dragged her deeper into the woods, closer to the pond. Troy started to pull her pants down, but I said we should get out of there.

MR. CRESS: Why did Troy want to pull her pants down?

WITNESS BANKS: Because we, uh, we had talked about— we planned to do things to her body.

MR. CRESS: You intended to rape her.

[witness nods head in affirmative]

MR. CRESS: Why did you tell Troy to stop? Why then? Why not stop him earlier, before it was too late?

WITNESS BANKS: I didn't want to stop the murder, but, uh, I was getting scared. It took too long, you know? I was afraid we'd get caught.

MR. CRESS: So you left Lily's body there, hidden in the woods near Breed's Pond. Almost eight weeks went by before you came forward and told your parents what you had done. To your knowledge, did Troy ever go back there?

WITNESS BANKS: Yeah, Troy told me he went back to her body a few times.

MR. CRESS: Why did he do that?

WITNESS BANKS: He said to, um—to finish what he started. He—he said he went there to, uh [inaudible]

MR. CRESS: He told you he had sex with Lily's corpse. Isn't that correct?

WITNESS BANKS: Yeah, he said he, uh—

[witness testimony is indecipherable due to the victim's mother crying in the gallery]

MR. CRESS: Hold on, Daley. Mrs. Pierce, you don't have to sit through this. Do you want to wait [inaudible]

THE COURT: Mr. Cress, perhaps a short recess would be appropriate?

MR. CRESS: We have no objection. I think that might be best, your honor.

Chapter 2

The worn stage planks of Boston's historic Orpheum Theater creaked beneath Rowan's measured steps. A solitary spotlight cut through the dusky theater as she approached the podium, her fingers clasping and unclasping at the hem of her dark blazer. The light framed her in a stark halo that set her ginger hair ablaze in the searing beam.

It had been three days since Rowan's failed attempt on Daley Banks' life. As she gripped the edges of the podium, her heartbeat was now a steady drumroll against her ribs. These public events always made her anxious, but ever since Lily's murder and the high-profile lawsuits that ensued, she had become the reluctant public face of victims of violence. It was an overwhelming responsibility, and she often wondered if recounting Lily's story over and over at these events made any difference. But she hoped that one day her work with organizations like Haven for Hope might give her a sense of purpose and fulfillment in a life otherwise scraped bare.

So far, all these speeches did was reopen old wounds.

The smell of wood varnish and musty velvet curtains

enveloped her as her gaze swept over the sea of faces—sympathetic, expectant—each pair of eyes an echo chamber for her grief. Everyone in attendance had one thing in common: violence and tragedy had touched them all. They had gathered here tonight to share their stories, to find hope amid their common pain and solace in music. Countless performances had graced the Orpheum's gilded arches and faded grandeur, but few were as harrowing as the soliloquy of loss Rowan was about to deliver. She cleared her throat; the sound amplified through the microphone, a jagged shard of static that pierced the pregnant silence.

"Good evening, everyone," she began, her voice brittle but gaining strength as she settled into her routine and found her confidence. "First, I want to thank each of you for being here tonight. Your presence means more than words can express—not just to me, but to every family affected by violence. Tonight, we gather not only to remember the victims but also to find hope, strength, and unity in the face of unimaginable loss."

Rowan's light green eyes swept over the captive audience, their features obscured by the relentless glare of the stage lights. "My name is Rowan Pierce, and I'm Lily's mom. Lily was everything to me—bright, vibrant, and full of life. She was just fourteen years old, with a heart as big as her dreams. She was the kind of person who saw beauty everywhere and in everyone. But seven years ago, my beautiful girl's life was stolen. Two of her classmates—boys she called friends and thought she could trust—lured Lily into the woods near our home. What happened next is something no parent should ever have to endure. They took her from me in an act of brutality so senseless, so horrific, it's hard to imagine. They claimed heavy metal music inspired them, but what it was is nothing less than evil. Pure and simple."

Rowan paused and drew a shaky breath. The hard part was over. She never mentioned that she'd been drinking that night. That she had suspected Lily was lying about spending the night at a friend's, but the whiskey made her too tired to put up a fight—to be a mom. That part of the story was too unbearable to confront, so Rowan pushed it down deep and never let it see the light of day.

"Since that day, my life has been a journey through grief, anger, and endless questions," she went on. "How could this happen? Why didn't anyone see the signs? What could I have done to protect her? These are questions I will wrestle with for the rest of my life.

"But tonight is not just about Lily's story. It's about the stories of so many others who have been taken from us by acts of violence. It's about the families left behind to pick up the pieces, the communities that rally together in the wake of tragedy, and the urgent need to create a world where this kind of pain doesn't have to be endured again.

"We are here tonight to honor the memories of those we've lost—not as victims, but as beloved sons, daughters, siblings, and friends. We're here to celebrate their lives and to channel our grief into action. Because while we can't bring them back, we can fight to ensure their legacies make a difference.

"Let's work together to educate our children about empathy and respect. Let's advocate for stricter measures to identify and address warning signs in young people. And let's hold each other accountable as a society to protect the innocent and cherish life above all else. Violence begins in hearts and minds that are lost and broken. Let's focus on healing those hearts and minds before tragedy strikes again."

A figure detached from the shadows near the end of the stage, tall and imposing, with eyes like shards of ice. Rowan's chest constricted at the sight of him, recognition slamming into her with the force of a freight train. She felt like the stage had dropped away from beneath her.

What the hell was *he* doing here?

There stood Cole Abel—a monolith carved from darkness. His steel-blue eyes fixated on Rowan with an intensity that belied his otherwise inscrutable demeanor. His imposing silhouette seemed jarringly out-of-place in the soft glow of the concert hall. His presence was an open wound; salt in the festering grief that still consumed Rowan.

She hadn't seen the ex-frontman of the notorious heavy metal group Haruspex in five years—not since their last court date—but Cole appeared ageless. Though likely in his late thirties now, he remained tall, muscled, and heavily tattooed. He had shaved his head to the scalp on all sides, leaving a straight swath of ink-black hair sweeping over to one side like the soldiers Rowan had seen in World War II movies. The tattoos on his throat—a pair of giant knives crisscrossing across his larynx like the swords of a pirate flag—were a silent reflection of a life forged in violence and survival.

In the span of a moment, the air between them crackled with an electric charge of mutual recognition, an invisible tether pulling taut as every shared second of their pasts collided.

The murmurs of the crowd hushed into silence, waiting for

Rowan to go on with her story. She gripped the podium tighter, her nails digging into the wood as she forced herself to continue, to ignore the simmering anger Cole's unexpected presence had ignited in her veins.

"To those of you performing tonight: thank you for using your talents to bring us together. Music has a unique power to heal, to inspire, and to remind us that even in the darkest times, there is light. Lily loved music, and I know she would have been moved by your songs tonight."

Rowan let her words hang in the air, an invisible arrow aimed straight at the heart of the man whose music Lily had truly loved.

Cole remained silent in the shadows, shrouded in the dark allure that had once crowned him the king of heavy metal. He leaned with his back against the wall, arms folded across his chest, muscles coiled beneath his ink-stained skin. His eyes never left Rowan, a silent battle of wills unfolding across the distance between them.

"To everyone here: thank you for standing with us," Rowan went on, undaunted, "for refusing to let violence have the last word. Your support reminds me that while grief is a heavy burden, we do not have to carry it alone. Together, we can honor Lily and all the others we've lost by building a world where love triumphs over hate, compassion over cruelty, and hope over despair.

"Lily used to tell me, 'Mom, the world is like a painting. Even if there's a dark spot, you can always add more colors to make it beautiful again'. Tonight, let's be the color in our world."

The applause faded to a dull roar in Rowan's ears as she left the stage, hair swaying like a battle flag, her eyes never leaving Cole's. He straightened as she marched toward him, his burly figure tensing beneath his black t-shirt as if bracing against the onslaught of a tempest. On stage, the first act of the night began their performance, a folksy duo of women obviously inspired by Indigo Girls and Ani Di Franco.

"*You*," Rowan breathed, the word barely audible over the music. She halted before him, close enough to see the defiance in his gaze, to smell the faint scent of leather and metal that clung to his skin. "What the hell are you doing here?"

Cole met her furious glare without flinching. "I'm just here for some quiet entertainment in support of a good cause, Rowan."

"How dare you," she hissed, fighting to keep her voice level.

Around them, the crowd began to take notice with hushed whispers and sideways glances. Rowan knew she should walk away, but the grief and rage that had been her constant companions for seven long years wouldn't let her.

"Your music poisoned their minds," she spat, the words dripping with venom. "Those boys... they worshipped you. And look what it led to."

Cole's jaw clenched, the sharp tips of the twin blades on his tattooed throat nearly touching his pierced earlobes. "I didn't put the knife in their hands," he growled, his voice low and dangerous.

"No," Rowan hissed. "You just gave them the idea. Fed their darkness. Nurtured it."

She could feel the eyes of the crowd on them now, could

sense the growing tension in the air. But she didn't care. Seven years of pain and sleepless nights had led her to this moment.

"Those boys... your devoted fans... they brutalized my daughter like she was nothing. They spilled her blood and carved her up while singing your filth. My *daughter*..." Tears stung Rowan's eyes, but she refused to let them fall.

Cole's face remained impassive, but something flickered in his gaze. Guilt? Regret? Rowan couldn't tell, and at that moment, she didn't care.

"You don't get to wash your hands of this," she snarled, jabbing a finger at his chest. "I won't let you hide from the truth. I won't let you deny that Lily's blood is on your hands."

Cole's expression hardened. He leaned in, his frame casting a shadow over Rowan. "I won't be your scapegoat, Rowan. I've been where you're standing, searching for a reason for depravity. There isn't one. My music is dark, yeah. But real. I didn't invent the evil in this world."

Rowan's hands clenched at her sides, nails digging crescents into her palms. The pain was a welcome distraction from the inferno raging in her chest. "No, you didn't invent it. But you glorified it. You sold it wrapped in screaming lyrics and loud guitars. Made it seem powerful. Desirable."

"I gave a voice to the voiceless," Cole countered, his eyes flashing. "To the kids society threw away. Like me."

Rowan wanted to scream, to lash out, to make Cole feel a fraction of her agony. "And what about the voice you silenced? The innocent girl snuffed out because of your... your poison?"

Cole's lips curled into a sneer. "Life's full of poison. I just put a beat to it."

Rowan felt something snap inside her. The carefully constructed walls of her composure crumbled, leaving only raw, primal fury. "You miserable, self-righteous bastard," she snarled, advancing on him. "You hide behind your art, your trauma. But you're just as guilty as those two boys. More so."

Their faces were inches apart now, two storm fronts colliding. Rowan could see the pulse throbbing in his neck beneath the knife tattoos. For a moment, she imagined her hands around that throat, squeezing until…

Whispers rippled through the crowd, faces turning towards the scene unfolding before them. Rowan felt the weight of their stares, but couldn't bring herself to care. Her world had narrowed to this moment, to the man who represented everything she'd lost.

Cole's shadow loomed over Rowan, the steel in his gaze unyielding. "I didn't come here tonight to fight with you, Rowan."

"Then why *are* you here? Can't you see you're not wanted?"

He leaned forward, and his voice dropped to a conspiratorial whisper that only she could hear. "I've seen the darkness that clings to you—I was there at the prison."

She stiffened, her fingers knotting into fists. "What do you mean?"

"Daley Banks," he murmured, his words slithering into her ear like smoke. "I know what you intended to do."

Rowan's blood ran cold. Her failed attempt at revenge, the moment of weakness that had nearly cost her everything—

how could he possibly know?

"You're not as subtle as you think," Cole said, answering her unspoken question. "I could see it on your face—and that pistol in your pocket was easy enough to spot for anyone who was paying attention."

Rowan stared at him, still trying to piece things together in her mind. How long had he been observing her, a silent witness to her private hell? She swallowed hard, her voice steadier than she felt. "Have you… have you been stalking me?"

A ghost of a smile played at the corners of Cole's mouth, a glimmer of something dark and dangerous in his eyes. "You can't let it go, can you? Your thirst for vengeance? But you're playing with blunt tools in a world that requires a keener edge. I can help you. There are… *other* ways. More effective ways."

The crowd's murmurs faded to white noise as Rowan struggled to process his words. "What are you talking about?" she hissed, torn between curiosity and revulsion.

"Not here," Cole replied with a furtive glance around. "Too many eyes, too many ears. But if you want true justice —the kind that'll make those boys wish for death—I can show you."

He pulled a crumpled piece of paper from his pocket and pressed it into Rowan's palm, his calloused fingers lingering for a moment too long. The contact made her skin crawl.

"Consider this an invitation," he said. "It's up to you, Rowan. When you're ready to unleash hell on your daughter's killers."

Rowan stared at the paper, her mind reeling. Unable to

focus, the numbers danced before her eyes. She looked up, a thousand questions on her lips, but Cole was already retreating, melting into the restless crowd.

On stage, the duo finished their song. As the crowd's applause rose around her, Rowan stood frozen, the paper burning in her hand like a fiery ember. What had Cole meant by "other ways"?

And more importantly, was she willing to find out?

Chapter 3

Rowan's boots crunched on the frostbitten grass as she trudged toward her modest clapboard house on Pennybrook Lane, its profile a darkened silhouette under the crescent moon. She kept her back to the black void that was the entrance to the Lynn Woods Reservation, just down the street. She couldn't bear to face it, to think of the terrible things that had happened to her daughter deep within that dark forest. No, not tonight.

Lynn was a coastal town north of Boston, steeped in history and legend. It sprawled along the Atlantic with a certain rugged charm, the old brick buildings, remnants of its once-thriving industrial days, standing in defiance against the modern developments creeping in, as if the past and future were in a constant struggle for dominance. Narrow, winding streets led to unexpected corners where time seemed to have paused, preserving whispers of the town's storied history in the cracks of cobblestones and the faded signs of its vintage shops.

The old house creaked and groaned as Rowan shut the

front door behind her, the click of the lock echoing through the empty rooms. She leaned back against the sturdy wood, eyes closed, letting the silence strip away the echoes of the concert that still lingered in her ears.

How long had it been since laughter and light filled these walls? Since Lily bounded down the stairs, ponytail swinging, calling out *Mom!* in that sing-song way of hers? Too long. An eternity.

Rowan pushed off the door and shrugged out of her coat, the weight of her solitude settling onto her shoulders once more. In this shrine of loss, every photograph and piece of furniture was a constant reminder of the life and joy that was snatched from her.

The evening weighed heavily on Rowan's bones as she sank onto the couch and closed her eyes, willing herself to clear her thoughts before memories came knocking at her door. The emotions of the past few days had exhausted her, and she knew sleep would elude her yet again tonight. So she sat there in the darkness, listening to the sounds of quiet suburbia outside—a lonely cricket chirping and leaves rustling in the November wind.

But her encounter with Cole kept clawing its way through her thoughts. It had been seven years. Seven years of navigating a world rendered foreign by grief, but Cole's presence had torn open her barely healed wounds.

"Damn him," she hissed, her voice slicing through the silence. Her fists clenched involuntarily. How could he stand there and speak of justice when he was the man who inspired her daughter's killers? How could he still not admit that his words, his music, had been the match that lit the fuse?

With her anger growing into a living entity writhing within her veins, Rowan rose from the couch and paced the floorboards from room to room. The creaking echoes bouncing off the walls only reminded her she was alone in this house that once bustled with life.

Candles and dried flowers were arranged on a lace cloth covering the dining room table—a table no one had sat around in years. There was no more laughter over shared meals. No love notes scrawled on napkins. Just four empty chairs.

In the kitchen, the refrigerator hummed. Rowan opened it, the harsh light spilling out and illuminating her weary face. Empty shelves stared back at her. When was the last time she'd gone grocery shopping? Days blurred together in an endless fog lately. She rummaged through the cabinets and drawers with a sense of detachment, hardly noticing the familiar sight of Lily's apron still hanging on a hook. The routine was automatic now—fill the kettle, turn on the stove, select a tea bag. Earl Grey, because it had been Alex's favorite. The memory of her husband's strong hands cradling a delicate teacup, his eyes crinkling with a smile, rose unbidden in her mind.

"I miss you," she whispered to the empty air. To Alex. To Lily. To the ghosts that populated her life more than the living.

The clock ticked away the seconds, indifferent to her turmoil.

It wasn't long before she stood before the open kitchen cupboard.

Rowan's hand hovered over the neck of the half-empty

whiskey bottle. Her fingers trembled ever so slightly as she fought the urge to take a swig. The bottle was a leftover from the years of self-destruction she had spiraled into after Alex's death in the fire. It would have been easier—maybe even smarter—to pour its contents down the drain the day she quit drinking, but she'd kept the whiskey as a reminder that she had the willpower to resist its allure. For now.

She had been sober for two years now, but tonight, the sight of the amber liquor still held a welcome promise of oblivion, a temporary respite from the onslaught of memories that screamed within her. It called to her, the glass cool, almost soothing against her fingertips.

Closing her eyes, Rowan took a deep breath and reminded herself of all the reasons she had quit drinking: for herself, for her sanity, for any hope of a future. She withdrew her touch as if scorched by a flame. No, she wouldn't let Daley Banks and Cole Abel do this to her. She wouldn't find solace at the bottom of a bottle—not tonight, and never again.

With a shuddering breath that seemed to drag the weight of the world through her lungs, she closed the cupboard and turned away.

The kettle whistled, shrill and insistent, as Rowan's mind drifted back to Banks and his release from prison. Her hand shook as she poured the boiling water, splashing some on the counter. The system had failed her, just like everything else in her damn life. They let one of Lily's killers walk free while her baby girl lay cold in the ground. Rowan had sat through every trial date, every hearing, reliving the nightmare over and over as Banks' defense negotiated the terms of his plea bargain with the D.A. Without his confession and testimony, the circumstantial evidence tying the two boys to Lily's murder was useless to the prosecutors—and Banks' lawyer knew it. The D.A. had no choice but to reduce the charges against him in exchange for his cooperation.

And now he was a free man.

Frustration and anger boiled within Rowan once again. How anyone could think seven years in prison were enough for what he did to her daughter?

He's no longer a threat to society, the parole board had reasoned. *He was just a boy when he committed his crime, a troubled teen easily influenced by his sociopathic friend, Troy Chapman. He confessed and showed remorse…*

And yet, Rowan knew that even if Banks had served his whole life behind bars, it would never be enough. It would never bring Lily back or heal the bottomless void in her heart.

Setting the cup down harder than necessary, Rowan turned her back on the kitchen. The rage was a living thing inside her, coiled and ready to strike. It terrified her sometimes, the depths of her own fury. She had thought she could bury it, lock it away and go on existing. But Cole Abel had torn the scab off, and now it bled, hot and hungry.

Rowan's eyes fell upon the stairs that led up to the bedrooms. Her feet moved without thinking, up the steps and down the hallway to the silent door guarding the reliquary of adolescent dreams that was Lily's room. She twisted the knob, the click of the latch sounding like a gunshot in the stillness. The door swung open with a soft creak, and Rowan stepped inside.

Time had frozen here. She had kept this space perfectly preserved since the night the two boys had lured her daughter into the woods down the street, never to return. But she hadn't mustered the courage to enter this room in… how many years? Three? Four? She had still been drinking then. The whiskey had given her the courage to face the ghosts that lingered here. Otherwise, the memories were too raw, too crippling.

Now, she moved through the bedroom like a sleepwalker, her fingertips grazing over the surfaces, stirring up dust. Moonlight spilled through the open curtains. Lily herself had painted the walls a delicate shade of lilac. Posters of heavy metal stars adorned their lengths, bands like Slayer, Sepultura, and Haruspex—their scowling faces a reminder of the only rebellion that had ever set Rowan at odds with her daughter.

The bed lay unmade, a tangle of dark sheets with a fading hint of Lily's shampoo. Near the headboard lay a pillow bearing the indent of a head that would never return. Rowan's fingers traced the spine of a book left on the nightstand, the copy of Anne Rice's newest novel, *The Queen of the Damned,* she had given Lily for Christmas the year she died. The title was now faded by time and neglect. A hairbrush still held strands of Lily's golden hair.

A few stuffed animals sat at the foot of the bed, gifts from friends and family over the years. Their glassy eyes reflected the moonlight. Lily had long outgrown playing with them, but she couldn't bring herself to part with the cherished keepsakes of her childhood.

Rowan picked up a worn teddy bear and held it close to her chest, feeling a burning lump flaring to life in her throat. After all this time, she didn't think she had any more tears to shed, but being in this room brought back so many memories —both happy and devastating—that she couldn't control her emotions.

She sank onto the edge of the bed, the mattress groaning softly under her weight. The rage was still there, simmering beneath the surface. But in this moment, a tidal wave of grief eclipsed it, as raw as the day she'd lost her daughter. The fabric of Lily's last worn shirt crumpled beneath her touch, the cotton still holding the curve of shoulders that would never shrug in indifference or tense in anger again. Her daughter's laughter seemed to echo off the walls, a cruel trick of acoustics and longing.

Rowan's palm grasped the silver charm she wore around her neck, the one that had belonged to Lily—the one by which Rowan had identified her body.

"My sweet girl," Rowan whispered, her voice brittle with tears. "I'm so lost without you."

The silence that followed was crushing; an answer in itself.

A desk covered in papers and books stood in one corner of the room. It was a habit of Lily's to study late into the night, often falling asleep in her chair with her textbooks in front of her. Rowan remembered having to rouse her and tuck her into bed before heading off to work in the morning. Rising from the bed, she went to the desk where her daughter's notebooks lay open, mid-sentence declarations of teenage angst and dreams cut short. Each scribble, each crossed-out word, was a remnant of a voice forever silenced.

Next to the desk was a bookshelf filled with novels and sketchbooks. Some of them still had sticky notes poking out from various pages. Rowan sifted through the artifacts of a life interrupted. She paused before the mirror above the desk, its surface a collage of concert tickets, photographs, and doodles. In the corner was a picture of Lily and Alex, their faces peeking out from beneath the frothing torrent of a waterfall.

The weight of the past pressed against Rowan's chest as she gazed at the photo, tracing the outline of her late husband's face with her eyes. Alex, who had charged into infernos with the courage of a mythic hero, only to fall in an act of ordinary bravery. A collapsed beam, a sudden flare-up—and the firefighter's fate had been brutally succinct.

Holding back sobs, Rowan reached out and touched the faces in the photograph. She remembered that day like it was yesterday—the camping trip up in the White Mountains and the afternoon they'd spent lounging in the waterfalls of Diana's Baths. They had been so happy then, their smiles bright and carefree. But now, their faces stared out at her with sad eyes, as if mourning the lives they could have had.

The memory of that terrible morning seven years ago crashed over Rowan like a rogue wave. The knock on the door. The grim-faced police officers. The world shattering around her.

"God, Alex," Rowan choked out. "You should've been here. You would've known what to do."

She set the photo down, her hands shaking. "I needed you to be the strong one. But you were gone, and I… I leaned on our little girl instead."

Lily had been just ten when Alex died. His loss ruptured her world, yet it was Rowan who had crumbled under grief's relentless siege. How many nights had Lily held her mother, stroking her hair while Rowan sobbed in the darkness? A child offering solace when she herself needed it most. The guilt of those moments clung to Rowan like the smoke that had claimed Alex, a smothering mantle she could never escape.

The room seemed to close in around her with every memory she reawakened. Rowan turned away from the mirror, her attention snagged by the square edges of a CD case protruding from beneath a pile of school notebooks. She hesitated before picking it up.

Haruspex.

The cover was a grotesque tableau of demonic figures and apocalyptic visions, a stark contrast to the innocence of the stuffed animals perched on the nearby bed. Rowan's first instinct was revulsion. This was the music Lily had drowned in, the soundscape to her secretive descent. Part of Rowan wanted to hurl the CD across the room. She had never understood Lily's fascination with that noise she called music —the screeching guitars and guttural vocals that set Rowan's teeth on edge. Her tastes tended toward more classic rock like Fleetwood Mac and Eagles, but she did enjoy some of those new Seattle grunge bands.

Yet, as she flipped the CD over in her hands, curiosity pricked at the edges of her mind. What was it that had drawn her bright and lively girl to such darkness? Was Cole Abel some voice in the dark offering understanding? A promise of control amidst the chaos of adolescence?

Rowan shook her head, her fingers tracing the edge of the CD as she wrestled with her emotions. She had been a graphic designer before Alex died and her life fell apart. She was all too familiar with the allure of escapism through music and art. But she refused to believe her daughter had been driven by something as trivial as teenage rebellion. She couldn't understand why Lily had hidden this side of herself, but she knew this music had been important to her daughter.

Standing there alone in Lily's silent room, Rowan was overcome by a deep sense of longing and an irresistible need to connect with her child. She couldn't deny the impulse as she clicked the CD into the tray of Lily's dusty stereo. She hesitated for a moment, her finger hovering over the play button as if it were a trigger that could unleash unknown demons from the depths of Hell—or perhaps from within her own soul. At last, she pressed play.

The first few notes were haunting, sending shivers over Rowan's skin. She closed her eyes, allowing herself to be enveloped in the dark and brooding melodies, until the room exploded in a torrent of sound, the speakers crackling under the assault of Haruspex's unbridled fury. Wave after wave of churning chords and pounding drums made the walls shake and the floor vibrate beneath her feet.

Rowan recoiled, hands flying to her ears as she went to shut it off. But something held her in place.

"Jesus," she whispered, her eyes widening as the guttural vocals kicked in. The lyrics were a blur of violence and pain, yet beneath the brutality, she sensed a desperate cry for understanding. She found herself leaning in, straining to make out the words.

And what she heard chilled her to the bone.

The raw edge of Cole's voice clawed through the thunder and latched onto something primal within her. At first, she stood motionless, a statue amidst the sonic tempest. Then, slowly, her foot began to tap, her head bobbing almost imperceptibly to the rhythm that was both alien and intimately resonant. She closed her eyes again, allowing the waves of aggression to wash over her. Cole's lyrics, searing and ragged with emotion, seemed to reach into her very soul, dragging forth the rage and anguish she had kept locked away for so long.

An instinctive disgust churned Rowan's stomach, the same she had felt when she first heard of the band years ago. How could this vile music, which once symbolized everything that had torn her life to shreds, now pulse through her veins like a drug? A riptide of confusion overwhelmed her, her mind grappling with her strange attraction to something so repellent.

And then it hit her—a jolt of lightning striking the iron core of her being. The music, this relentless outpouring of rage and pain, it mirrored the storm that had raged within her all these years. Each snarled verse, each pummeling riff, spoke to the darkest parts of her, the places where her grief and fury intertwined. The lyrics were haunting and introspective, filled with themes of death, violence, and despair. But there was also an undercurrent of understanding and acceptance that pricked at Rowan's heart. They spoke of vengeance and loss, of the fire that consumes and the ashes left in its wake. It was her story, set to a brutal backdrop of thunderous melody.

Listening now, Rowan opened herself to the possibility that Cole Abel wasn't glorifying death. He was acknowledging its inevitability and offering solace to those who struggled with it.

Surrounded by the remnants of her daughter's life, Rowan let the music envelop her. Cole's voice roared with a throat full of glass. Each scream from the stereo was a release of her pent-up fury, each searing lyric a cathartic exorcism of the violence that seethed beneath her skin. For the first time since the fire claimed Alex and two teenage boys murdered Lily, Rowan felt the shackles of her sorrow break, giving way to an unfathomable sense of liberation. In the eye of this sonic hurricane, she found a twisted solace, a darkened mirror reflecting the blackest depths of her soul. And it was there, in the maelstrom of Haruspex's unrelenting onslaught, that she tasted a bittersweet feeling of peace.

Rowan finally understood. This is what Lily had been drawn to—this purifying sense of catharsis. This is how her little girl had dealt with the grief of her father's death and the burden of her mother's spiraling addiction.

The crushing realization that it was Cole Abel who had been there for her daughter when she needed it most was too much to bear. A lump formed in Rowan's throat as she listened to each song, feeling like a voyeur peeking into Lily's innermost thoughts and feelings. As the last notes faded away, Rowan sat back on the bed, wiping tears from her cheeks. The barrage of churning guitars and roaring screams from the stereo had ceased, leaving a ringing silence in Lily's room. In its wake, Rowan remained motionless and spent, her fingers trembling as they clutched the jewel case of the Haruspex CD. The listening experience still resonated, stoking an inferno of emotions she couldn't extinguish.

She rose from the bed and crossed to the window, her

reflection a ghostly figure in the dark glass. The street below was empty, silent as a tomb.

With every fiber of her being screaming against it, Rowan acknowledged the truth: Cole Abel, the man who authored the soundtrack to her nightmares, might just hold the key to extinguishing the blaze of injustice that seared her soul.

Rowan's hand fished in her pocket and found the folded paper he had given her. Her palm hovered over the phone on the desk, her fingers trembling like aspen leaves in a storm. The room now felt heavy with indecision, the air thick with the ghostly echoes of Cole's music. Before she could stop herself, she snatched the receiver, fingers punching numbers with mechanical precision.

One ring. Two. Then a gravelly voice answered.

"Abel," Rowan said, her voice a taut steel cable.

"Rowan Pierce," Cole replied. His tone carried an edge sharp enough to slice through the dense fog of her mind. "Didn't expect to hear from you so soon—or at all."

"It's time we talked," she said. "Face to face."

A low chuckle crackled through the line. "Brave or foolish?"

Desperate was the first word that came to mind, but Rowan would never admit it. Not to this man.

"Curious," she replied.

TRANSCRIPT OF PROCEEDINGS

In the matter of:
Case #9036CR001031
People of Essex County v. T. Chapman

Pages: EXTRACT (236-241)
Place: Salem, MA
Date: Aug. 17, 1995

WHEREUPON, the proceedings in the above-entitled matter commenced

BEFORE: THE HONORABLE NOAH L. COBBETT, JUDGE

DR. CALVIN MOSS, M.E.

called as a witness for the Commonwealth of Massachusetts, having first been duly sworn, was examined by Assistant District Attorney NELSON CRESS and testifies as follows:

DIRECT EXAMINATION:

MR. CRESS: How long have you been a medical examiner for the Commonwealth of Massachusetts, Dr. Moss?

WITNESS MOSS: Twenty-three years.

MR. CRESS: Did you examine the body of Lily Pierce?

WITNESS MOSS: I did. Given that her remains had been left exposed to the elements for two months, they were in an advanced state of decomposition.

MR. CRESS: How advanced?

WITNESS MOSS: Soft tissues were mostly gone and there was ample evidence of animal predation.

MR. CRESS: Nevertheless, you were able to positively identify the victim as Lily Pierce?

[witness nods head in affirmative]

WITNESS MOSS: The victim's mother identified her through dental records and a necklace that was found on the girl's remains.

MR. CRESS: What did you discover in your examination of her body?

WITNESS MOSS: The victim had been stabbed twelve times in the neck and torso, likely with a blade at least six inches in length, as there were distinct notches in her rib bones. There were abrasions on her throat, consistent with strangulation. The C3, 4, and 5 vertebrae in her neck had also been crushed and the spinal cord severed, likely by extreme blunt force impact.

MR. CRESS: Are these wounds consistent with Daley Banks' testimony that Troy Chapman stomped on Lily's neck while she lay bleeding on the ground?

WITNESS MOSS: They are, yes.

MR. CRESS: Did you find any evidence of sexual assault?

WITNESS MOSS: The victim's remains were too decomposed for us to make a determination.

MR. CRESS: Based on your examination, what did you conclude to be the ultimate cause of Lily's death?

WITNESS MOSS: None of the stab wounds were fatal, nor was the trauma to her neck. She would have been rendered paralyzed instantly when her spinal cord was severed, but in my determination, the victim bled to death, likely over an extended period.

MR. CRESS: So she was still alive when the boys started mutilating her?

WITNESS MOSS: Yes, she was still alive. Perhaps even still conscious.

MR. CRESS: In your opinion, this wasn't a quick and painless death, then. Was it Dr. Moss?

WITNESS MOSS: I'd say the poor girl suffered quite a bit.

Chapter 4

The windshield wipers fought a losing battle against the deluge, smearing Rowan's view of the winding coastal road that led to Cole Abel's isolated retreat. A flash of lightning illuminated the turbulent ocean below. Thunderstorms like this were rare in early November, but the remnants of a late-season tropical storm were still churning up from the south. Another few weeks and a storm like this would be a snowy nor'easter.

Rowan gripped the steering wheel tighter, her knuckles white. Her headlights cut through the darkness, revealing glimpses of treacherous drops mere feet from the edge of the route that wound around the town of Marblehead.

From the moment Cole had given his address over the phone, a prickly sensation had taken root in the pit of Rowan's stomach. It churned with questions, refusing to let her relax. How likely was it that a rock star like Cole Abel had settled down less than an hour away from her own town? Had he always lived in this picturesque, rocky peninsula jutting into the sea northeast of Boston? Was it just some cruel coincidence that his home was mere miles from where Lily had been brutalized and left for dead? Or had he deliberately chosen to settle here for some twisted reason? The thought sent a shiver through her flesh and she shook her head, trying to dislodge the paranoid notion.

The steady rhythm of wipers and thrumming rain on metal provided an apt soundtrack to Rowan's grim thoughts. Despite her curiosity about Cole's mysterious offer, part of her dreaded this meeting and the old emotions it would stir up. What could he want from her after all these years? After all she had put him through?

When Daley Banks admitted that Cole's lyrics had inspired him and his friend, Troy Chapman, to torture, rape, and sacrifice Lily, Rowan took action and sued both Cole and his record label for wrongful death. She wasn't the first grief-stricken parent to sue a heavy metal artist after losing a child—lawsuits against Ozzy Osborne and Judas Priest were both thrown out on First Amendment grounds years earlier. But Rowan and her lawyer had taken a novel approach. She didn't want to censor Cole or restrict his band's creative freedom. Instead, she held them responsible for knowingly *promoting* violent material to vulnerable minors and exploiting troubled kids like Daley and Troy for financial gain. It was the same strategy that had proven highly effective against big tobacco companies. In Rowan's eyes, if teens weren't mature enough to buy cigarettes, alcohol, guns, or porn, they shouldn't have access to music with violent themes like Cole's.

Ultimately, the judge didn't find Cole's lyrics obscene enough to warrant such restrictions, and dismissed the case.

But the damage was done—Rowan and Cole emerged from the trial as bitter enemies. Now, she couldn't stop replaying the courtroom confrontations with him, his piercing blue eyes always veiling a storm beneath.

The rain-drenched road snaked through the darkness as Rowan steered toward Peaches Point at the furthest tip of the peninsula. Here, the secluded mansions distanced themselves from each other, their silhouettes jagged against the night sky as they loomed over their expansive grounds.

Rowan's unease only intensified when she pulled up to the gated entrance of Cole's sprawling property and saw the high walls. She still couldn't help but wonder why someone like Cole would choose to settle down out here on this windswept coast. Was there some deeper connection to Lily's death that she was missing?

Intricate designs and the letter "A" adorned the large wrought-iron gates. Rowan reached out into the rain to press the intercom button. Windblown raindrops sprinkled through the open window and spattered her face as she waited for a response. After a few moments, Cole's deep voice crackled through the speaker.

"Rowan?"

"Yeah, it's me," she replied, hoping he could hear her over the pounding rain and the sound of the sea churning below the nearby cliffs.

The gates swung open and Rowan drove through, following a long and winding driveway through the property. As more of Cole's imposing mansion came into view, the rain lessened to a spiteful drizzle, and the clouds parted just enough for a sliver of moonlight to illuminate the estate.

The structure was a fortress of stone and shadows, perched on the craggy cliffs like some living, brooding dragon guarding its territory.

So this is what blood money can buy you, Rowan mused as she parked the car. She killed the engine, sitting in silence as rain drummed on the roof. She remained there for a moment, collecting herself while her stomach churned with dread. This was crazy. What the hell was she doing here? She recalled snatches of news reports detailing Cole's arrest for assault and attempted murder in his band's early years. Evidently, he'd attacked the lead guitarist of their tour's headlining band and sent him to the hospital. Although authorities eventually dropped the charges against Cole and the matter was quietly settled out of court, it didn't stop the tabloid-fueled frenzy painting him as a monster.

Rowan shuddered. What was she about to walk into?

Stepping out of the car, she felt the cold bite of the wind and the salted sting of the ocean. The air here tasted of brine. She wrapped her coat tighter around her frame and huddled against the drizzle, her hair whipping about her face as she approached Cole's massive front door.

She paused at the threshold, her finger hovering over the doorbell. To confront this man, to hear him out despite their history, revealed the true depths of her desperate hunger for revenge.

The door creaked open before she could announce her presence, and there he stood, expecting her. Cole regarded her with those intense blue eyes and an unreadable expression on his face. He wore a black t-shirt and jeans, and with his tattoos and imposing physique, he looked more like a paramilitary soldier than a musician. The knives on his throat stood out like macabre reminders of the violence that lurked beneath his skin. Again, Rowan wondered what had possessed her to come here alone.

"Rowan," he said, his voice a low rumble. "I wasn't sure you'd come. Come in." He stepped aside to let her pass.

The interior of Cole's home was a living, breathing entity that exuded a sense of dark and brooding energy. As Rowan stepped inside, the sound of her footsteps echoed through the grand hallway, bouncing off the high ceiling.

Cole took her coat and led her further into the house. She found herself admiring each room they passed through. Large classical paintings depicting macabre scenes of death and despair lined the walls of rich, dark wood panels. Rowan soon noticed a common theme among the art: all the paintings in Cole's impressive collection were images of Hell. She had taken art history while studying graphic design and was surprised to discover the lurid renderings of doom and the Last Judgment were remarkably similar to John Martin's famous illustrations of *Paradise Lost*. Could any of these actually be authentic works by the British master?

The presence of such cultured taste took Rowan by surprise. What had she expected of Cole? Framed gold records and magazine covers? Did he even understand or appreciate the rare quality of these paintings? How much they were worth?

The hollow echo of Cole's footsteps on the polished hardwood created an eerie ambiance, accompanied by the soft crackle of a fireplace burning somewhere in the house. Outside, the crashing waves rumbled, a constant reminder of the turbulent ocean below.

"The house is one of the oldest in all of Marblehead," Cole explained without any hint of conceit. "One of Salem's wealthiest ship-owners built it as a retreat in the 18th century."

A native New Englander, Rowan was well acquainted with the wealthy history of the notorious "witch city" across the bay to the west. She gave a vague nod as she took in more of her surroundings. The furniture was all ornate and carved from blackened wood, with plush velvet upholstery in deep shades of red and purple. Gothic-style chandeliers hung from the ceiling, casting a dim glow over the rooms. Heavy damask drapes framed large windows that offered sweeping views of the dark and stormy sea. The musty scent of old wood and book leather permeated the house, and a lingering aroma of candles or incense added a mystical quality to the atmosphere. The air itself seemed to carry a sense of foreboding, as if the walls held dark secrets and the shadows whispered of past deeds.

At last, they entered a conservatory that was a glass cathedral to excess. It was a grand room composed entirely of tall windows that allowed for a panoramic view of the churning ocean. Vines snaked up the back wall, adding a touch of nature to the otherwise extravagant setting. The air was sweet with the fragrance of exotic flowers mingling with the musty scent of damp earth and the tangy aroma of saltwater.

As they stepped inside, the gentle trickle of water on the glass roof greeted them, creating a soothing white noise. The occasional clap of thunder rattled the window panes, adding to the sense of being sheltered beneath a grandiose sanctuary. Lightning forked across the sky, bathing the room in a stark light and revealing Rowan's pale reflection in the glass against the backdrop of the tempestuous sea.

Cole motioned her to a pair of high-backed chairs that faced the raging waves, their silhouettes dwarfed by the vastness beyond.

Rowan sat in silence for a moment, too enrapt by the dramatic seascape to realize she had already let her guard down while Cole studied her. She caught herself, and despite her best efforts, couldn't keep her eyes from straying to the deadly knives tattooed across his throat as he took the chair opposite her.

"They're a reminder to always keep my chin up," Cole explained, as if reading her thoughts. "No matter what."

Rowan nibbled her lip and looked away, determined not to reveal her discomfort. Her eyes roamed around, searching for… what? A trap?

Cole's voice again pierced the patter of rain against the glass roof. "Can I get you something? A drink?"

Rowan shook her head, a curt dismissal. "I don't drink."

Cole shrugged and poured himself a glass of water instead. "I've been sober for years now," he said. "Just like you."

Rowan's gaze snapped to his face, surprise eclipsing her wariness. "How did you—"

"Takes one to know one," Cole interrupted, tapping his temple with a tattooed finger. "We've both been through some shit, haven't we?"

"Is that supposed to be our common ground?" Rowan's voice was a sharp whip crack in the relative silence of the conservatory.

"Maybe," Cole allowed, those steel-blue eyes not wavering. "It might be the only thing we have in common."

Rowan pressed her lips together, acknowledging the fact with a nod. "Let's cut the bullshit, Cole," she said. "You said you could help me. I'm listening. Why did you invite me here?"

"It wasn't to apologize, if that's what you're looking for."

Rowan was on her feet and heading for the door before she even realized it, her blood simmering beneath her skin as she crossed the room. This was a mistake. She should never have come here.

"I can help you kill your daughter's murderers."

Cole's words froze her where she stood. She swiveled around and found him gazing back at her from across the room.

"That's what you want? Isn't it?" he said.

"How?" she demanded, her tone leaving no room for evasion. "How does a washed-up rock star like you pull off something like that?"

There was a glint in Cole's eyes as her sharp words hit him. Was it anger or amusement? Was there a part of him that secretly enjoyed the barbs they exchanged? The undisguised enmity she harbored for him?

Cole motioned to her empty chair. "Please… sit."

He waited for her to rejoin him, and when he spoke again, his voice seemed to resonate with the thunder outside. "What do you know about the power of sound, Rowan?"

She frowned, unable to hide her impatience. "I don't have time for riddles, Cole."

"It's no riddle. Sound has the power to heal, to soothe… but it can also destroy. You were right about us. Our music *is* evil… just not the songs we put on our records." Cole leaned back. "We were always drawn to the occult. Over the years, we tapped into something ancient, something dark. And we found… *power* in the dark arts."

"You're talking about what? Black magic?" Rowan's voice was flat, disbelieving.

"Call it what you want," Cole replied. "Since primitive times, music has always been at the heart of any sacred ritual. It's the only truly transcendent language, and when wielded with intention, it's capable of tearing the veil between worlds and summoning those who dwell beyond."

"Summoning?" Rowan let out a cynical laugh. "Summoning what? Demons?"

A grim smile played across Cole's lips. "Now you're catching on. We can make those bastards pay, Rowan. Both of them."

"Have you lost your mind out here by yourself?" Rowan scoffed.

Cole's eyes hardened, all pretense of pleasantry vanishing. He set down his glass with a sharp clink. "No, clarity is what I've found. The kind that only comes when you've got nothing left to lose. You know how that feels, don't you, Rowan? I can show you. I can give you the closure you so desperately need."

"By invoking what—Hell itself?"

"Vengeance demands a vessel," Cole said. He rose from his seat to stand before the giant windows. "And Hell has no fury like that which we can unleash together."

Rowan swallowed hard as a heavy silence fell, broken only by the howling wind and lashing rain. She knew what he was proposing was insane. Demons? Vengeance rituals? And yet, part of her wanted to believe him, that it was possible to see that Lily's killers got what they deserved.

"Why are you so eager to help me?" Rowan asked. "We've been at each other's throats for years. After everything I put you through, you can't expect me to believe you've suddenly had a change of heart. And don't expect me to believe this is about your conscience."

A muscle in Cole's jaw twitched. "You think I don't want revenge too? Those sick fucks who killed your daughter didn't just destroy your life, Rowan. They destroyed mine, too. My music was all I had. And now... it's gone. The media crucified me. My career was ruined and my band was blacklisted. I lost everything... and I want to see them suffer for it."

Rowan watched him, a flicker of understanding dispelling some of her distrust. She knew all too well the consuming hunger for retribution, the need to make someone pay for the pain they'd caused.

"Why me, then?" she asked. "If you want revenge so badly, why not perform this summoning yourself?"

"I tried," Cole replied. "But these forces are unlike anything I've ever invoked. They're drawn to anger and wrath... and I suspect no one hates those motherfuckers more than you do."

"I don't know, Cole," Rowan said. "This all seems too... unreal. Say I believe you. How can I be sure this ritual of yours will even work?"

Cole's lips curled into a mirthless smile as he stepped toward her, closing the distance between them. "I expected you would have your doubts. If the ritual fails, if I'm lying, I'll sign over my entire music catalog. You get everything. Every song, every lyric that Haruspex ever produced. It's worth millions."

"Millions..." Rowan echoed, as if she hadn't heard correctly.

"Millions for you to burn, to erase every chord and verse that inspired those monsters," Cole continued. "If the summoning fails, you can dismantle my legacy, ensure it never influences another soul. It's what you always wanted, isn't it?"

Rowan stared at him, the weight of the offer sinking in. With Cole's music under her control, she could bury it forever, ensuring no one else would ever be inspired to commit such atrocities again.

But if the ritual succeeded...

She could have something far more valuable. The chance to bring Lily's killers to true justice, to watch them suffer as her daughter had suffered.

Rain lashed at the panoramic windows, blurring the world outside into a shifting tapestry of shadows and light. Rowan sat motionless, her eyes tracing the rivulets that raced each other down the length of the glass.

She was just laying there, crying for help—crying for her mother. That was the worst part, hearing her begging for her mom like that...

Daley Banks' testimony and the vivid images they conjured burned in Rowan's memory, filling her with a fiery rage. If only he hadn't said those words, she might have somehow found a way to move past Lily's death and heal. But knowing that her frightened little girl had cried out for her mother while she suffered was an unending torment that only blood could purge.

"Revenge or ruin," she murmured to herself.

Lightning illuminated the room as Cole watched her, his eyes glinting with the flash. "It's your call, Rowan."

She turned from the window, her gaze meeting his. "Can we really do this?" The question slipped from her lips, barely above a whisper.

"You wouldn't believe the wonders I've witnessed," Cole responded solemnly. "Such beautiful and terrifying wonders. They're not about belief, Rowan—they're about desire. How badly do you want justice for Lily?"

Rowan's hands clenched into fists. What were her options? The courts had failed her, and here was an opportunity— however fantastical—to balance the scales.

"Justice," she echoed, tasting the bitterness of the word.

"Or closure," Cole added, stepping closer. His presence was magnetic, the darkness he exuded both repelling and enticing.

"Or damnation," she countered, her light green eyes hardening with the steely glint of a woman who has nothing left to lose.

"Sometimes damnation is a small price to pay for peace."

Rowan's breath fluttered in her chest. *Peace.* The concept felt alien, a distant shore she had long since stopped believing she could reach.

"If I do this," she said. "I'm not doing it for you. I'm doing it for Lily."

Cole gave her a wry smile. "I wouldn't expect anything else."

Rowan hesitated a moment longer, the decision ripping from her like the roots of an ancient tree torn from the earth. "Alright, fuck it," she said. "I've spent seven years chasing ghosts. What's one more leap into Hell?"

COMMONWEALTH OF MASSACHUSETTS

Case #9036CR001031
People of Essex County v. T. Chapman

Government Exhibit: #23

Lyrics to the song "Veil of Decay"
Performed by the band Haruspex
Written by Cole Abel
From the album "Fleshbound Apocalypse"
Published by Armageddon Music, 1989

(Verse 1)
Moonlight drips through shattered stone,
Calling me back to the place you've gone.
Six feet deep, but I hear your name,
Whispered in the wind like a lover's shame.

(Pre-Chorus)
No chains can hold, no grave can bind,
Through blood and death, you're still mine...

(Chorus)
Through the veil of decay, I reach for you,
Frozen lips, pale hands, murder so cruel.
Time can't steal what the dark won't betray,
I'll find you beyond the veil of decay.

(Verse 2)

Roses blacken, wilting in your hair,
Hollow eyes still pull me there.
Cold embrace, skin turned to stone,
But I won't let you rest alone.

(Pre-Chorus)
No chains can hold, no grave can bind,
Through blood and death, you're still mine...

(Chorus)
Through the veil of decay, I reach for you,
Frozen lips, pale hands, murder so cruel.
Time can't steal what the dark won't betray,
I'll find you beyond the veil of decay.

(Bridge)
Drenched in the stench of decay, no remorse in sight,
A desecration of the flesh, in the dead of night.
Bound by the darkness, in this vile affair,
In the arms of the dead, I lay my soul bare.

(Chorus)
Through the veil of decay, I reach for you,
Frozen lips, pale hands, murder so cruel.
Shadows rise, and the cold winds say,
We are one beyond the veil of decay...

(Outro)
We are one... beyond the veil...

Chapter 5

Thunder rumbled ominously, shaking the foundations of the old mansion as Cole led Rowan up the winding staircase to the attic studio that crowned the entire top floor. Rowan's pulse skittered like leaves chased by an unseen wind, a mix of trepidation and anticipation stirring in her veins. She still couldn't quite believe she was here, following a man she detested into the heart of his private sanctum.

At the top of the narrow steps, Cole pushed open a heavy wooden door, revealing the dimly lit expanse beyond. The studio was a cavernous space, its walls draped in shadows. Occasional bursts of lightning penetrated the thick curtains, but the room's exceptional soundproofing kept the thunder at bay.

Rowan entered, her eyes widening as they adapted to the gloom. Inside was an eccentric blend of modern technology and ancient mysticism. Guitars lined the walls like obsidian totems—some glossy with the sheen of careful use, others the scarred relics of Cole's past performances. A massive mixing board dominated the center of the room, its array of knobs and sliders bristling like the back of some reptilian beast. Among the amplifiers, pedals, and recording equipment was an assortment of rare and exotic instruments: vintage keyboards with ivories yellowed by time, drums with skins that whispered of pagan ceremonies, and stringed oddities whose origins were lost to the mists of history.

But it was the other items that captured Rowan's attention. Leather-bound tomes crammed the shelves, their spines etched with symbols that she didn't recognize. Crystal skulls and statuettes of deities long forgotten by modern faith stood guard over the room, their features cast in grotesque detail. A massive pentagram was meticulously painted on the wooden floor. The cloying sweetness of incense and candle wax filled the room. It was both repellant and engaging, much like the man who guided Rowan through it.

"This is... intense," she murmured, her fingers ghosting over a strange metallic object that looked part tuning fork, part sacrificial dagger. It struck her that, like the rest of the house, there was nothing here that paid tribute to Cole's success. Not a single memento of his time with Haruspex, or even a hint that he'd once been the frontman of the biggest and most influential band in his genre. It was as if that era in his life had simply never happened. Cole, it seemed, was not one to celebrate his own fame or dwell on the past.

His lips quirked into a humorless smile as he ran a loving hand over the fretboard of a nearby guitar. "This is where the magic happens... Literally."

Rowan's heart thudded in her chest, not entirely from the climb. She swallowed hard, trying to ignore the unease prickling at the back of her neck. She'd come this far; there was no turning back now.

"Magic," she repeated, unable to hide her skepticism. "Is that what you call it?"

"Call it what you want. All I know is that when I'm in here, when I'm making music… anything becomes possible. And that's a kind of magic, isn't it?"

Cole fixed her with a piercing gaze, and Rowan felt herself caught in the pull of his charisma, the sheer force of his belief. Despite her doubts, she couldn't deny the flicker of curiosity that his words ignited within her. What if there truly was power in the music he made? What if it could somehow help her achieve the closure she so desperately craved?

"So this ritual," she said, her voice sounding small in the cavernous space of the studio. "You really think it will work? That it can… summon something?"

The intensity in Cole's eyes seemed to burn brighter at her question. He took a step closer, his presence filling the room, filling her senses. "I don't think, Rowan. I know. Sound is a primal force. It's the key that unlocks doors we're not supposed to open. And what comes through…" He shook his head, a look of dark wonder on his face. "There's nothing else like it."

Rowan bit her lip. "I'm not sure I believe in any of this," she admitted. "You've done this before? Summoned things to serve you?"

"We didn't claw our way to the top of the metal kingdom with talent alone," Cole replied, his pale eyes gleaming. "We had something… *else* on our side—a power that other bands couldn't match."

A troubling possibility entered Rowan's mind. "These incantations. You swear you never put them in your recordings?"

"No," Cole smirked. "That would be far too dangerous. It was our little secret. Now… are you ready to dance with the devil?"

Rowan's breath caught in her throat, her mind spinning with the implications of his words. She thought of Lily, of the gaping wound her death had left in her own soul. If there was even a chance that this ritual could help her set things right…

"Tell me what I need to do," she whispered, fear and determination warring within her. "I'm ready."

Cole's smile widened—a white slash in the shadows—and he reached for a guitar. It was sharp and custom-made, with intricate occult symbols etched into its body. His hands wrapped around the neck with a tenderness that seemed at odds with the darkness of his purpose. His fingers danced across the fretboard, coaxing forth a sinister melody that pulsed through the air and vibrated in Rowan's bones.

"The key is in the sound frequencies," he explained, his voice barely audible above the hypnotic drone of the guitar. "All universes are governed by vibrations. Each frequency is unique, and when layered just right, they unlock realms beyond our own."

Rowan leaned in, mesmerized by the eerie tones. "How is that possible?"

"Think of it like a cosmic combination lock." Cole replied, his eyes gleaming. "Each note, each frequency, is a number. Get the sequence right, and…"

"The door springs open," Rowan said.

Cole's gaze locked onto hers as he plucked the guitar strings. "Most of these frequencies are hidden away beyond the capacity of human perception in the realm of something known as *infrasound*."

"Like the frequencies that dogs can hear, but we can't?"

"Yeah, like that. But thanks to this…" Cole gestured to the complex soundboard. "We can capture those secret frequencies and layer them over each other, each building upon the last, entering the right combination and resonating with the fabric of reality until the veil between worlds is at its thinnest."

"And what comes through?" Rowan whispered, both dreading and craving the answer.

Cole's lips curled into a knowing smirk. "That, Rowan, depends on what we invite."

He stopped playing and held out the guitar to her. Rowan hesitated, her fingers trembling as they brushed the polished wood.

"Your turn," Cole urged. "I'll teach you the basic melodies. But the real power comes from what's inside you."

Rowan cradled the instrument, its weight unfamiliar yet somehow right. "I've never played before."

"You don't need to be a musician," Cole said, positioning her fingers on the strings. "This isn't about technical skill. It's about tapping into your pain, your rage, your grief. Let it flow through you and into the music, and together we can channel it into something powerful."

Rain pelted the windows as Rowan's fingers hovered over the guitar strings, a quiet hum issuing from the amplifier. The weight of the instrument felt alien in her hands, a live wire with its energy coursing through its core, waiting to be unleashed. The possibility of avenging Lily, of finding justice in a world that had abandoned her daughter, tugged at her heartstrings. She clenched her jaw, feeling the rage boiling within her.

Can I really trust him? she wondered. But if there was even a shred of truth in what Cole claimed, she had to try.

Cole watched her with an intensity that could cut glass. "It has to be you, Rowan," he said, his voice low and gravelly. "It's your path to tread. Your chance to make them pay."

He held her gaze, his eyes piercing through her uncertainty. Rowan's fingers trembled as she positioned them on the strings, her heart pounding in her ears. She thought of Lily's smile, of the last time she'd held her daughter in her arms, her head thick and fuzzy with whiskey. The grief surged through her like a tidal wave, threatening to pull her under, drowning her with the knowledge that she had failed to protect her only child.

She closed her eyes, surrendering herself to the unknown. For Lily, she would walk through fire and crawl through glass. She would descend into Hell itself.

"Teach me," she said.

A dark smile flickered across Cole's face as he reached for another guitar, a sleek black instrument that seemed to absorb the dim light around it. "This melody is the foundation of the incantation," he explained, demonstrating the notes. "Channel your sorrow, your rage, your wrath. Pour it all into the notes and let it guide you."

As Rowan's fingers touched the frets and strings, she felt a sudden connection to the instrument, as if it were an extension of her own grief-stricken soul. She watched intently as Cole played the haunting melody, committing it to memory.

"Now you try," he prompted, stepping back to give her space.

Rowan inhaled, thinking of Lily's laughter, of blood-stained crime scene photos, of sleepless nights and tear-soaked pillows. When she struck the first note, it rang out like a scream.

The melody began tentatively, as if afraid to fully bloom. The sounds that emanated from the guitar were raw and primal, echoing through the room like a mournful cry. Rowan felt her emotions surge through her veins, the memories of Lily's life and death flooding her mind as she poured her heart into each note. Soon, the music seemed to take on a life of its own, her fingers moving of their own accord. Beneath her sorrow, something else stirred—the simmering rage that had been building for seven long years. She latched onto it like a lifeline, letting it flow through her and into the guitar. The sound was untamed, the room vibrating with a frequency that felt both strange and intimately familiar. The studio faded away, and all that existed was the fury and the all-consuming need for vengeance.

Cole nodded approvingly as he turned to the soundboard. His fingers flew over the controls with a sorcerer's precision, shaping the noise into a dark symphony. His voice seemed to come from far away, guiding her through the complex patterns of the incantation.

"Keep playing," he instructed. "Feel it build inside you."

The guitar became an extension of her being, each note clawing its way from the depths of her shattered heart. As she played, the boundaries between herself and the instrument blurred, her emotions bleeding into the melody, weaving a song of sorrow and wrath.

"Yes," Cole urged, his eyes alight with a feverish intensity. "Just like that. Let it all out, Rowan. Invite them in."

An unexpected exhilaration flooded Rowan's senses, a wild, intoxicating rush that reminded her of listening to Cole's music in Lily's bedroom—the raw power, the defiance, the cathartic release of pent-up emotions. It was a sensation so intense it bordered on euphoria, mingling with her grief to forge something potent and indescribable. The sound spoke directly to her pain, giving voice to the anger and heartache that had consumed her for years.

"Feel it, Rowan. Let it become you," Cole stood back, his silhouette dark against the lamplight, watching the transformation unfolding before him.

With every chord she played, Rowan felt the fabric of reality thinning, the veil between worlds fraying under the pressure of her sound and fury. Each pluck of the strings seemed to summon an otherworldly energy that thrummed with power and dark intent. And in that moment, her heart pounded with the rhythm of revenge, every beat a step closer to the justice she sought for the blood spilled and the innocence lost.

The serrated notes clawed at the air, a raw, wild sound that vibrated through Rowan's body as her fingers danced across the strings with a feral grace she didn't know she possessed. The guitar hummed with life, its vibrations a siren song to the demons of vengeance that swirled within her soul.

Cole loomed over the soundboard, his tattooed hands moving with deft precision as he manipulated dials and sliders. He layered Rowan's guitar tracks, applying distortion and reverb, twisting and warping the sound until it became a malevolent drone that filled the studio like the heartbeat of some ancient, slumbering beast. Its hypnotic cadence wove itself into the very fabric of Rowan's being.

"More," he prompted, his voice a low growl barely discernible over the maelstrom of sound. "Give it more of your pain."

Rowan obliged, pouring every shard of her shattered heart into the strings. The music swelled, dark and all-consuming, wrapping around her, permeating her senses until she was nothing but the instrument in her hands and the haunting symphony they created.

The drone took on a life of its own. It spiraled outward from the amplifiers, resonating off the walls, past the eerie glow of the occult artifacts that crowded the shelves. It was as though the entire room conspired to amplify their ritual, to carve open a pathway for the darkness to enter.

"Let go," Cole commanded, his eyes fixed on Rowan with an intensity that burned. "Let it consume you."

And she did. The drone seeped into her pores, infiltrating her mind, a hypnotic serpent coiling tighter with every note she played. Rowan felt a whisper of frost creeping up her spine—a sensation of cold tendrils seeping into her mind, ensnaring her thoughts. She fought the urge to resist, allowing the pulsing rhythm to wash over her. She felt herself slipping, her mind untethering from her body as her consciousness drifted. Her vision blurred, reality distorting as the sound carried her away from the physical confines of the studio, away from the storm that raged outside.

"Lily," she whispered, her voice breaking. It was for her daughter that she embraced this madness, for Lily that she would traverse Hell itself. The drone promised power, promised retribution, and she clung to it, letting it drag her consciousness wherever it wanted.

With each passing second, she felt herself tumbling down deeper into the void, her mind spiraling away from the gloom of the studio and toward some unknown destination. She could no longer discern where the guitar ended and she began —they were one, bound by the dark harmonies they created together. The music swelled around her, a vortex of sound and emotion. And as the last notes faded away, Rowan felt a sudden, wrenching shift in her consciousness, as though she were being pulled out of her own body and into something else entirely.

"Find him," Rowan thought, her resolve crystallizing amid the tumultuous drone. "Find Daley Banks."

And somewhere in the pitch-black depths, something ancient and malevolent stirred in response.

Rowan closed her eyes, giving herself up to the hypnotic power of the drone. The sensation was disorienting, like being pulled underwater by a powerful riptide. She was adrift, lost in a sea of darkness and despair, struggling to find her way back to herself. The sound washed over her in waves, each one carrying her further away from the confines of Cole's studio and into a realm of shadows.

In her mind's eye, she saw a dimly lit street, its rain-slicked pavement glistening beneath the sickly glow of street-lamps. She moved forward, her footsteps soundless, propelled by a force that was not her own. She could feel something inside of her, something black-hearted and bloodthirsty. Or was it the other way around? Had her body remained behind in Cole's studio even as her consciousness ventured forth and became one with whatever dark force they had conjured?

Vengeance demands a vessel...

Cole's words came echoing back to her, and she understood why it had to be her. *She* was vengeance. And this malevolent entity she had summoned—this demon—was guiding her.

Rowan's heart slammed against her breastbone. She could feel the demon's power coursing through her, the rage and grief that had driven her for so long now amplified by its unholy strength.

A flash of lightning tore through the sky, illuminating the street. Rowan caught sight of her reflection in a nearby window and staggered back, suddenly breathless. The face looking back wasn't that of a demon, or even her own.

It was Lily. Her Lily.

Her daughter's innocent eyes—once brimming with life— were now glowing crimson orbs devoid of warmth. The demon had stolen her form, a cruel disguise that twisted the knife of Rowan's grief. She felt like she was standing on a frozen lake, hearing the crack but unable to move. The downpour seemed to quiet, leaving only the hollow echo of her own disbelief.

"Lily..." The name was a strangled whisper. A wave of vertigo washed over Rowan as she struggled to comprehend what she was seeing. She raised a hand to her face, watching in horror as Lily's reflection mirrored her movements.

And then she understood. This was the form the demon had chosen for her vessel.

Lily.

Resurrected as a creature of wrath.

The demon wearing Lily's face tilted its head, regarding Rowan with a mixture of curiosity and cruel amusement. When it spoke, it was with her daughter's voice, distorted by an otherworldly echo.

"Isn't this what you wanted, Mom?" it purred. "To see me again? To make them pay?"

"No," Rowan moaned, her voice trembling with revulsion. "This can't be happening. This isn't what I wanted."

But even as the words left her lips, she knew they were a lie. This was exactly what she had wanted, what she had been working toward for the past seven years. Part of her thrilled at the power that coursed through her veins. The ability to at last punish those who had taken her child was intoxicating; the chance to make them suffer, to inflict upon them the same pain and terror that they had inflicted upon her daughter.

And now, through the power of Cole's music, she had finally achieved it. A cruel satisfaction bloomed in her heart. She was the demon now, an avenging force come to deliver justice to those who had taken everything from her.

As the realization washed over her, Rowan felt a grim sense of purpose settle into her bones.

Lily, forgive me, she thought, as the demon in her daughter's form turned away from its own reflection.

Rowan blinked, disoriented, until her vision focused on a dilapidated house at the end of the street. She thought she recognized the neighborhood, one of the sketchy ones south of Boston that she used to drive by on I-93. Dorchester? The house had peeling paint, broken shutters, and a sagging porch —all illuminated by the sickly glow of a single streetlamp.

As the rain continued to pelt down upon her, the demonic figure of Lily that now served as Rowan's vessel slinked along the shadow-streaked pavement. The streetlights cast a yellow hue on the rundown homes that lined the block, their rotting facades like gaping, toothless maws ready to swallow anything that dared to venture too close.

The demon crept forward with Rowan's consciousness tethered to its own, moving with an unnatural fluidity. Its gaze locked on a flickering light from an upstairs window.

This was Daley Banks' home. He was in there—the man responsible for tearing her world apart—somewhere within that festering place.

Once he's gone, your soul can finally rest, Rowan thought. *And maybe… just maybe… I can too.*

Rowan's voice was a guttural growl that resonated through her dead daughter's lips. "Time to face your demons, Daley."

Chapter 6

Rowan tried to pull away, to wrench her consciousness free from the demon's grasp, but its hold was too strong. She was a passenger in her own mind, helpless to do anything but watch as the demon-Lily stalked toward the house. Its hunger coursed through her veins, a primal urge that simmered in her blood. The rain pelted her skin and the wind howled in her ears, but she hardly noticed. Her senses were no longer her own. She perceived the world through eyes that belonged to something far more ancient and wicked than anything human.

But the rage that smoldered in her flesh was entirely her own.

The decrepit house loomed ahead, its silhouette a jagged wound against the stormy night sky. Paint peeled from its facade like leprous skin and thick shadows enveloped the porch of the cheap apartment in Dorchester where Daley Banks had taken refuge in the days following his release.

A shiver of anticipation—or was it dread?—shot through Rowan as Lily moved closer, her movements now driven by the demon's predatory grace.

Where are you?

The demon's voice slithered into Rowan's consciousness, the sound a guttural growl that vibrated with malice. She could feel the demon's impatience as Lily prowled the periphery of the building, a shadow stalking through the torrential downpour, waiting for the opportune moment to strike. A dim light flickered through the rain-streaked windows of the house, betraying life within the rotting walls.

Rowan's heart pounded like the drums in one of Cole's songs. Anticipation and revulsion coursed together through her being. Lily's hand trembled as she reached out to the grimy windowpane. Faint smudges clouded the glass as she sought her prey.

A figure passed behind the foggy windowpane—a silhouette that sent a jolt of hatred so profound through her veins that Rowan gasped with the intensity of it. Through Lily's eyes, she saw Banks moving about his apartment, oblivious to the horror that awaited him. A cruel smile twisted Lily's lips, a look that seemed ghastly on her face.

Close now... so close...

Rowan felt power swell within her borrowed form, the demonic strength coalescing with her wrath. This was the moment she had yearned so much to achieve—the chance to face her daughter's killer, the opportunity to exact the justice that had eluded her for seven agonizing years.

End him...

The demon's whisper mingled with the drone still reverberating in Rowan's mind. Tonight, there would be no mercy, only the final, cathartic release of blood for blood.

And in that moment, as she prepared to unleash the full fury of her vengeance on the man who had destroyed her life, Rowan found she didn't care. She didn't care about Banks' childhood of neglect, or that it was his own conscience that had eventually prompted him to confess and lead the police to Lily's body. She didn't care that his parents had begged Rowan to allow them to do anything they could to atone for what their son had taken from her. Only the justice she'd been denied mattered. She would now take it, regardless of the price.

Rowan peered into the window through Lily's eyes, her breath fogging the glass. She could feel the demon's hunger, its desire to tear into Daley's flesh and make him suffer as Lily had suffered. She felt a surge of exhilaration, a dark thrill that was both intoxicating and terrifying. The intensity of the demon's bloodlust shocked her, but a part of her relished the dark anticipation that coiled in her gut.

Rowan's heart pounded as she watched Daley move about his squalid apartment. The flickering light of the television cast eerie shadows through the living room, illuminating piles of empty beer cans and overflowing ashtrays. The squalor of the place assaulted Rowan's senses. Nicotine stained the walls, the peeling wallpaper hanging in ragged strips over the mold. Discarded pizza boxes and porn magazines littered the floor, the detritus of a life in ruins.

Daley sat hunched on a threadbare couch, his greasy hair dangling in his face as he focused on the screen, unaware of the malevolent presence lurking outside his window. He was a pitiful sight, his face gaunt and unshaven, his eyes sunken and haunted. The weight of his time behind bars seemed to press down on him, bowing his shoulders and draining the life from his features. For a moment, Rowan almost felt sad for him. He'd been just a boy, just a year older than Lily, the night his own life had changed forever.

She was just laying there, crying for help—crying for her mother. That was the worst part, hearing her begging for her mom like that...

Remembering the atrocity Daley had inflicted on her daughter, Rowan felt the demon's power surging within her once more, feeding off her darkest emotions. It was a sickening, intoxicating sensation, one that both repulsed and enticed her.

Look at him, the demon whispered, its voice a sinister caress in her mind. *So oblivious, so vulnerable. He has no idea what's coming for him.*

Rowan watched as Daley reached for another beer, his movements sluggish and uncoordinated. She wondered how many nights he had spent like this since his release, drowning his freedom in alcohol and mindless television, trading one prison for another. Did he ever think of Lily, of the life he had stolen from her?

A wave of stench assaulted Rowan's senses. Her stomach churned as Lily's nostrils flared, the demon savoring the miasma of body odor, stale cigarettes, and something darker —hopelessness. She pressed closer to the window, Lily's nails leaving scratches on the weathered frame.

Let me in, the demon hissed, and Rowan could almost feel its hot and foul breath in her ear. *Let me make him pay for what he's done.*

Rowan hesitated, torn between her desire for vengeance

and the knowledge that she was teetering on the brink of something irrevocable. If she let the demon take control, if she allowed it to carry out the violent retribution she craved, there would be no going back.

But then she thought of Lily and how her bright light had been extinguished too soon. She thought of the years she had spent consumed by grief and rage, of the hollow ache that had taken up residence in her chest. And in that moment, her resolve hardened into something cold and merciless. The road to healing was paved with the ashes of the damned.

"Do it," she whispered, her voice barely audible over the drumming of the rain. "Make him suffer."

She felt Lily's lips grin, a feral expression that sent chills rippling over her skin like wind across a still pond. Lily began to claw at the window, her fingers now sharp talons that sank into the rotting wood as she sought to gain entry.

Inside the house, Daley remained oblivious, lost in his own world of numbing intoxication.

Rowan watched through her dead daughter's eyes. Her breath came fast and heavy now, as Lily's efforts grew more frenzied. The window creaked and groaned under her assault, the glass beginning to crack. And then, with a final, violent wrench, she tore the window from its frame and hurled herself into the room.

Daley's head snapped up, his eyes widening in terror as he saw Lily's form standing before him. He opened his mouth to scream, but no sound escaped his lips.

He knows now, Rowan thought, relishing the terror in Daley's eyes. *He knows what's coming for him.*

The demon's power pulsed within her, urging her forward.

She could feel its hunger, its desire to inflict suffering and claim another soul. And for the first time since Lily's death, Rowan felt a twisted sense of purpose, a dark satisfaction in knowing she would be the instrument of Daley's death.

"L—Lily?" The name rasped from Daley's dry lips.

Rowan's mouth curled in a mockery of Lily's shy smile. "Hi, Daley." Her voice, tinged with a demonic growl, slithered from the vessel of her murdered daughter.

"I… I… I didn't…" Daley's voice trailed off into a feeble whimper, as if a simple denial could wipe away seven years and the blood on his hands.

"Oh, but you did," Rowan purred, "and now it's time to atone."

Daley scrambled backward, his eyes darting around the room in search of an escape. But there was none. Even while wearing Lily's skin, the demon's presence filled the apartment, suffocating and inescapable.

"Please," Daley croaked, his voice cracking with fear. "I'm sorry. I didn't mean to—"

"Didn't mean to what?" Rowan snarled in the demon-Lily's voice. "Didn't mean to murder my daughter? Didn't mean to rip her away from me forever?"

Lily took another step forward, the floorboards creaking beneath her feet. The demon's energy crackled around her, a tangible force that seemed to suck the air from the room.

This is for Lily, she thought, her veins humming like high-voltage wires. *This is for every moment of pain and suffering he caused her.*

The demon reached into the depths of Daley's mind, dredging up his most traumatic memories and forcing him to relive them again and again. In the darkness of his subconscious, he was once again trapped in the suffocating walls of his prison cell. The stench of fear hung heavy in the air, like a smothering fog. He saw himself surrounded by menacing figures, experiencing the brutal and degrading attacks that had scarred him for life. He felt the sharp sting of metal against his skin, heard his own piercing cries reverberating through the prison walls. No one came to help him—the guards reviled him for what he'd done to Lily. The cold metal bars pressed against his skin and he heard the echoes of his fellow inmates laughing at his anguished wailing. He could still feel the blood trickling down his inner thighs after they'd violated him and left him sobbing like an infant on the concrete floor.

"No," Daley moaned, clutching at his head. His body trembled and his vision blurred as he relived those horrifying moments. "Make it stop. Please, make it stop."

But Rowan felt no pity, no mercy. She watched as Daley writhed on the floor, his face contorted in agony. The demon's laughter echoed in her mind, a sinister cackle that froze the blood in her veins.

He deserved it, she told herself, even as a small part of her recoiled from the sheer brutality he had endured. *He deserved to suffer as Lily suffered.*

Daley's screams rose in pitch as the demon's torment intensified, its insidious whispers crawling through his mind.

More, Rowan thought, and Lily's lip curled in a cruel smile. *Make him feel the pain he inflicted on my Lily.*

The demon was only too happy to oblige. Rowan watched, transfixed, as Lily's hands reached for Daley and clawed their way into his head, conjuring images of the fiery hell that awaited him as a punishment for his sins. Flames withered his skin, leaving behind blistered marks, and the air was thick with the acrid smell of sulfur. The landscape was a desolate wasteland, with jagged rocks and burning pits. Fire crackled through the air, accompanied by the hissing of roasting flesh. The screams of the tortured souls echoed endlessly, a haunting and nightmarish chorus.

Daley's eyes rolled back in his head, his body convulsing as the barrage of horrific images assaulted him. He could see it clearly now—the hellish landscape that would be his eternal prison.

And through it all, Rowan watched with eyes that were cold and merciless. She was dimly aware that there would be consequences for what she was doing, but in this moment, she didn't care. All that mattered was that Daley was suffering, just as Lily suffered in her final moments. Rowan felt the demon's satisfaction mingling with her own, a dark and heady cocktail of emotions. She reveled in the power coursing through her, the knowledge that she was finally giving Daley a taste of the hell he deserved.

"Please," Daley moaned. "I'm sorry. I'm so sorry."

But his pleas fell on deaf ears. Rowan's anger surged, white-hot and all-consuming. She remembered the way Lily looked when they found her body, and any lingering doubts burned away in an instant.

This is justice, she thought. But a small voice in the back of her mind whispered that it was anything but. She felt herself being pulled deeper into the darkness. The boundaries between her own consciousness and the demon's blurred until she could no longer tell where she ended and the creature began. Its thoughts became her thoughts, its desires her desires, until all that remained was a singular, overpowering need for blood.

Rowan's chest tightened as she watched Daley stumble through the apartment, his eyes darting from one imagined horror to another. He crashed into a rickety table, sending empty cans clattering across the floor before he reeled backwards. His back hit the peeling wallpaper as he slid to the floor. He let out a scream as Lily closed in on him. Rowan felt herself moving in tandem, a passenger in this unholy pursuit. The demon's borrowed form towered over Daley.

"No more," he sobbed, "Please, God, no more."

The demon's snarling voice slithered through Lily's lips. "There is no God here, only us. You took her life from her. You took her innocence, her future. And for what? To play guitar?" Lily's claws extended, gleaming in the flickering glare of the television.

Daley shook his head frantically, tears streaming down his face. "No, no, it wasn't like that. I didn't mean to—"

"*LIAR!*" The word tore itself from Lily's throat. She surged forward, her claws outstretched, ready to rend and tear and destroy.

In that moment, Daley's eyes meet Lily's, and Rowan saw the full extent of his terror. He knew, beyond any doubt, that he was going to die here, in this squalid little apartment, at the hands of the innocent girl he had defiled. The realization was scrawled across his face; a mask of pure horror.

And Rowan felt nothing. No pity, no remorse. There was

only the darkness, cold and all-encompassing, and the sickening crunch of bone and sinew as the demon began its grisly work.

Lily reached out with a clawed hand, her fingers curling around Daley's throat. Rowan could feel the young man's pulse racing beneath his skin as her dead daughter's grip tightened, her claws puncturing Daley's flesh and sending rivulets of blood cascading down his neck. Blood sprayed in graceful arcs, painting the walls like some ghastly artwork. Daley's screams echoed through the apartment, a cacophony of agony and terror that seemed to stretch on for an eternity.

Rowan witnessed it all through Lily's eyes, mesmerized by the brutality unfolding before her. She felt the demon's savage joy, the twisted pleasure it took in every blow, every rending of flesh. The scent of copper and viscera flooded her senses, overwhelming and nauseating, and as she watched, she felt a dark satisfaction welling up within her, mingling with the revulsion and horror. She had craved this for so long. To see her daughter's killer suffer, to see him consumed by the same terror and despair that he had inflicted upon her little girl.

And yet, even as the demon exacted its vengeance, Rowan felt a flicker of something else deep within her soul. This was wrong, so wrong. A line that could never be uncrossed. The catharsis she thought she would feel was conspicuously absent, replaced by a hollow ache that threatened to swallow her whole.

Daley's eyes, wide with terror, locked onto Rowan's. In that moment, she didn't see the monster who had taken her daughter, but a broken man facing his own mortality. This was what she had wanted, what she had summoned the demon to do. And yet, as she witnessed the depths of its cruelty, she couldn't help but wonder if she had gone too far.

"Stop," she whispered, her voice trembling. "This isn't… I didn't…"

But Lily's assault continued, relentless and savage. Bones cracked like gunshots, tendons snapped like overstretched guitar strings. Daley's cries grew weaker, gurgling through a throat filled with blood.

"Please," he croaked, blood bubbling from his lips. "I'm sorry… I'm so sorry…"

With a final, sickening crunch, Lily crushed Daley's windpipe. His body convulsed, a last, agonized shriek tearing from his ruined throat before he went limp. His eyes stared blankly at the ceiling as his lifeless form crumpled to the floor. The sound reverberated through Rowan's very being, a haunting note that she knew would echo in her nightmares for years to come.

Lily stepped back as the demon admired its handiwork. What was left of Daley lay in a pool of his own blood, his body a ruin of shattered bone and pulped flesh.

Rowan, trapped in her daughter's form, stared at her blood-soaked hands. Her vision swam, the room blurring as conflicting emotions battled within her. A sickening thrill of satisfaction coursed through her veins, mingling with revulsion at the carnage she had just witnessed.

What have I done? she thought. *What have I become?*

But even as the thoughts entered her mind, a darker part of her yearned for that rush again. The intoxicating sense of control, of righting an unforgivable wrong. After all, hadn't

Daley and Troy taken everything from her? Hadn't they robbed Lily of her future, her chance at life? Deep down, in the darkest recesses of her soul, Rowan knew that a part of her would always revel in this moment.

And the night was not yet over.

Chapter 7

Rowan's eyelids snapped open, her vision blurred and her mind adrift in a disoriented haze. It was as if her consciousness and body were untethered, floating on a foggy, endless sea. When the jolt of reality hit, it was a bolt of lightning breaking through a thick layer of clouds.

Where the hell was she?

The soft, unfamiliar sheets beneath her fingers felt like a distant dream; the plush pillow cradling her head a stark contrast to the cracked and rain-drenched streets of Dorchester. Fighting off a wave of panic, Rowan blinked and struggled to focus. The room swam into view, her senses seeping in like water into a sinking ship. Ornate wallpaper, antique furniture, heavy brocade curtains framing leaded glass windows.

Unfamiliar. Wrong.

The lavishness of her surroundings did nothing to diminish the pounding dread within her skull. Gray slants of morning sunlight filtered through the curtains, casting pale rays over the opulent bedroom. Dark roots of unease burrowed deep into Rowan's gut. She was still somewhere in Cole's mansion.

How did I get here?

A dull throbbing pulsed behind her temples as she pushed herself upright, the room tilting sickeningly. She pressed a hand to her forehead, willing the vertigo to subside and feeling the clammy sheen of sweat that coated her skin. Her body ached, as if she had been through a physical ordeal rather than a nightmare.

A sudden fear gripped her as she considered what Cole could have done to her in her vulnerable state. She struggled to piece together her fractured memories of the ritual in his studio and the trance she had fallen into. Flashes of her vivid dreams, of her violent fantasies of slaughtering Daley Banks, filled her mind. They *had* been dreams, hadn't they? None of that really happened. Those horrific images, they were some nightmarish vision induced by the hypnotic drone she and Cole had produced. What else could they have been?

Rowan tried to ignore the wave of dizziness that washed over her. Her hands trembled as she ran them through her disheveled hair, the strands damp with sweat and clinging to her face. She still wore her clothes and was lying on the bed's plush duvet. Her eyes darted around, taking in the extravagant decor—a far cry from the spartan existence she had embraced since Lily's death.

Think, Rowan, think! What happened last night?

She pressed her palms against her temples as if to squeeze the memories from her foggy mind. The last clear recollection she could grasp was that haunting drone and the lightning flickering in Cole's studio. She remembered playing the guitar, her melodies taking on a life of their own as Cole layered them into an otherworldly cadence. Then, a surge of power so intense it had scorched her soul, and after that… the suffocating darkness that had engulfed her as she slipped into the trance.

Her heart thrummed, a relentless pounding she could feel in her spine. God, how long had she been out? Hours? What had happened during those unguarded moments? Cole must have drugged her and done—what? Was this all some sort of set-up to get back at her for dragging him through the ordeal of her lawsuit years ago?

"Focus, damn it!" Rowan's whisper was sharp, a blade cleaving through the haze.

She swung her legs over the side of the bed, her feet sinking into the thick rug beneath. The room swayed around her as she stood, her legs unsteady beneath her weight. She stumbled to a gilt-framed mirror, searching her reflection for signs of something she couldn't name. Violation? Possession? The woman in the mirror barely resembled the one she knew —ginger hair disheveled, haunted green eyes staring back, ringed by dark circles.

Rowan gritted her teeth, willing herself to push through the disorientation and the pounding in her head. She needed answers, and she needed them now.

She staggered toward the door, hand outstretched, fingers grazing the cool metal of the handle. She hesitated, a flicker of uncertainty crossing her features. Was she still a guest in this place? Or a prisoner?

"Time to face the music," she whispered, steeling herself for whatever lay on the other side of that door.

With one last glance at the stranger in the mirror, she

turned the handle and was relieved to find it unlocked.

"Cole?" she called out, her voice hoarse.

No answer.

Her footsteps rang on the hardwood as she marched down one empty hallway after another, searching the mansion. The corridor opened up into the grand foyer, the vaulted ceiling disappearing into the gloom above. Rowan paused, her eyes scanning the room for any sign of life. But the mansion remained silent.

She found him in the conservatory.

Cole stood with his back to her, his tattooed form silhouetted against the towering windows. Cold gray light bathed the room, the overcast sky casting an eerie pallor over the lush foliage.

Rowan's footsteps echoed on the marble floor as she strode toward him, her anger building with each step. He turned at the sound of her approach, his icy eyes locking onto hers with an intensity that prickled her skin.

"You're awake."

"What the hell did you do to me?" Rowan demanded, her fury shattering the fragile serenity of the room. "Tell me what happened!"

Cole's lips curved into something like a smirk. "You're asking the wrong questions, Rowan."

"Don't fuck around with me, Cole," she snapped. "How'd I end up on that bed and what did you do to me while I was out?"

A flicker of annoyance crossed Cole's face, but he quickly composed himself. "You collapsed after the ritual. I carried you there and made sure you were comfortable. Nothing more."

"What exactly happened last night?" she pressed. "Did you hypnotize me or something? I had these dreams of—"

"Dreams? They weren't dreams, Rowan."

Rowan stared at him. "What—what are you saying? That what I saw was real?" Her voice faltered, the image of Daley's mutilated body flashing before her eyes. The metallic scent of blood still lingered in her memory, too vivid to be imagined. "You can't be serious."

Cole's silence hung heavy in the air, neither confirming nor denying the bloody reality of her vengeance. And in that moment, Rowan understood the true cost of her grief-fueled rage, a price paid not in flesh and blood, but in the tattered remnants of her own humanity.

"What did we do?" she whispered, her plea a blend of hope and horror. "What did *I* do?"

"Nothing you didn't ask for." Cole's gaze locked with hers, his voice a low rumble that reverberated through the stillness of the conservatory. "The ritual… it worked, Rowan. You did it. Daley, Troy—they're dead. Both of them."

Rowan's stomach churned, bile rising in her throat. She had wanted this, yearned for it with every fiber of her being, yet now, the confirmation sliced through her like an ax.

"Impossible," she uttered in disbelief. "Troy was locked up, guarded—"

"Dead," Cole interrupted. "It's all over the news. Both of your daughter's killers butchered in one night—one of them behind bars, his guards untouched, unaware. The police don't even know where to start, but we… we know the answer, don't we?"

Rowan felt the world tilt beneath her feet. She gripped the edge of a nearby pedestal, her knuckles turning white. "No," she whispered, even though part of her felt a perverse thrill at the news. "I don't believe you. I need proof. I need to see it for myself."

Cole studied her for a long moment, his expression unreadable. Then he brushed by her and left the conservatory. Rowan got the impression she should follow. She trailed after him down a winding hallway and through a set of double-doors to a large home theater.

A faint electric buzzing whispered in her ears as she entered. It grew into a low hum as she approached the massive projection screen that took up an entire wall. Plush, burgundy carpeting, soft and bouncy underfoot, lined the floor, and leather chairs with gently yielding armrests filled the room. Unlike the oil paintings in the mansion's other rooms, impeccable woodcut engravings, reminiscent of Gustave Doré's work, decorated this room. Rowan noticed they all featured the same subject…the devil.

Cole moved to a control panel, his tattooed fingers dancing over the buttons. The massive screen flickered to life, bathing the room in an eerie glow. He flipped through the channels until he reached a news anchor mid-coverage—CNN's Tom Earnshaw looking grim-faced.

"…a chilling story of mystery and intrigue that has left two communities reeling. Two men, both connected by a dark chapter in their pasts, were found dead under suspicious circumstances this morning—despite being miles apart. Let's hear more from Rene Carroll at our Boston affiliate, WCVB."

The coverage cut to a junior reporter with hair like Rachel from *Friends*. She stood in front of the police tape surrounding the crime scene that was now Daley Banks' apartment.

"Good morning, Tom," she said, her breath misting in the cold air. "The deaths of Daley Banks and Troy Chapman are sending shockwaves through Massachusetts this morning. Both men were infamously convicted seven years ago as teenagers in the brutal murder of their classmate, Lily Pierce—a crime that horrified the city of Lynn and captivated national attention. Now, in a grim twist, both men are dead under mysterious circumstances."

A split screen of Banks and Chapman's sullen teenaged faces filled the screen while the reporter's voice-over continued. "Daley Banks, 22, was discovered in his apartment here in Dorchester early this morning. He had been granted early parole just last month and released from MCI Shirley earlier this week, following a controversial decision by the state parole board. Police have not confirmed the cause of death but describe the scene as 'disturbing.'"

The coverage cut to a sound bite of a recorded interview with a grizzled man outside Banks' apartment. The chyron at the bottom of the screen read LEO STANKEY, VICTIM'S NEIGHBOR.

"It's scary," the man said, rubbing a hand over his chin. "He just moved in a few days ago. I mean, this isn't the greatest neighborhood, but I can't believe something like this happened right here."

The reporter's live feed took over again. "Meanwhile, thirty miles away at Bridgewater State Hospital, Troy Chapman—

Banks' co-defendant in the Pierce murder case—was found dead in his locked cell early this morning. Following his conviction and sentencing to life without the possibility of parole, Chapman successfully petitioned the court for a transfer to the secure facility Bridgewater for mental health treatment in 1992. Authorities are calling his death 'suspicious' but have not elaborated further."

The feed switched to a wide shot of the police action outside Bridgewater. Flashing squad car lights and detectives coming and going. "Sources inside the facility describe heightened security measures and an intense investigation underway. Chapman's death has left fellow inmates and staff shaken."

Rowan felt her legs giving way beneath her and she sank into a chair, her eyes transfixed on the screen. Distant memories of the crime scenes flashed through her mind, the blood-soaked walls and the twisted, mangled remains of the men who had taken her daughter from her. Horror washed over her, seeping into her bones and chilling her to the core.

Oh God, it's true. It's all true...

The broadcast returned to the reporter. "This morning, authorities are remaining tight-lipped about whether these deaths are connected. No details have been released regarding suspects, motives, or the circumstances surrounding the scenes. Both the Boston Police Department and investigators at Bridgewater declined to comment on ongoing investigations."

The screen split to include Tom Earnshaw in the CNN studio. "So many unanswered questions this morning," he said. "And as you said, Rene, the timing and connection between these two men cannot be ignored."

"That's right, Tom. The eerie synchronicity of these deaths has left many wondering: Was this a coincidence, or could someone be targeting these men for their role in Lily Pierce's murder? We'll continue to follow this story closely and provide updates as they become available."

"Thank you, Sarah," Earnshaw said. "A disturbing and mysterious story indeed. Coming up next, the latest on—"

"Turn it off," Rowan whispered, unable to bear the sight any longer. Cole obliged, silencing Earnshaw's voice and plunging the room into silence once more.

"God, what have we done?" Rowan gasped.

"We've balanced the scales," Cole replied, his eyes flashing with a mixture of triumph and something darker. "An eye for an eye."

She turned to face him. "Balance? This isn't balance, Cole. It's butchery."

"Is it?" His gaze bored into her. "Tell me you don't feel a shred of relief knowing they can't hurt anyone else."

Rowan shook her head. She remembered Banks as she saw him in his apartment—a pitiful, broken man shattered by his years behind bars. He wasn't a threat to anyone, not anymore.

"No, this… this isn't what I wanted," her words came out in a choked whisper. "I never meant for it to happen like this."

"Ah, but you did," Cole countered. His presence was overwhelming, the intensity of his gaze making Rowan's skin tingle. "Don't pretend you didn't want this, that you didn't pray for their suffering every goddamn night. You made a choice, Rowan. You chose wrath over forgiveness, darkness over light. There's no coming back from that."

Rowan flinched, but she couldn't deny the truth in his words. She had dreamed of this moment, fantasized about it in the darkest corners of her mind. But now that it was here, now that it was over, she felt only a sickening sense of horror and regret. She wanted to believe him, wanted to embrace the righteousness of their actions. But the guilt was too strong, the mortification too overwhelming.

"I wanted justice," she murmured, more to herself than to Cole. "But this… Is this what Lily would have wanted? To have her mother making pacts with—what? Demons? What the fuck did we summon, Cole? What was that thing?"

Cole crouched beside her, his presence both comforting and unsettling. "Rowan, it's not easy to explain—"

"Try!" Her anger boiled over, frustration and fear fueling her outburst. "How can you act so calm? We *butchered* people, Cole. We called on something unholy to slaughter two men. How am I supposed to live with that?"

The weight of her actions pressed down on her, suffocating her. She had blood on her hands now, the blood of the men she had wished dead for so long. But instead of the satisfaction she had hoped for, all she felt was a hollow emptiness, a void that could never be filled.

"No," Rowan said, her voice barely above a whisper. "I made a mistake. This isn't what Lily would have wanted. This isn't who I am."

Cole tilted his head. "Who you were, maybe. But trauma changes us, Rowan. It's time to embrace that change."

Rowan's eyes slid shut, the weight of his words settling on

her shoulders like a physical burden. He was right—she had made her choice, and now she had to live with the consequences.

"How is this even possible, Cole?" she sighed. "Demons, magic, supernatural vengeance—these things don't exist. They can't."

Cole's mouth twitched into a grim smile. "The old ways have power, Rowan. You offered your pain, your rage… and something answered. The occult isn't just smoke and mirrors. It's real, and it's ancient. And now you've seen it for yourself."

Rowan shuddered, remembering the dreadful sensation of being intertwined with her dead daughter while she tore men limb from limb. She had wanted this, hadn't she? But now, faced with the gruesome reality…

"I don't know how to do this," she whispered, her voice cracking. "I don't know how to be the person I've become, the one who conjured a creature who could do this."

Cole's hand found hers, his fingers lacing through her own. "You'll learn," he murmured, his breath ghosting across her cheek. "I did."

Rowan's eyes fluttered open, meeting Cole's gaze. In that moment, she saw a flicker of understanding, a recognition of the shared pain that bound them together. They were two lost souls, adrift in a world that had taken everything from them.

"I… I can't…" Rowan stumbled to her feet, her vision blurred by tears. She needed to escape, to find a way to make sense of the chaos that had engulfed her life.

Cole reached for her. "Rowan, wait—"

But she was already gone, fleeing the room without

another word. She didn't know where she was going, only that she needed to leave Cole and the devastating truth behind her.

Chapter 8

The sea air whipped at Rowan's face and stung her eyes as she fled across the manicured grounds to the rocky shoreline, her feet carrying her away from the mansion and the horrifying reality of what she had done. A salty wind clawed at her skin, its icy fingers like an angry sea creature. The sky was a heavy and foreboding gray—a perfect mirror to the storm raging within her.

I'm a murderer. I took their lives, just as they took Lily's…

Each word was a knot around her heart.

Yet despite the turmoil threatening to drown her, a small voice whispered in the back of her mind—a voice that sounded achingly like Lily's. It spoke a truth Rowan couldn't admit to herself—that her remorse was an act. She was saying the right things; what she imagined a decent person should think and feel after taking someone's life. But secretly, she knew Cole was right about her. After all, just days ago, she'd been determined to shoot Daley Banks dead in public. She may have lost her nerve in the moment, but she hadn't stopped believing that Daley and Troy deserved to die for what they'd done to Lily.

No. What disturbed Rowan the most wasn't that they were dead—it was the *pleasure* she had taken in their slaughter.

In her darkest fantasies, she always saw herself avenging her daughter with the detached composure of a hangman. It was nothing more than a task that required fulfillment, the righting of a wrong so that Rowan could move on and start healing. Good people weren't supposed to take pleasure in killing—only monsters like Daley and Troy did that.

So what did that say about her now?

The weight of her self-loathing bore down on her. And it wasn't just what she had done that horrified her—it was *how* she did it. She still couldn't believe any of it was real. Her head spun with the revelations Cole had thrust upon her, the reality of the occult powers they had unleashed. She had always been a woman of logic, of reason. She had smiled politely at the funerals when well-wishing mourners assured her Alex and Lily were *in a better place*. But she'd never actually believed it. Until last night, she had been certain there was no heaven or hell except the ones we made for ourselves.

But now, she found herself adrift in a sea of the impossible. It still seemed too fantastical to believe. She'd practiced black magic—and it had worked. What did that make her? Some sort of witch? And if demons were real, what else lay hidden beyond the realm of human perception? Did Heaven exist? Were Lily and Alex there? And what if Hell existed? What would that mean for Rowan's own eternal fate?

Her pace slowed, her shoes crunching on the pebbles as she reached the water's edge. The wind fluttered her wool sweater and the briny scent of the ocean filled her lungs, displacing the metallic tang of blood that lingered in her nostrils. With each thunderous crash of the waves, fragments of the ritual flashed before her eyes—the lighting flickering in the studio, the haunting melodies that held her spellbound, the otherworldly presence that had answered her call.

Through blurred vision, Rowan watched as the sea foam gathered and retreated. She shivered from a chill that seemed to come from within, a bone-deep cold that no amount of clothing could chase away. The waves crashed with a deafening roar that drowned out the chaos of her thoughts. She stood there on the damp sand, her body trembling as she felt something inside her begin to fracture.

Was there no other way?

The question thrashed within her like a living thing desperate to escape. There was no simple answer, only the painful recognition that some wounds may never heal, and some ghosts may never be laid to rest.

"Your mom really fucked up, kiddo," she whispered, a bitter laugh escaping her lips. Her words dissolved into the salty mist that rose like wraiths from the churning sea. "I thought this would bring us peace. But this… this feels like something else entirely."

Above her, the sky was a tapestry of gray, the clouds hanging low and mournful. Rowan's gaze traced the tumultuous waves crashing against the shore. The ocean's fury seemed to beckon her, inviting her to cast off the shackles of her anguish and disappear beneath the frothing crests.

Instead, she bent her thoughts toward the pragmatic. What would the cops make of the murders? Without a doubt, they'd already realized that the simultaneous executions of two of the most heinous and notorious murderers of the past decade were too perfectly timed to be a mere coincidence. Would they eventually trace the killings back to Rowan? She was an obvious suspect—who else had such a powerful motive to see the pair of convicts dead?

More questions flitted through her mind. Had she left any evidence behind at the crime scenes? And what was there to leave? Any fingerprints they found would belong to—who? Lily? A razor-taloned demon? And then there was the fact that Troy had been safely locked up and guarded in a state facility. It's not like Rowan could have simply walked in and slaughtered him in his bed. The police would have to assume it was an inside job.

But Daley Banks was a different story.

Rowan suspected she could at least expect a visit from the police asking about her whereabouts. She could only imagine the scene currently unfolding back at her house on Pennybrook Lane. Were the cops already there, knocking at her door? What would she tell them when they tracked her down? That she'd spent the night with Cole Abel, her hated nemesis? What kind of alibi would that be? And would Cole even back up her story? Or would he wash his hands of the whole affair and dodge accountability yet again?

Rowan stared out at the horizon, where the gray waves met the gray sky in a seamless curtain of desolation. There was no comfort here, no absolution—only the stark reality that her life had irrevocably changed yet again.

Cole had promised her vengeance, a way to silence the screams that haunted her nights. But in their wake, the quiet was oppressive, heavy with the ghosts of the two men she had massacred. As she watched the ceaseless dance of the waves, she understood that her quest for retribution had bound her to Cole in ways she had never expected, weaving their fates together with threads darker than any metal anthem he had ever sung.

Another shiver coursed through her body, though whether from the cold or the dawning realization of her actions, she couldn't tell. She wrapped her arms around her sweater as if to hold together pieces of herself that threatened to shatter.

Maybe Cole was right. Maybe she would learn to live with herself.

Or maybe they were just dragging each other further into the darkness.

The wind whipped around her, tugging at her hair and stinging her eyes as she stared into the distant horizon. The sea before her roiled with untamed power, vast and relentless.

Then, a glimpse of something out of place in the ocean's fury caught her eye—a figure flailing helplessly amidst the towering waves.

Rowan's heart skidded.

Someone was out there, arms thrashing, struggling desperately against the water's wrath.

"Damn it," Rowan cursed under her breath. The raw instinct to rescue surged through her, eclipsing her own turmoil. "Hey!" she shouted over the roar of the waves. Could her voice even carry across the distance? "Hold on!"

The figure was a mere speck against the vastness of the ocean. Rowan stole a glance back at the mansion. There was no sign of Cole. Every second mattered; there wasn't time to get help. Adrenaline shot through her veins and her heart surged like the ocean waves crashing against the shore. She tried to remember what Alex had taught her about hypothermia. In water that cold, she would last —what? About thirty minutes? She sized up the distance to the figure. She was a strong swimmer, but in those waves, the current might sweep them both out to sea.

Still, she had to at least try. She couldn't stand there and watch a person drown. She'd seen enough death, and now she was being offered a shot at redemption. And after all she'd been through, she wasn't sure if she cared if she lived or died.

The frigid shock of the water pierced her skin like a thousand needles as she kicked off her shoes and plunged into the churning waves. She gasped, her breath stolen by the icy embrace, but she pushed on, driven by the same unwavering force that had compelled her husband to rush headlong into burning buildings.

"Keep fighting!" she yelled, her voice straining against the roar of the surf. The waves battered her body, saltwater filling her mouth and nose. Her strokes were long and purposeful as she fought against the current, timing her exertions with the rise and fall of the crests.

The figure bobbed helplessly, a pale hand slicing through the violent waves. Rowan's arms cut through the churning water, her relentless pace pushing her to the brink of exhaustion. She felt her strength waning in the freezing water, her burning muscles threatening to give out, but she refused to give up. Not now. Not when she was so close.

The figure came into clearer view—a girl struggling to stay afloat. She was close now, but not close enough to make out her face. How did she get out here? Did she slip off the rocks somewhere further up the point? Swept overboard from a boat?

Closer now, the struggling form became clearer.

"Take my hand!" Rowan shouted when the girl was within arm's reach.

The girl grasped her outstretched hand with the desperation of the drowning. She spun around in the water.

Rowan's blood froze, the icy grip of horror sinking its teeth deep into her soul. "No," she gasped, her voice lost to the roaring waves. "It can't be."

But there was no mistaking the familiar face.

It was Lily.

A grotesque semblance of her daughter's visage stared back at Rowan as they bobbed and tossed in the surf. Malice twisted Lily's features, and her lips curled into a sinister smile, revealing rows of razor-sharp teeth. She opened her mouth, and Lily's voice poured out, distorted and layered with malevolence.

"You can't save me, Mommy," she hissed, mimicking Lily in a cruel mockery that sent a cold tide through Rowan's veins. Her eyes glowed red, her mouth stretching into a wicked grin. "You're too late. You're always too late."

Rowan recoiled, the shock crashing over her like the relentless waves. This wasn't her daughter, the girl she had loved more than life itself.

This was the demon. The abomination wearing Lily's face.

Rowan's heart shattered anew, the jagged pieces lodging in her throat. She treaded water, paralyzed with terror. The demon laughed, a sound that chilled Rowan to her core. In a heartbeat, it lunged at her, fingers elongating into razor-sharp claws.

"Christ!" Rowan gasped, throwing her arms up instinctively. The claws raked across her forearms, drawing blood that mixed with the churning sea. She reeled back and swung her fist, aiming for the grotesque parody of her daughter. But the creature was swift, ducking beneath the water with serpentine grace. Rowan's knuckles sliced through empty space, and she felt the cold grasp of hands—too many hands—around her ankles, pulling her down into the abyss. She thrashed wildly, fighting both the demon and her own rising panic.

The pressure increased as they sank deeper, squeezing Rowan's chest like a vice. Her lungs burned, screaming for air. In the murky depths, she could just make out the Lily's twisted grin, a promise of oblivion.

This is how your daughter felt. The demon's voice slithered through her mind, unbidden and cruel. *Alone. Helpless. Terrified.*

Rowan's movements grew sluggish, her strength ebbing. How long had she been in the frigid water? Ten minutes? Fifteen? The sea seemed to whisper, offering an end to her pain, her guilt. For a moment, she was tempted to give in and let the darkness claim her.

But something within her rebelled. A spark of the same determination that had driven her for seven years flared to life. She would not die here, not like this.

With a silent roar, she summoned every ounce of strength left in her battered frame. She kicked violently, her heel connecting a solid blow. The creature's grip loosened, just enough for Rowan to break free.

She kicked away, her lungs burning as she propelled herself upward. Hope, fragile but fierce, bloomed in her chest. The surface shimmered above, tantalizingly close.

Rowan reached… reached… reached…

Her fingertips just grazed the surface when Lily surged up from the depths, her ghastly face now twisted with fury. Water churned around them as she lashed out, her claw-like fingers reaching for Rowan's throat. Lily's nails dug into her flesh with an iron grip, drawing pinpricks of blood that swirled in the murky water.

No! Rowan's mind screamed, her body thrashing. The brief moment of hope crashed into soul-crushing despair as the depths reclaimed her.

She kicked desperately, her movements growing weaker with each passing second. Together, they sank deeper and deeper into the inky water. Lily's face loomed before her, a hideous mockery of her girlish features contorted in malicious glee. The saltwater stung Rowan's eyes and blurred her vision, darkness creeping at the edges as the thing inside her daughter constricted her throat. She clawed weakly at Lily's wrists, her strength fading. But it wasn't enough. Lily's grip only tightened, her fingers digging into Rowan's windpipe, cutting off what little oxygen remained. Every cell in Rowan's body screamed for air and her lungs felt ready to burst. Her pulse roared like a waterfall, drowning out every thought. The cold embrace of the sea became her world, the icy depths pulling at her consciousness, threatening to drag her into oblivion.

I'm going to die, Rowan realized with a sickening certainty.

Just like I deserve.

But something snapped deep within her. A spark ignited—a fierce, primal need to survive. With a surge of adrenaline that set her nerves ablaze, she reached out and raked her nails across Lily's face, furrowing the skin from eyes to chin.

The demon inside her daughter let out a furious roar and recoiled. Rowan seized the moment and wrenched herself free from the creature's grip. She kicked frantically, driven by pure terror, propelling herself upwards, toward the distant glimmer of light that promised salvation. Closer and closer she swam toward a surface that seemed to dance just out of reach. With a final, desperate lunge, she broke through, gasping and choking.

The taste of salt and bile mingled on her tongue as she heaved and gulped lungfuls of precious air. The relentless waves slammed into her, tossing her around like a rag-doll. Every muscle in her body ached and burned from the brutal struggle. The sea threatened to swallow her again as she fought with every last ounce of energy she had left. But her limbs felt heavy and wouldn't respond to her will. She was starting to feel the first effects of hypothermia, and she knew she would drown if she didn't get back to shore soon.

Suddenly, strong arms encircled her waist from behind. The grip was firm, human. With a powerful surge, Rowan felt herself being pulled through the surf, further away from the submerged creature that wore her daughter's face like a grotesque mask. Through the haze of wild panic, she heard a familiar, gruff voice.

"I've got you," Cole grunted, his tattooed arms keeping her afloat. "Just hold on."

Rowan's fingers dug into Cole's skin as they battled against the churning sea, inching toward the safety of the shore. Rowan's muscles screamed in protest, but she kept pushing, driven by a determination that surprised even her.

As they neared the beach, a strong wave propelled them forward. They stumbled onto the sand and Rowan's legs gave way beneath her. She collapsed against Cole, her chest heaving as she shivered uncontrollably and struggled to catch her breath. The adrenaline that had fueled her during the fight was dissipating now, leaving her feeling drained and vulnerable. For a moment, she allowed herself to lean into his strength, her heart quaking like the ground before an earthquake, trembling on the brink. Then, with a shuddering breath, she pulled away.

"What the fuck was that, Cole?" she sputtered through her chattering teeth. "What is happening?"

Cole didn't answer. His gaze remained fixed on the restless waves, alert and searching. But there was no sign of Lily. When he faced her, Rowan saw something in his eyes that she didn't think he was capable of.

Fear.

"We opened a door," he said, his words heavy with grim realization. "And something far worse than we imagined came through."

Chapter 9

Water dripped from Rowan's clothes and formed a growing puddle on the floor around her as she stood by the raging fireplace in Cole's spacious library. Her hair clung to her cheeks in wild, wet tendrils. Her teeth chattered uncontrollably, the heat of the flames slowly melting away the cold that had settled deep in her bones.

"Tell me," she demanded, her voice a low growl barely heard over the crackle of firewood. "What did we summon last night? What was that thing, and why did it try to kill me?"

Cole's eyes reflected the firelight as he handed her a thick towel and wrapped another around his own broad shoulders. Gray sunlight filtered through the large windows, casting a pale glow on the rows of books and arcane curios displayed in glass cases throughout the library. A rolling ladder propped against one wall allowed for easier access to the higher shelves.

A muscle clenched in Cole's jaw as he weighed his words. The tattoos on his neck twitched as if the blades had a life of their own. "It's... ancient," he said, his voice low and strained.

"Like what, then? Satan?"

Cole's lip bent with a sneer. "Christianity is a myth, Rowan. Only the Church would be so arrogant to believe it invented evil. This… this is much, much older. Older than anything in existence. A demon of immense power and malevolence that enforces the will of the underworld gods and punishes those who try to escape their fate."

"Like Daley and Troy," Rowan said.

Cole nodded. "We simply gave it a target to focus on."

Rowan closed her eyes and thought of Daley Banks and the terrible memories the demon had pushed into his mind and forced him to relive. She heard the echoes of its voice taunting her in the water, the dreadful things it had accused her of. "I saw her face," she choked out, the image of Lily's ghastly visage burning behind her eyelids. "It wore my daughter's face."

Cole frowned. "This thing… It's not just some mindless force. It's intelligent, calculating. It's not enough for it to drag the souls of the guilty to Hell. It needs to punish its victims first, to torment them."

A chill that had nothing to do with her wet clothes ran through Rowan. "Then why did it turn on me?"

"I don't know," Cole admitted. "The demon was supposed to be your vessel, but for some reason, it's hungry for more than we'd ever intended to give. I didn't think—"

"Clearly," Rowan cut in, her green eyes hardening like shards of glass. "You never do!"

Cole squared his shoulders as if bracing against a blow. "Rowan, I—" he began, only to be silenced by the sharp slice of her hand cutting through the space separating them.

"Because of you," she spat out each word with venom, "my daughter—"

Her throat constricted, choking off the rest of the sentence. Damn him. Damn his secrets and his lies. She had trusted him, let him lead her down this wicked path. And for what? More questions than answers. More darkness than light.

"You never once stop to consider the consequences of your actions, do you?" Rowan's fists clenched at her sides. She stalked closer, so close she could smell the salt on his skin. "All you do is cause chaos and destruction everywhere you go, without a care for who gets hurt. Summoning a demon, glorifying violence to kids—and let's not forget the man you nearly killed! Is there any line you won't cross?"

She shoved him hard, her palms striking his chest as if it were a block of granite.

He flinched as the sudden burst of aggression caught him off-guard. His jaw tightened and his face darkened as something sharp and angry flashed in his eyes. His fists balled at his sides, and Rowan could see the angles of his knuckles jutting out. It was an instinctive reflex, lasting barely an instant before it vanished. But something about that look in his eyes suddenly made her feel uneasy being alone in this house with him. For the first time, she saw the danger lurking in the former metal frontman. Cole might have just saved her life, but he'd also already been charged with attempted murder once before. What could he be capable of if she pushed him too far?

She stepped back, wondering what had triggered him. Was it that she had struck him? Or that she had brought up his dark past? Her gaze raked over him. The knives inked across his throat seemed to mock her, a silent reminder of the sharp edge they both danced upon.

"You said you knew what you were doing," she hissed. "You promised me answers, but all you've done is unleash hell on both of us. It's not done with me, is it? I can feel it. Like part of us is still linked."

Cole met her gaze and ran a hand over his stubbled jaw. The tattoos on his forearm rippled like dark snakes in the firelight. "I didn't know this would happen, Rowan. I swear it. I told you these forces were unlike any I've ever invoked."

Rowan squeezed her eyes shut, trying to block out the horrifying memories of the demon's attack. But they still came flooding in behind her eyelids in vivid detail. The icy grip of Lily's fingers pierced her skin, sending a jolt of terror through her body. She gasped for air, feeling the burning sensation in her lungs as she struggled to break free from her daughter's grasp. Even with her eyes closed, she could still feel every terrifying moment, the images swimming and swirling, taunting her with the memory of that dreadful encounter and the awful certainty of another.

When she opened her eyes again, the green of her irises was hard as stone. "I blamed myself for so long, Cole," she said. "I carried the guilt of Lily's death like a goddamn anchor around my neck, dragging me down into the depths of despair. But now I see the truth. *You* brought this darkness into our lives. You and your damn music. And now you've damned me as well."

Cole reached out, as if to bridge the chasm that had opened between them. "Rowan, please. I never wanted to hurt you or anyone else. I was lost without my music, trying to find a new way through the pain, just like you."

Rowan slapped his hand away, the sound cracking like a whip in the room's stillness. "Don't you dare compare your pain to mine. You have no idea what it's like to lose a child, to have your entire world ripped away from you in a single, horrific moment."

She turned from him, her shoulders shaking with the force of her emotions. The firelight cast her shadow on the wall, a looming, distorted figure that seemed to embody the darkness that had consumed her life.

"I want answers, Cole," she said. "I want to know how to stop this demon from coming after me again. And if you can't give me that, then I swear to God, I'll find someone who can, even if I have to walk through the gates of Hell itself to do it."

Cole looked into the fire and slicked his hair back from his face, the black strands still wet with saltwater. Silence stretched between them, taut as a hangman's noose.

"Devin might know," he said at last.

"Devin?" Rowan's brow furrowed, her mistrust of him simmering beneath the surface like a festering wound.

"My old guitarist," Cole explained. "If anyone has the answers, it's him. He's the only one who might know what went wrong… and how to stop this thing."

"Then we need to see him. Now."

Cole shook his head, a humorless laugh escaping his lips. "It's not that simple. Devin and I haven't spoken in years. After the band broke up, he disappeared. Went off the grid."

Rowan's lips twisted into a bitter smile. "Of course he did.

Nothing can ever be simple, can it?"

"Nothing worth doing ever is," Cole quipped.

Rowan stepped closer, mere inches away now as he towered over her, his presence an imposing wall of muscle and ink. "You don't have a choice, Cole. We need him. I need him. And if you can't find him, then I will."

Cole hesitated, his blue eyes clouded with doubt as he stared into the fire. Its flickering light cast shadows across his face.

Devin...

The name conjured images of smoky bars and screaming crowds and thundering stadiums, of sweat-soaked nights spent pouring their souls into the music that had become their lifeblood. But it also brought with it the bitter taste of betrayal, of bridges burned and friendships shattered.

"Devin... he might not want to be found," Cole said. "And even if we do, there's no telling if he can—or will—help us."

"Then we have no choice but to make him," Rowan countered, her jaw set in a hard line. She paced in front of the hearth, her feet splashing through the shallow puddles on the hardwood.

"Convincing a man who's turned his back on the world won't be easy," Cole said

"Neither is being hunted by the ghost of your child."

Cole's expression softened, the fight draining from him as the weight of Rowan's sorrow bore down upon him. "Alright," he said, but the word was heavy with reluctance. "But remember, Devin's no saint. He's got his own demons. He was into some heavy occult shit. Went further down the rabbit hole than any of us and never came back up. Last I heard, he was a junkie living in his cabin up in the White Mountains."

"Then that's where we'll start," Rowan said. "We'll drag him into the light, one way or another." She let out a shaky breath. It wasn't much, but it was a start.

A little over thirty minutes later, Rowan marched through the corridors of the mansion, her shoes pounding against the cold stone floor with a purpose that matched the fury in her heart. She had changed into a dry pair of ripped black jeans Cole had given her. At first, she flatly refused, shuddering to imagine who had owned them, why they were at his house, and if they had ever been washed. But he had convinced her that the two-hour drive to Devin's last known address would be more comfortable if she wasn't still sodden with seawater. He'd also given her a black Haruspex t-shirt and hoodie, the band's jagged and imposing logo now emblazoned across her chest.

She felt like a groupie.

If only Lily could see me now…

Her mind conjured images of the dangers ahead, of the horrors they might face. But she pushed them aside. Beneath the fear, a flicker of hope burned within her. If Devin could help them, if they could find a way to stop the demon…

Cole followed close behind, his shadow looming large and foreboding as they approached the heavy oak doors of the mansion. Their previous clash still hung heavy in the air between them, but the gravity of their situation had finally sunk its fangs into their pride.

Together, they pushed open the doors. The chilly air

brushed against their skin, carrying with it the scent of impending rain and the distant peal of thunder. The door slammed shut behind them with a resounding finality.

A dense fog had settled over the sprawling estate. The gravel crunched beneath their feet as they crossed the circular driveway, passing Rowan's car on their way to Cole's massive garage.

"Keep your eyes open," Cole whispered, his voice barely rising above the rustle of the leaves that trembled in the gloom.

Rowan nodded, her jaw set. "This place feels alive," she said, the words tinged with unease.

The garage doors stood open, revealing a trio of impressive vehicles. The first was a sleek custom chopper motorcycle, its chrome glinting in the light. Next to it sat a classic Dodge Challenger R/T, its curves and lines gleaming with an air of muscular power. But the most imposing presence was commanded by the new Land Rover Defender, jacked up and armed to the teeth with menacing features that seemed custom-built for urban warfare. All three machines were uniformly dressed in jet black, accented with bold pops of fiery red detailing that added a dangerous edge to their already impressive appearance.

A hidden smile tugged at Rowan's lips despite herself. Cole's impressive taste in art had thrown her, but this brawny temple of testosterone was exactly what she expected from him. There was nothing flashy here—no exotic European coupes or speedsters—just raw power. Rowan's late husband, Alex, had been a gear-head; he would have drooled over these machines.

Cole's eyes scanned the murky fog as he led the way to the Land Rover and unlocked the passenger door. Rowan paused, her hand on the door handle. She looked back at the mansion, its windows dark and empty. For a moment, she could have sworn she saw a flicker of movement, a shadow darting across the glass.

"Did you see that?" she whispered, her heart pounding in her chest.

Cole followed her gaze, his brow furrowed. "See what?"

Rowan shook her head, trying to calm her racing thoughts. "Nothing. It's just… I feel like we're being watched."

Cole's expression hardened, his hand tightening on his keys. "I feel it too."

Rowan swallowed hard, her mouth suddenly dry. The reality of their situation crashed down upon her, the weight of it almost too much to bear. They were facing an enemy they barely understood, a force that seemed to defy all reason and logic.

"Do you really think Devin can help us?" she asked, her voice low and uncertain.

"Maybe," Cole shrugged. "Or he might lead us straight to our graves."

Chapter 10

The Land Rover's windshield wipers slashed through the rain as it cut a path through the White Mountains, its headlights nothing but dim beacons in the relentless downpour. Cole's hands gripped the steering wheel, his knuckles bone-white against the dark leather. Rowan sat silent and brooding beside him, her eyes fixed on the blurred forest beyond the rain-streaked glass.

The truck's luxurious interior felt like a cramped cocoon of tension that shrank with every mile they covered. Rowan's thoughts churned with every misgiving that spiraled unchecked through her mind, a maelstrom of conflicting emotions. She could still hear the demon's whispers echoing in her memory, insidious and alluring, promising power and retribution. She shuddered, the memory of its touch lingering like a cold caress. How could something so vile feel so familiar, so intricately connected to her very being?

And then there was Cole, a man she had once despised, now an unlikely ally. His revelations had shaken her, opening her eyes to possibilities she could never have imagined. She couldn't deny the growing bond between them, forged in the fires of their shared pain and purpose.

A sharp gust of wind buffeted the truck, jolting Rowan from her reverie. Cole corrected the vehicle's course with a firm hand and shifted in his seat, the tattoos on his throat flexing with a swallow. His presence was a constant challenge, a question mark that loomed over her ability to trust him. Not for the first time, Rowan got the impression he was hiding something from her. Did he know more about the demon than he was letting on? She remembered the stark look of fear on his face back on the beach. Was he more frightened than he was willing to admit?

"Storm's getting worse," Rowan said, the first words she'd voiced in over an hour. "How much further?"

"Not far," Cole replied, his tone steady despite the raindrops pelting the windshield. His gaze remained locked on the road, but he seemed acutely aware of Rowan's scrutiny, of the possibility that she might glimpse the apprehension he was working hard to conceal.

"Should we even be driving in this?" Rowan asked.

"We don't have a choice," Cole grumbled. There was no turning back, not until they had figured out the strange link between Rowan and the demon they had conjured.

"Feels like we're driving through purgatory," Rowan muttered. She could feel the tension coiled like barbed wire within her.

"Or heading straight for it." Cole flicked the wipers to their maximum speed, slicing through the opaque wall of rain that veiled the mountain road ahead.

Thud. Thud. Thud.

The truck's powerful engine hummed a low dirge, harmonizing with the thrum of water against metal. Each swerve around the mountain's curves was a delicate brush with danger. Cole's hands remained steady on the wheel, but the cab was feeling like a coffin, the silence hanging as heavy as the storm clouds above.

Rowan glanced sideways at Cole, taking in the rigid set of his jaw. His daunting presence filled the confined space, and she felt a sudden need to break the suffocating silence again. She glanced down at the jagged logo blazing across her own chest.

"Haruspex," she said abruptly, the word cutting through the drone of the downpour. "What does it mean?"

Cole's eyebrows lifted slightly. He was quiet for a moment as he shifted in his seat. "It's an ancient Etruscan practice," he replied. "A haruspex was a priest who would divine the future by examining the entrails of sacrificed animals."

Rowan's stomach churned at the image. "Charming," she muttered, imagining dark rituals and innocent blood spilled upon pagan altars. The macabre imagery conjured memories of her daughter's brutal murder and she swallowed hard, pushing down the rising tide of grief.

Cole's lips twitched in a humorless smile. "It fit the music. The darkness. The search for meaning in chaos and pain."

Rowan studied his profile, noting the tension in his jaw. "And the occult connection appealed to you?"

"I've always been drawn to the shadows," Cole admitted. "The forbidden. I found power there when I had none."

"And now?" she asked, unable to keep the edge from her voice.

Cole's gaze remained fixed on the road ahead. "Now I know the price."

The conversation lapsed into silence once more. Rowan turned to stare out the window, her mind a whirlpool of conflicting emotions. The occult influences that had driven her daughter's killers, the twisted beliefs that had fueled their violence—how could his music not have played a role in their descent into savagery?

As if sensing her thoughts, Cole spoke again, his tone softer, almost apologetic. "I never intended for our music to inspire violence," he confessed, his gaze distant. "It was a way for me to confront my own demons, to channel the pain and anger that had defined my life. But sometimes, I wonder if we did call out to something we couldn't control."

Rowan shuddered with something that had nothing to do with the rain-soaked air. His words resonated with her own inner darkness, the bottomless grief that had swallowed her light and hope in the years after Alex's death and Lily's murder.

"Intention doesn't always dictate outcome," she said, her voice steady despite the turmoil that churned within her. "Sometimes, we create our own demons without meaning to."

"Exactly," Cole replied, his eyes reflecting an inner conflict that rivaled her own. "And once unleashed, those demons can be hell to put back in chains."

In the space between heartbeats, Rowan sensed the fragile thread connecting her to Cole—two souls adrift in the eye of a storm wrought by loss and regret. She wondered if Cole, too, had found a twisted form of comfort in the darkness that surrounded them both, a strange kinship born of their mutual suffering.

Cole seemed to sense Rowan's gaze on him, probing, reassessing. "You're wondering if you can trust me," he said, his voice a low growl. "If the guy who nearly beat a man to death can be trusted to save your life."

Rowan shifted in her seat. "The thought had crossed my mind."

Cole's laugh was bitter, humorless. "Join the fucking club."

The truck fell into silence again. The wipers swept back and forth, smearing raindrops across the glass in hypnotic arcs.

Thud. Thud. Thud.

Rowan's thoughts drifted to the demon that had possessed her, the insidious presence that had become both her curse and her salvation. She pushed the memories aside and focused on the road ahead, a ribbon of black glistening in the headlights. The silence stretched on, broken only by the rhythmic swish-thunk of the windshield wipers and the distant rumble of thunder.

After a time, Cole shifted in his seat, his body language betraying a growing unease. "Ricky Barnes was a piece of shit and a predator," he said unexpectedly, his voice low and rough. He glanced at Rowan from the corner of his eye. "He's the guy I almost killed, the guitarist for Doomsday."

Rowan looked at him as he hesitated, his jaw clenching as he struggled to find the right words.

"It was back in '86, in the early days of Haruspex," he went on. "It was our first tour, and we were the opening act. Word got around about what Ricky liked to do to girls, but I didn't pay it much attention. Dudes say a lot of stupid shit on tour and we were rock stars—who was I to judge if some girls liked it rough? But Ricky, he seemed to think his fame gave him permission… entitlement. One night in Detroit, I heard these screams coming from his dressing room backstage—not the usual kind. These were screams of terror, of panic. I looked at the security guy guarding the door and he looked at me, and his eyes told me everything." Cole's fingers tightened on the steering wheel as his words lingered in the air, thick with disgust and an anger that hadn't diminished. "So I let myself in."

Rowan sat rigid in her seat, absorbing his story as if it were a physical blow.

"The girl could have been sixteen or twenty-two—it's hard to tell sometimes with how they dress. Ricky had her pinned against the wall, his hand over her mouth and her underwear around her knees. She was struggling and crying, terrified."

Rowan's stomach churned, bile rising in her throat. She could picture the scene all too clearly, the helplessness and fear in the girl's eyes. "What did you do?"

"I grabbed the nearest thing I could find. A guitar. And I swung it at Ricky's head with everything I had." Cole's voice was flat, devoid of emotion. "A Gibson Les Paul weighs about ten pounds… and I'm a big guy."

Cole trailed off, his gaze distant.

"Ricky spent a couple months in a coma with a fractured skull, and I was charged with attempted murder. Might have gone to prison for it too, if the record label hadn't gotten involved. Doomsday was their biggest moneymaker and they couldn't have their star arrested for rape. Turns out the girl's parents were only too willing to take a payoff in exchange for her silence, and the label would make the charges against me go away if I signed a non-disclosure agreement and kept my mouth shut about what I saw. I was young, an entire career ahead of me... so I did."

Rowan's mind raced, trying to reconcile the image of Cole as a violent savior with the man she had come to know. She could see the toll the memory had taken on him, the guilt and anger that simmered just beneath the surface.

"You saved her," Rowan said softly. "You did what you had to do."

Cole shrugged, his eyes haunted. "Maybe. But it changed something in me. I didn't have to hit Ricky with that guitar. I could've just hauled him off her. But when I saw that look on that girl's face, something just snapped and I *wanted* to hurt him. I saw that look of terror in her eyes as she looked at me, pleading for help, and I thought... that's how my mother must have looked."

The raw honesty of this revelation hit Rowan like a punch to the gut. She felt a jolt inside her chest at the vulnerability that lay beneath his hardened exterior. It was a mirror to her own soul's dark corners—places where grief morphed into rage. She understood now—perhaps more than she wished to —the allure of violence as retribution, the visceral need to protect, to punish. She felt something shift within her, a grudging respect taking root where only bitterness had lived before. Cole was flesh and blood, scarred by traumas of his own, seeking solace in the only way he knew how. She didn't want to feel for this man, didn't want to acknowledge the pain that had shaped him into the person he was today. But in that moment, they were no longer two strangers bound by circumstance and necessity. They were just two broken souls, adrift in a sea of their own making, desperately seeking a way back to shore.

"Sometimes I think we're all just trying to survive our histories," she said, the words spilling out before she could stop them.

Cole turned to look at her, his steel-blue eyes capturing hers with an intensity that made her breath catch. "Survive, sure," he murmured. "I'm not trying to justify what we did last night—but sometimes... violence is the only language left to speak."

"Is that what we did, Cole? Or were we just feeding our own demons?"

"Maybe it's both. Maybe we need the demons to fight the monsters."

His words stayed with her, a truth Rowan couldn't deny. Her thoughts tumbled through memories of Lily's laughter, the roaring flames that had claimed her husband, the stony silence of the courtroom where justice had slipped through her fingers like smoke. Her fingers drummed against her thigh, the cadence syncing with the rhythmic swish-swish of the wipers. It was a metronome to her indecision, a countdown to the moment she would have to trust Cole completely or sever this uneasy alliance they had forged.

"Your intentions, Cole—what are they, really?" she asked. "Why are you helping me?"

He leaned back against the seat, his silhouette etched over the backdrop of the rain on his window. "Reckoning," he said simply. "For all the wrong notes I've played in my life."

The simplicity of his answer struck her—a chord of

sincerity that resonated deep within. Torn between her years of anger at him and the creeping tendrils of doubt, Rowan felt the edges of her hostility soften, just a fraction.

"Then let's make sure it's a fucking symphony," she said.

Rain lashed the windshield mercilessly as Cole pressed down on the accelerator, the wipers slashing back and forth in a futile attempt to clear the torrential blur. The truck plowed on through the storm, headlights carving a feeble path through the gloom. Rowan flinched with every flash of lightning. She stared out the window at the droplets splintering into fragmented lines of light that streaked across the glass. Each passing mile brought them closer to their destination, to the man who could have the secret to severing this unholy bond she had unwittingly forged, but the weight of her uncertainty clung to her.

"Devin's house should be just around the bend," Cole muttered, his voice barely audible over the hammering of the rain on the truck's roof. The truck's headlights sliced through the downpour as it snaked along the narrow woodland road, the dense canopy above choking out the desperate tendrils of gray light.

Rowan nodded. The forest seemed to press in on them, an ominous presence that sought to crush the truck in its grasp. She imagined the trees were like sentries, guarding the secrets that lay ahead, and she felt the tension between her and Cole coil tighter, a spring wound to its breaking point.

Finally, the truck slowed to a stop, gravel and pine needles crunching beneath the tires as they pulled up to Devin's secluded home. A mingling of anticipation and dread flooded Rowan's veins at the sight of it. To her surprise, what Cole had called Devin's *cabin* was actually a massive timber lodge. It loomed before them, a dark silhouette against the rain, its windows like empty eye sockets staring into the void.

Cole killed the engine, and for a moment, they sat in silence, each caught in their own contemplations. Raindrops pelted the truck with relentless force, a staccato drumming against the metal roof that had been their shelter. The world outside was a blur of gray and green, trees swaying like mourners at a funeral march.

"Here we are," Cole said at last, breaking the silence with the solemnity of a man walking to the gallows.

"Here we are," Rowan echoed. She was doing her best to keep her voice steady, despite the maelstrom of emotions roiling within her.

A sudden flash of lightning illuminated the scene, and for a split second, Rowan swore she saw something move among the trees—a shadow flitting at the edge of her vision. She jerked away from the window, her heart hammering.

"Did you see that?" she asked in a whisper.

Cole's eyes flicked to the rearview mirror. "Just the rain."

But Rowan remained unconvinced. She pressed herself against the door, nails digging into the plush upholstery.

It's not real, she told herself. *The demon can't be here. Don't let it in your head.*

Yet Lily's hideous face swam before her eyes, every gust of wind carrying her dead daughter's fetid breath.

"You okay?" Cole's gruff voice cut through her spiraling thoughts.

Rowan swallowed hard. "Fine," she lied, her words clipped and brittle.

Cole grunted, unconvinced. "We need to be ready for anything," he said. "Devin's involvement with the occult runs deep, and there's no telling what he might have uncovered since I last saw him."

Rowan turned to face him, her light green eyes searching his. "What if this is all for nothing?" she whispered, her voice barely audible above the patter of rain against the truck. "What if Devin can't help us? What if—"

"Rowan," Cole said. "Whatever happens in there, I got you into this; I'll get you out."

Rowan looked at him, her fingertips unconsciously toying with her necklace, thinking of Lily's face, forever frozen in time. "Sure," she said with a sigh. "I've been fighting my own demons for years. What's one more?"

Cole nodded, and with a flick of his wrist, his door swung open, releasing him into the storm's embrace.

As she watched him dash through the downpour, Rowan found herself reassessing him. The demonic presence that stalked her loomed large in her mind, but for the first time in hours, she felt a flicker of hope. Cole, with all his darkness and scars, might just be the ally she needed in this fight.

Chapter 11

The icy rain fell in relentless sheets as Rowan sprinted across the muddy stretch to the sprawling timber lodge. Lightning split the sky, illuminating the looming structure for a heartbeat before plunging it back into the gloom. Her chest heaved as she joined Cole beneath the shelter of the covered porch. The waterlogged wood overhead groaned under the weight of the downpour.

Cole slicked his black hair back from his forehead and shook the water from his leather jacket. He hesitated a moment, drawing himself together before rapping his knuckles hard on the front door.

They waited a minute.

Then another.

No answer.

Just an eerie silence and the sound of the rain hammering the roof.

"He probably can't hear us," Rowan suggested with little actual conviction.

Cole reached for the doorknob and turned. The door

creaked open, revealing a yawning darkness.

"Devin?" he yelled. His voice cracked like a whip through the quiet, rebounding off the walls and meeting nothing but silence.

Rowan glanced at him. There was something wrong with this place—something *off*. And she sensed Cole felt it, too.

The moment he pushed the door wider, a pungent miasma of decay punched the air from Rowan's lungs. The vile scent of rot assaulted her senses and clung to the back of her throat like a physical presence, threatening to choke her with its invisible, ghastly fingers. She recoiled instinctively and pressed her wet sleeve over her nose and mouth, trying to block out the sickly sweet reek.

Cole stood beside her, his imposing figure filling the doorway, the cords of his neck shifting with tension. He drew a sharp breath through clenched teeth, his face set into a grim mask. Yet Rowan caught a slight flinch as he, too, registered the odor.

"God," she managed with a strained gasp. "It smells like death."

"Because it probably is," Cole replied uneasily, his gaze sweeping the dim interior. "Devin!" he called again, his voice bouncing through the gloom. "It's Cole!"

Still nothing.

The timber walls creaked under the battering force of the rain.

Rowan felt it then—the tickle of anxiety curling like smoke around her heart. Every unanswered shout left her more unnerved. The shadows inside the lodge seemed to grow claws that scratched at the edges of her courage.

"This doesn't feel right," Cole grumbled, echoing her thoughts. "Come on. Let's find what we came for and get out of here."

"And what exactly are we looking for?"

"If we can't find Devin, then we need to find the Tablet of Ereshkigal."

"The *what*?"

"Let's call it an ancient spell-book," Cole replied. "Ereshkigal was the Sumerian goddess of the underworld. Her cult created stone tablets inscribed with the invocation for the demon we summoned. The originals are locked away in a museum in Damascus, but we got our hands on parchment rubbings. Devin kept them when he disappeared."

Rowan nodded, her determination pushing back the wave of nausea that threatened to overwhelm her. "Sumerian goddess. Like Gozer the Gozerian."

Cole shot her a glance. "*Ghostbusters*?"

"It was Lily's favorite movie."

"This is more like *Evil Dead*. These demons are nasty sons of bitches."

"Yeah, I spent last night living in one while it wore my daughter's face and slaughtered people."

Cole frowned. "I still don't know why it turned against you, but the tablet might give us the key we need to send this fucker back to Hell."

They moved through the foyer and into the lodge's massive great room. The wide planks of the floorboards creaked beneath their feet, announcing their presence to anyone who was listening. An impressive fieldstone fireplace dominated one side of the room, the ashes on its grate sitting gray and cold with disuse. Shadows clung to the corners of the high ceiling. The silence felt ominous, as though the very air was waiting to breathe out a scream.

Cole flicked on a lamp and they split up, each taking a side of the room. Rowan's eyes scanned the walls and shelves, noticing every detail. Photographs hung crooked, faces frozen in time, staring back at her. Dust motes danced in the dull slivers of daylight that penetrated the grimy windows.

"The tablet could be anywhere," Cole's voice cut through the stillness. "Devin had a massive occult collection, but he was also unpredictable. It wouldn't surprise me if he hid something like the rubbings in plain sight."

"Got it, Egon," Rowan replied. Moving a stack of old newspapers with the toe of her boot, she found nothing but the scarred wooden floorboards.

"Nothing here," Cole called from across the room, his words loaded with frustration.

"Then we keep looking." Rowan's voice had a hardened edge.

"Kitchen's this way," Cole said, gesturing toward a doorway. His usual confidence now betrayed a tremor of uncertainty.

"Oh God," Rowan choked out as they entered.

The counters were a battlefield of rot and decay. Maggots writhed in what might have once been fruit, while mold bloomed across forgotten dishes. A half-empty bottle of whiskey stood like a watchman over the chaos.

"Looks like Devin left in a hurry," Cole muttered, his eyes scanning the room. "Or something made him leave."

Rowan swallowed hard. The unease that had been building

since they entered the lodge was now simmering in her chest, a rising tide of dread that set her nerves on edge. "We need to find that tablet and get the hell out of here," she said. "This place... It's not right."

Cole gave a grim nod and led the way from the kitchen, his boots crunching on the debris littering the floor. Rowan followed as they returned to the great room and ascended the creaking staircase to the second floor. The stench grew more pungent as they climbed, the timber groaning under their weight like the very bones of the house were protesting their intrusion.

At the top of the stairs, they paused, straining to hear over the muted sounds of the storm. The landing stretched out before them, a yawning void that seemed to swallow the gray light from the windows. Doors lined the hallway, gaping mouths waiting to devour the unwary trespassers.

Rowan's skin crawled with the certainty that something waited in that dusky gloom, something hungry and patient.

"Keep your eyes peeled," Cole muttered. His gaze flitted across faded photographs and abandoned memorabilia that stood as silent testaments to Devin's life here. "Every bookshelf, every drawer."

Dust motes danced and swirled around them like restless spirits as they moved from one room to the next. The ghastly odor of decay clung to the air like a malignant fog, a physical barrier that seemed to squeeze Rowan's chest. They searched room by room, rifling through drawers and cabinets, finding nothing but the detritus of Devin's reclusive life.

Rowan shook her head, a sense of hopelessness washing over her. They were searching for a needle in a haunted haystack, chasing a relic that might not even exist. And all the while, the specter of Devin's absence loomed large. Where was he and what happened here?

They continued down the corridor, searching each room, finding only emptiness and abandoned belongings. With each failure, Rowan's frustration mounted, mingling with the dread that coiled in her gut. They were running out of time, running out of options.

Soon, there was only one room left—the master bedroom at the end of the hallway. A palpable sense of unease settled over them as they drew near. The stench of decay was overwhelming here, a cloying sweetness that oozed into their lungs. Rowan fought the urge to gag, her eyes watering. They hesitated before the door, Cole's hand hovering over the knob.

Rowan's skin prickled with a premonition. Fear had honed her instincts like a blade, each new trauma sharpening the edge. And right now, she knew something awful awaited them on the other side of that door. She could feel it.

With his breath drawn tight into his lungs, Cole pushed the door. It swung open with a long, drawn-out creak.

The curtains were drawn and shadows shrouded the room except for a sliver of light spilling in from the hallway, casting long fingers across the floor. It took a moment for their eyes to adjust, for the scene before them to coalesce into a nightmarish clarity.

Rowan's stomach lurched, and she reared back a step.

Inside, the decaying carcass of what used to be Devin lay sprawled on the bed. His mottled and sunken flesh clung to his skeleton like melted wax. His sallow skin stretched taut across the jutting bones of his face. The empty holes of his sockets stared up at the ceiling, his eyes having putrified into his head. A tarnished spoon and used syringes littered the bed. The needle that had delivered his last high, still clutched in his rotting hand, glinted in the faint light.

"Damn…" Cole exhaled, his voice low with revulsion and pity.

Rowan stumbled back out of the bedroom, her palm clamped over her mouth, forcing down the urge to vomit. She'd seen death before, had stared into its hollow eyes and felt its icy touch, but this… this was something else entirely. The stench curled on her tongue, conjuring unwanted memories of the smell that lurked beneath the formaldehyde in the morgue where she had identified Lily's remains. Her stomach churned, bile rising hot and acrid in her throat, as the sight before her dredged up images of Lily's corpse—the horror, the helplessness. She swallowed hard against the onslaught of grief that threatened to break her facade of composure. She wanted nothing more than to flee this godforsaken place, to put as much distance between herself and this house of horrors as possible.

"Jesus, let's get out of here," she gasped. "We need to leave. Call the police."

She started for the stairs when Cole stopped her with a firm grip on her arm.

"No," his voice cut through her panic, steel-edged and unyielding. "We can't leave. Not yet."

Rowan stared at him in disbelief. "Are you insane? We just found a dead man, Cole. We can't just—"

"If we call the police, they'll lock this place down to

investigate, and we'll have no chance of finding the tablet. We need to keep looking."

Rowan closed her eyes, taking a deep, shuddering breath. He was right. They had come too far to turn back now, no matter how much every instinct screamed at her to run.

She nodded and waited in the hallway while Cole searched the bedroom. He rummaged through the closets and drawers with a ruthless efficiency, until he slammed the last one shut, the sound echoing in the chamber of death like a judge's gavel.

"Nothing," he grumbled in frustration as he reemerged into the corridor.

Rowan's mind churned, trying to make sense of it all. She had never met the man, but Devin had been their only hope. He was the key to unlocking the secrets that would allow her to undo what she had done and free herself from the demon. But now he was gone, and with him, any chance of finding the tablet.

She clenched her fists, the familiar anger welling up inside her, threatening to overwhelm her. She wouldn't let it end like this, not after everything she had sacrificed.

"There has to be something," she said, refusing to give in to the despair clawing at her soul. "A clue to where he might've hidden them."

"Devin was paranoid," Cole replied, his gaze lingering on the open door to the dead man's room. "We need to think like him—guarded, distrustful."

"The cellar," Rowan suggested, her gaze flicking towards the stairs.

Cole shrugged. "Maybe."

Together, they descended the creaking stairs and searched the ground floor until they located the door to the cabin's underbelly. Cole reached out and twisted the doorknob, the screech of the hinges sounding like a mournful ghost. The way down was nothing but a yawning mouth of darkness.

Cole's boots thudded on the splintered treads as he led the way, the air growing colder and more dank with each step. The scant light streaming over their shoulders from above cast long shadows across the steps, the darkness seeming to press in on them from all sides. The upper levels had offered nothing but dust and disappointment. Now, as they descended deeper into the dark bowels of the lodge, each step felt heavy with dread.

Rowan's nostrils flared, trying to dispel the cloying scent of decay that had infiltrated the upper floors. She felt the hairs on the back of her neck rise as they reached the bottom of the stairs. Her eyes strained to make out the shapes in the gloom. The cellar was a vast pit that reeked of mildew. Darkness seemed to cling to the very air they breathed. Her heart pounded in her chest, not from fear—she was too familiar with that emotion—but from anticipation of the secrets this grim crypt might yield.

Cole found an old light switch, and with a flick, a series of bare bulbs sputtered to life, casting a sickly yellow glow over the expanse. The cellar stretched on further than it had any right to, a labyrinth of shelves and crates, the musty smell of old books hanging heavy in the air. The dim light from the bulbs carved paths through the darkness, illuminating the cobweb-strewn corners and the damp stone walls that seemed to pulse with an unspoken history.

"Holy shit..." Rowan murmured, struck by the scale of Devin's underground vault. Laden with esoteric tomes and arcane artifacts, it was like stepping into a witch's laboratory.

They split up and moved slowly, methodically, searching for any sign of the parchment tablet rubbings. Long minutes crawled by, the silence broken only by the soft rustling of papers and the occasional trickle of water through unseen cracks in the foundation stones. The scent of mildew and old leather mingled with the lingering odor of rot drifting from upstairs.

Rowan's pulse rippled through her like a stone dropped into still water. Her heightened senses made every shadow a potential threat; every sound a possible forewarning of danger.

Amidst the cobwebbed shelves, Cole's silhouette was a dark smudge against the faint light. His broad shoulders hunched over, his fingers pausing on the spines of the volumes. The tattoos on his knuckles stood out like brands in the dimness. A surge of something—hope, fear, desperation—rose as he plucked a tome from a shelf and opened the cover, only to plummet back down into a pit of frustration.

"Dammit," he muttered under his breath, his voice a low growl resonant with pent-up rage. He slammed the book shut, the sound a sharp crack in the still air. He had known loss, known the bitter touch of abandonment, but this—this helpless flailing in the face of an ancient evil—this was a new kind of torment.

"Keep looking!" Rowan called from across the cellar, her voice steady despite the despair that was seeping deeper into her heart. "It has to be here."

And with that, they plunged further into the search, seeking the one relic that held the key to their salvation or their doom.

Cole's hand hovered over the spines of the ancient tomes, unwilling to admit to the growing fear that their efforts might be in vain. With each book he discarded, a sense of desperation coiled around his ribs like a constrictor.

"Nothing," he said, the word slicing through the silence. "It's not here, Rowan."

The cellar seemed to absorb his dejection, the flickering shadows mocking them as they danced along the walls. It was as if the very darkness they stood in was alive, feeding on his disappointment.

"Shit." Cole exhaled, pressing his palms against the cool stone wall as if to keep himself grounded in reality.

Rowan rounded a corner in time to see him slump against the shelves, defeat etched into the lines of his face. Her gaze darted around the cellar again, desperate for any sign they had missed something, anything.

And then, as if drawn by an invisible thread, her eyes snagged on a book that seemed slightly out of place, its spine less dusty than the others. She reached out, her fingers brushing against the leather-bound cover. A subtle irregularity in the shelving's woodwork caught her attention. She probed around before feeling the unexpected give of a mechanism hidden behind the book. A glimmer of hope sparked within her as she traced the outline of a secret latch cleverly disguised by the bookshelf's ornate carvings.

"Cole," she whispered, urgency threading her voice.

He looked up, the dim light casting deep shadows under

his eyes. "What is it?"

"Here," she said. She tugged at the latch concealed behind the ancient volume. It gave way with a soft click that reverberated through the silence, a sound so minute yet so pregnant with possibility that it sent a shiver through her flesh.

The shelf began to creak and groan. Rowan held her breath, watching as a section of the shelving swung slowly forward, revealing a secret door that opened into another realm of darkness.

"Christ," Cole breathed out, pushing away from the wall to join her. They both peered into the revealed space, their hearts pounding with a mix of fear and anticipation.

Inside was a small chamber built into the lodge's stone foundation. Cole figured it must have been the root cellar or a coal shoot before Devin had it concealed with the trick bookshelf. A solitary lightbulb flickered within, its feeble glow casting an eerie dance of shadows against the damp stone walls. The air was thick with the scent of mildew and rot.

"Are you fucking kidding me?" Rowan said. "Are we in an episode of *Scooby-Doo*? Who the hell has something like this in their cellar?"

"I told you Devin was paranoid," Cole replied. "Money, fame, and drugs are a dangerous combination that can make you do weird shit."

He bent his shoulders and squeezed into the secret chamber, the single flickering bulb illuminating Devin's true collection—a trove of ancient tomes and occult paraphernalia.

"Anything?" Rowan asked from outside the narrow door.

"Come see," Cole called back. "You will not believe this."

Rowan stepped over the threshold, the chill of the hidden room curling around her like the breath of something long buried. She found herself surrounded by ancient spell-books, skulls, blackened candles, and grisly artifacts that sent spiders tap-dancing down her spine.

Cole's eyes blazed with triumph. In his hands, he held a stack of parchments etched with archaic script and cryptic glyphs. Rowan's breath caught at the sight. She leaned closer, the musty scent of the ancient paper mingling with the faint odor of sweat and leather from Cole's jacket.

"Is that…?" she began, her voice trailing off.

"The tablet," he said with a nod. He was rigid with tension, like a coiled spring ready to unleash.

Rowan traced her fingers over the delicate parchments. She could almost feel the thrum of their dark power.

"Can you read it?" she asked. "What does it say?"

Cole shook his head. "It's written in cuneiform. But there's a book back at the house that can help translate it. It'll take some time, but we can decipher this."

"Could this really work?" There was an edge to Rowan's voice, a mixture of hope and doubt that echoed the turmoil raging inside her.

"We'll make it work," Cole replied. "Whatever it takes, we'll send this thing back where it—"

A heavy thud from above cut him off mid-sentence, slicing through the concentrated silence like a knife through flesh.

Rowan's blood turned to ice, her eyes meeting Cole's in a moment of shared terror. The cellar suddenly felt like a trap, the darkness pressing in around them.

"What was that?" Rowan breathed.

Cole's throat bobbed as he swallowed hard. "Nothing good," he growled, his eyes fixed on the ceiling above. "Someone's here."

Chapter 12

Rowan's mind was a maze with no exit, each turn leading deeper into panic as she stood motionless in the dank chamber. The musty air filled her lungs with each shallow breath. Her fingers curled into her palms and her nails bit into her flesh as the slow creaks and groans of the footsteps crept through the lodge above them. Every thump sent a fresh jolt of fear through her veins. A muffled shuffling preceded each footfall, as if whoever was upstairs slowly dragged their feet across the floorboards.

Thump... Swish... Thump... Swish...

Something about that slow and steady tread sent a cold ripple up Rowan's spine. It was the sound of something sinister. Of something stalking.

Cole shifted his weight beside her. His presence was a taut bowstring, quivering with unreleased force. His eyes flickered with apprehension in the scant light. The tattoos on his throat rippled with every swallow, betraying the adrenaline surging through him.

He felt it too. Something malevolent was up there.

"Don't move," he murmured, his voice a nervous rumble in the stillness of the secret chamber. His hand brushed against Rowan's arm, and she felt a flicker of gratitude cut through her overwhelming dread. She wasn't alone. They were in this together.

Thump…. Swish… Thump… Swish…

The footsteps above grew louder, closer, and Rowan sucked in her breath. The unseen presence was directly over their heads now, the floorboards creaking under its weight. Rowan's heart quaked like the ground before an earthquake, trembling on the brink. She froze as the footsteps paused just above her, her lungs aching as a sprinkling of dust showered down upon her. A bead of sweat trickled down her brow, her entire body rigid with fear. In the suffocating silence of the cellar, she could hear the blood rushing in her ears, the wild drumming of her heart. She prayed to a God she had long since abandoned, pleading for the footsteps to move on, for the danger to pass.

A long moment dragged on in silence. Then the footsteps moved again. Slowly. Deliberately. Receding into the distance.

Rowan exhaled a shaky breath, her body sagging with relief. The floorboards uttered a final complaint and fell ominously quiet. The footsteps ceased, leaving an eerie silence that pressed down upon them.

Rowan's senses remained razor-sharp as she prepared for whatever came next. The absence of sound was more unnerving than the footsteps had been. Who was up there? The nearest neighbor was miles away. Was it the police? Squatters? Thieves? Or something worse?

The silence stretched, broken only by the distant rumble of thunder. Rowan's skin prickled, goosebumps rising along her arms. *The calm before the storm*, she thought. Her pulse thrummed in her temples. What was going on up there? Had the unseen intruder left the lodge?

She glanced at Cole and saw the tension etched into his features, his jaw clenched tight, his throat stretching taut. They exchanged a glance and he leaned closer, his whisper barely audible over the pounding of her heart.

"We can't stay here, Rowan," he said. "We need to move. This might be our only chance. If we're going to make a break for it, it has to be now. It's only a matter of time before they find us."

"Before *who* finds us?" Rowan asked. "We don't know what we're up against. What if it's the demon?"

In that moment, she couldn't shake the memory of the creature wearing Lily's skin, its baleful eyes searing into her, dragging her down into the frigid, watery depths of the ocean. The image was a knife to her heart.

"It might be," Cole conceded. "But staying down here waiting to be discovered is a guaranteed dead end. We have to take the risk."

"Could be a trap," she said. "What if it already knows we're here, and it's up there waiting for us?" But she knew Cole was right. Every fiber of her being screamed at her to run, to put as much distance between herself and this house as possible. But her rational mind, honed by years of grief and anger, warned her to be cautious. If they stayed, they risked being discovered, trapped like rats in a maze with no escape. But venturing upstairs meant facing the unknown, the possibility of walking straight into the demon's clutches.

She took a deep breath, the damp air filling her lungs. "Okay," she whispered. "But we need a plan. We can't just run out of here."

Cole scanned the secret chamber, searching for anything that he could use as a weapon. His fingers curled around a piece of rusted steel rebar that stood discarded in a corner.

"We head straight for the truck," he said, his voice low and deadly. "And I take care of anything that gets in our way."

In the dim light of the cellar, his face was a mask of grim determination, the shadows accentuating the hollows of his cheeks. But there was also a cold glint in his eye that suggested he was almost delighting in the prospect of violence.

Rowan found her own makeshift club—a splintered wooden plank—and held it at the ready. It was a poor excuse for a weapon, but it was all she had. She clutched it tightly, drawing strength from its solid weight.

"Ready?" Cole whispered.

Rowan gave a shaky nod, not trusting herself to speak. Fear clawed at her throat, threatening to choke her, but she pushed it down. There was no time for fear now. Only survival.

Together, they emerged from the hidden chamber and crept through the cellar toward the stairs, their footsteps muffled by the damp earth. The muted sounds from above had long ceased, yet the silence bore down on them with the gravity of a thousand screams. Her mind was a wildfire, leaping from one spark to the next without pause. A thousand scenarios flashed before her eyes, each more horrifying than the last. What if the demon was waiting for them at the top of the stairs? What if they were walking straight into a trap? The doubts swirled in her mind, but she forced them aside. There was no turning back now.

The stairs creaked beneath their weight as they ascended, each groan of the dry wood sending a jolt of terror through Rowan's veins. She held her breath, certain that the sound would give them away.

But no attack came. The only sound was the pounding of her own heart and the ragged breathing of Cole beside her. Step by step, they climbed, the darkness pressing in around them like a physical force. Time itself seemed to hold its breath, the world reduced to the space between heartbeats. The cellar door loomed above them, a gateway to the unknown danger that awaited beyond.

At last, they reached the top of the stairs. Cole pressed his ear against the rough wood of the door, listening for any sign of movement on the other side.

Nothing.

Cole's knuckles were white with tension as he rested his hand on the doorknob. He glanced back at Rowan, eyes glinting in the dimness. Her hand trembled, but she held her makeshift weapon raised and ready. She nodded, and Cole turned the knob.

The click of the latch echoed like a gunshot in the stillness. Cole winced as he eased the door open, inch by painstaking inch, revealing a sliver of the great room beyond.

Rowan emerged from the cellar, her senses on high alert, the wooden plank steady in her calloused grip. The fading light streaming through the windows did little to dispel the shadows that clung to the corners. The room appeared empty, but the hairs on the back of her neck prickled, a primal warning of unseen danger.

Beside her, Cole scanned the room for any sign of movement, straining his eyes to pierce the gloom. His muscular frame tensed like steel cables drawn tight.

But the room was still, the only sound the patter of rain against the windows and the creaking of the old lodge being lashed by the wind.

Rowan could hardly hear Cole's whisper above the rain. "We need to move. Now."

She nodded, her throat too tight to speak. They edged toward the front door, eyes darting from shadow to shadow, anticipating an attack from any direction. Each step felt like an eternity, the distance to the door stretching out before them like a gaping chasm. The floorboards groaned beneath their feet, betraying their presence in the deathly quiet.

Rowan's grip on the wooden plank loosened slightly, a flicker of hope igniting in her chest. Maybe, just maybe, the mysterious intruder had left the lodge. Maybe they'd make it out of there without facing whatever it was.

"I think we—"

A sudden movement in the gloom cut her words short, a blur of motion that sent a bolt of terror through her veins. Her blood turned to frost, freezing her from within as a figure peeled from the shadows by the cold fireplace and lurched into the light.

It was Devin, but not Devin.

The dead man's reanimated corpse was a walking abomination. Its skin was a sickly, mottled gray, stretched taut over jutting bones and withered flesh. A rictus grin spread across its face, its rotting lips pulled back in a snarl, stretching the dead flesh to impossible limits. The hollow holes of his eyes smoldered with malice.

"No," Cole whispered, his voice thick with horror. "It can't be." He put himself between the walking corpse and Rowan, brandishing the heavy piece of rebar to meet the threat head-on. "Stay behind me."

"Like hell I will," Rowan snapped back, unwilling to cede even an inch of ground. "We fight this bastard together."

The corpse's head snapped toward them, the movement so abrupt, so violently unnatural, that it seemed its neck might snap. Its soulless eye sockets fixed on them with a predatory intensity that held no trace of humanity.

It lunged with inhuman speed.

Cole reacted first, swinging the steel bar in a wide arc. The thing inside Devin dodged, its twisted limbs propelling it through the air like a feral beast. It surged at Cole, clawed hands grasping for his throat.

Rowan swung the plank, and the wood connected with the corpse's skull with a sickening crack. The blow was enough to buy them a moment, but it wouldn't stop the thing for long. It stumbled but quickly recovered, its empty eye sockets now fixed on her.

"You can't save him," the thing hissed through Devin's lips, its voice a guttural snarl that sent shivers down Rowan's spine. "Just like you couldn't save your slut of a daughter."

A glacial wind swept through Rowan's soul. She knew that voice.

Instead of wearing Lily's face, the demon had reanimated

Devin's corpse.

Rage and grief surged through her, a tidal wave of emotion that threatened to drown her. She channeled it into her next swing, putting every ounce of her strength behind it. The blow connected with the corpse's shoulder, but it barely flinched.

The thing inside Devin laughed, a sound that chilled Rowan to the bone. It caught the plank in its hand, wrenching it from her grasp with supernatural strength.

Cole tackled the corpse from behind, his arms wrapped around its waist. They tumbled to the ground in a tangle of limbs, grappling for dominance.

Rowan searched frantically for a weapon. Her eyes landed on the fireplace poker and she snatched it up, the metal cold in her grip.

The corpse threw Cole off, slamming him against the hard stones of the fireplace with a sickening crack. Rowan watched in horror as Cole slumped to the floor, his eyes glazed with shock and something deeper—a frailty she'd never seen in him before.

The corpse's rotting lips curled into a twisted sneer. "Poor little Cole," it taunted, its voice a horrific blend of Devin's and something far older. "Always fighting, always angry. Mommy didn't love you enough, did she?"

Cole's face contorted with rage and pain as he roused himself from the floor. "Shut your fucking mouth!"

"Oh… You're nothing but a scared little boy," the demon inside Devin went on, its words slithering into Cole's mind. "Your music, your anger—it's all just a mask for the weak, unloved child you really are."

The corpse drew back and turned to Rowan, its eyes soulless pits.

"You think you can save her, Cole?" the demon sneered. "You've never saved anyone but yourself. You'll betray her in the end, just like you always do. You left your friend to die alone, didn't you? Abandoned him when he needed you the most, just like you abandon everyone. Too wrapped up in your own selfish desires to spare a thought for anyone else!"

The words cut like a serrated blade, and Cole flinched as if physically struck. "You're not him," he grunted. "I didn't know what would happen to him."

The demon laughed, a sound like the cracking of bones. "Liar," it hissed. "You knew. You just didn't care."

Rowan saw the words hit home, saw the way Cole's shoulders slumped under the weight of his remorse. All at once, she understood. Understood the depth of the bond these two friends had shared, and the pain of its severing.

But there was no time for sympathy, no room for anything but the fight.

Rowan stood her ground, the poker gripped tight in her hands as the corpse advanced. It measured its steps, savoring the anticipation of the kill.

Time seemed to slow, each heartbeat an eternity. Rowan waited, poised on the edge of action, as the walking dead man drew closer. The broken holes of its eyes burned with malice.

"I am the abyss that swallows all light and hope," the demon snarled, its words dripping with venom. "You should be thanking me—I'm finally giving you a way to end your suffering. Your daughter wasn't so lucky. She begged for death long before it came for her."

Rowan's vision flashed red, a surge of rage boiling up from the depths of her grief-stricken soul. She lunged forward, the poker raised to strike, a scream of fury tearing from her throat as she aimed for the corpse's head.

But the demon was faster. It ducked, the metal whistling harmlessly over its rotting skull.

"Rowan, watch out!" Cole's warning sliced through the chaos just as the corpse's hand shot out, fingers elongated into talons aiming for her throat.

She twisted away at the last second, feeling the rush of air as the claws missed her by mere centimeters. Instead, they raked across her arm, leaving deep furrows. Blood welled up like dark, accusing eyes. Pain flared bright and hot. The corpse's hand whipped out one more time. This time, it closed around Rowan's throat. She gasped for air, the corpse's hideous face inches from her own, its fetid breath hot against her skin. She stared into those hollow eyes, into the soul of an evil not of this world. And in that moment, she knew true terror, an all-consuming dread that threatened to shatter her will.

Cole rushed forward with a snarl of defiance, a shard of broken glass clutched in his hand. He plunged it deep into the corpse's back, twisting it with a savage fury.

The corpse staggered, and the demon inside it let out an unearthly screech. Rowan wrenched herself free, stumbling back as the corpse rounded on Cole. Its surprise at his sudden attack gave her the opening she needed.

She snapped up the iron poker and surged forward. The rusted point found its mark, piercing the corpse's chest with a sickening crunch. The demon screamed, an otherworldly sound of rage and pain, as she drove the makeshift spear deeper, putting all her grief and fury behind the blow.

For a heartbeat, the corpse faltered, its malevolent eye sockets widening in shock. Rowan held fast, her knuckles white on the poker's haft, as the creature's claws scrabbled uselessly at the embedded iron.

"The door," Rowan ground out through clenched teeth. "Go, now!"

She grabbed Cole's arm, his breath coming in ragged gasps. Blood spattered from a gash across his brow, the crimson streaks painting his face. Together, they ran, stumbling and half-falling in their haste, the promise of escape lending desperate speed to their movements. The demon roared somewhere behind them, a sound that shook the very foundations of the lodge. But Rowan didn't dare look back. Her focus narrowed to the front door, to the slim chance of survival that lay beyond.

Faster, faster, Rowan's heart pounded in time with their frantic footfalls. The door was close now, so close, Cole's hand already reaching for the knob. Rowan risked a glance over her shoulder, just in time to see the corpse rip free of the poker with a howl of triumph. It charged, a living nightmare of flailing limbs and gnashing teeth, its eyes promising a thousand hells.

"Hurry!" The word tore from her throat, raw and desperate.

Cole yanked open the door, the cold air rushing in like a blessed tide. They plunged forward, out onto the rain-slick porch. The rain pelted their skin like icy needles as they stumbled down the steps, feet slipping on the wet wood in a final, gasping sprint for freedom.

"Move!" Cole barked, grabbing Rowan's arm to pull her along.

Behind them, the demon roared, the sound echoing through the night. It was a promise of retribution, a vow of vengeance.

They dashed to Cole's Land Rover as the wind howled its fury, whipping at their faces and tearing at their hair. But Rowan barely felt it, her entire being focused on the truck, on escape, on survival.

"Don't stop!" Cole shouted, his voice cutting through the pounding rain. "It's right behind us!"

Rowan's lungs burned, and her muscles screamed. She could feel her pulse throbbing in the cuts and bruises that marred her body. Each step sent a fresh wave of agony through her, but she gritted her teeth and pushed harder, faster, until her hand closed around the passenger door handle. She wrenched it open, hurling herself inside, Cole a heartbeat behind her.

"Keys!" she gasped, her voice barely audible over the roar of the rain on the roof.

Cole fumbled in his leather jacket, his fingers clumsy with cold and fear. The seconds stretched, an eternity of dread. "Got 'em!" his triumphant shout cut through the tension, the keys glinting in his hand like a talisman against the dark.

He jammed them into the ignition, his hands shaking, breath coming in unsteady bursts. The powerful engine roared to life, the vibration thrumming through Rowan's bones.

Cole threw the truck into gear, his foot slamming down on

the accelerator. The tires spun in the mud and…

Rowan's door ripped open.

She let out a gut-wrenching scream as the snarling corpse grabbed her arm and dug its nails deep into her flesh, intent on dragging her back out into the downpour. Wild with panic, she fought with all her might to break free, thrashing in her seat as Cole shifted into reverse and floored the pedal. The engine roared and the big tires spun in the sodden earth before finally finding traction and sending the big Land Rover lurching backward.

But the corpse wouldn't let go. It held Rowan tight in its iron grip, its snarling face twisted with malice as the truck picked up speed, dragging it along.

With her last burst of strength, Rowan wrenched her arm just as Cole jerked the wheel and swerved. The sudden shift in the truck's momentum ripped the corpse free and sent it tumbling away through the mud. It rolled a few times before springing back to its feet, howling with fury.

Hands wrapped tight around the wheel, Cole glared through the windshield. He could have swung around and kept driving, leaving the hideous perversion of his former friend behind. Instead, he floored it and the truck shot forward.

"Hold on," he growled over the roar of the engine and the pounding of the rain.

Rowan screamed and had just enough time to brace herself before the charging Land Rover slammed into the corpse with a sickening crunch of metal and bone. Its rotting body burst open like an overripe fruit, exploding like a grotesque fireworks show of blood and guts. Black ichor spewed over the windshield, creating a gruesome pattern against the rain. Organs and pulpy chunks of flesh flew out in all directions, some landing on the hood of the truck while others were strewn across the front grill.

The impact sent a shockwave through the cab, the force of it slamming Rowan back against her seat. The demon's howls ceased with the impact, replaced by the revving engine and the crunch of the gravel under the big tires as the Land Rover plowed through what was left of Devin's corpse.

When the truck finally shuddered to a halt, Rowan forced her eyes open, blinking away the spots that danced across her vision. The windshield was a spiderweb of cracks, the hood dented and dripping with gore. And there, splayed in the mud like a broken doll, was the mangled heap of rotting flesh and splintered bone that was Devin's corpse.

Rowan let out a shuddering breath, her hands trembling in her lap. "Is it... is it dead?" she asked, her voice hoarse and strained.

Cole shook his head, a grim certainty etched on his face. "No," he whispered. "We only destroyed its vessel. The demon itself... It's still out there."

Rowan saw the tension in his face, the haunted look in his eyes. "It's not over then," she said. "This... this is just the beginning, isn't it? That thing... it won't stop."

Cole nodded and gunned the engine. The tires spun, caught, and then they were moving, heading for the long driveway that snaked through the woods.

Trembling and bleeding in her seat, Rowan cast a glance back at the lodge, its outline now just a darker patch in the gathering gloom as it receded into the rain-soaked distance.

Her brain was a skipping record, fragments of the fight with the demon replaying over and over in her head. The creature's taunts, its accusations, the way it had looked at her with Devin's empty eyes—all of it coiled around her gut like a nest of snakes. She shuddered and struggled to push the thoughts aside, but the chill that settled in her bones was one not even the downpour could wash away. It was the realization that what lay behind them was just a prelude.

And if they couldn't fight this thing, what hope did they have?

COMMONWEALTH OF MASSACHUSETTS

Case #9036CR001031
People of Essex County v. T. Chapman

Government Exhibit: #24

Lyrics to the song "Defile the Innocent"
Performed by the band Haruspex
Written by Cole Abel, Devin Mill
From the album "Rituals of Annihilation"
Published by Armageddon Music, 1987

(Verse 1)
Awakened by the shadows, crawling deep inside,
A bitter taste of vengeance, no place for saints to hide.
The serpents coil around me, whispering deceit,
In this kingdom of corruption, where innocence retreats.

(Chorus)
Defile the innocent, shatter their purity,
Twisted sanctity, in the grip of obscurity.
Defile the innocent, let the darkness reign,
Righteousness devoured by a storm of endless pain.

(Verse 2)
A sacrifice of virtue, on the altar of disdain,
The fires of perdition, burning every chain.
Souls consumed by madness, in the heart of night,
The light of hope extinguished, in the raven's flight.

(Chorus)
Defile the innocent, shatter their purity,
Twisted sanctity, in the grip of obscurity.
Defile the innocent, let the darkness reign,
Righteousness devoured by a storm of endless pain.

(Bridge)
Beneath the veil of carnage, whispers of the lost,
Their cries for mercy echo, as the line is crossed.
No salvation for the fallen, in this realm of sin,
The final rites of torment, as the end begins.

(Breakdown)
Rise from the ashes, let the chaos spread,
In the name of vengeance, paint the world in red.
The innocent are broken, their cries a bitter song,
In the symphony of darkness, where the damned belong.

(Chorus)
Defile the innocent, shatter their purity,
Twisted sanctity, in the grip of obscurity.
Defile the innocent, let the darkness reign,
Righteousness devoured by a storm of endless pain.

(Outro)
In the wake of desolation, shadows claim the night,
The remnants of the innocent, lost without a fight.
In this world of darkness, where the serpents dwell,
We defile the innocent, and cast them into hell.

Chapter 13

Rowan sat hunched over on the edge of the claw-footed bathtub, her fingers trembling as they daubed the angry claw marks that marred her skin. The white cotton bloomed crimson with each touch and the antiseptic stung, drawing a hiss from her lips. But part of her welcomed the pain—a bitter reminder that she wasn't dead. Not yet.

"Steady," she muttered, her voice a hoarse whisper in the opulent space. "You've survived worse."

But had she?

The wounds the demon had left were deep red furrows carved into her pale flesh. She wound a strip of gauze around them, her fingers still trembling as she tied off the ends. The bathroom was thick with silence except for her quavering breath and the slow patter of water dripping from the faucet to the bottom of the porcelain tub.

Rowan's surging adrenaline had blurred much of the ride back to Cole's mansion. After fleeing Devin's cabin, he had wanted to take her to a hospital, but she refused. How would they explain her wounds? An animal attack? Not likely. Who would believe them if they told the truth? And even if Rowan could somehow muster the mental focus and energy to come up with a convincing lie, what about the gruesome mess of human remains splattered across the grill of Cole's truck? How would they explain that? No, Rowan wasn't about to waste any time dodging questions she couldn't answer. She wanted Cole to translate the tablet immediately so they could find some way of ridding themselves of this demon and end this nightmare.

Now, while Cole studied the tablet rubbings in his library down the hall, Rowan stood from the edge of the tub and braced her hands on the cool edge of the vanity. In the unforgiving glare of the overhead lights, Rowan met her own haunted gaze in the mirror. It reflected a woman she barely recognized, a stranger worn down by pain, fear, and exhaustion. The eyes that stared back were those of a woman teetering on the knife's edge between determination and despair. Her face was pale and gaunt, her green eyes sunken and ringed with dark circles. Her bare shoulders slumped beneath the strings of her bra straps, and her body seemed to sag with weariness. Long tangles of her limp red hair hung around her face, adding to her defeated appearance.

How many more battles could her battered body and fractured psyche endure? Rowan knew she couldn't keep going on like this. Eventually, she would need to sleep, but she hadn't been able to close her eyes since her encounter with the demon in the water that morning. Every time she tried, all she saw was Lily's grotesque face staring back at her.

Everything Rowan had witnessed in the past twenty-four hours left her reeling in disbelief. She had grown up in a family of skeptics—a family that believed in science and logic, not magic and spells. But here she was, taking refuge from a bloodthirsty demon in a mysterious mansion with a rockstar who understood ancient texts and performed occult rituals to commune with beings from other worlds.

God, could it really have only been a day since they unleashed that evil thing together? Since it had reached out to Rowan and carried her along while it slaughtered her daughter's killers? She couldn't believe it had only been a day since her life had so suddenly been ripped from its foundations.

But really, how strong had those foundations actually been? Rowan knew her life had been a ruin ever since Lily's death.

As she gazed at the haunted reflection staring back at her in her mirror, her mind drifted back to those terrible moments in Devin's cabin and the demon's attack. Those soulless eyes, filled with malevolent hunger. The sulfurous stench of its breath. The bone-chilling screech as its talons raked across her skin.

For the first time, a horrifying possibility took root in Rowan's mind: she might not survive this.

She and Cole couldn't run forever, and they couldn't hide from what they had summoned. The demon wouldn't relent until it had claimed her—claimed them *both*. The realization hit her like a punch to the gut, stealing her breath away and chilling her to the core. Her hands stilled, gauze dangling in the air.

No, Rowan vowed. *I won't let it end like this. I can't.*

But doubt had already wormed its way in, feeding on her

fear. What if they failed? What if they couldn't overcome this demonic entity? Were they just delaying the inevitable? The growing sense of doom threatened to crush what little hope remained. Rowan could almost feel the specter of death looming close, its icy breath a ghostly caress upon her neck.

Since losing Lily, she'd come to believe she no longer feared dying. In time, she'd even welcomed the prospect—a blessed release from the unending grief that haunted her with each passing day. She could recall at least a dozen drunken nights when she'd sat on the edge of her bed with Alex's pistol in her lap, trying to find the courage to press its muzzle to her head and pull the trigger. The temptation to end it all was overwhelming, but something always held her back. She was torn between the desire for escape and the fear of causing pain to those she cared about. It was a never-ending struggle that consumed her every waking moment. Eventually, she'd gotten sober and resolved to turn the gun on Daley Banks instead, but she couldn't honestly say that she'd ever really renewed her will to live.

So why was she so afraid now?

Because it's not death that frightens you, she thought. *It's Hell...*

Rowan shuddered and did her best to push the chilling thoughts from her mind as she turned from the mirror and shrugged back into the black Haruspex hoodie Cole had given her. The creak of the bathroom door echoed throughout the hallway as she cracked it open, the only sound in the eerie silence of the mansion. Night had fallen hours ago. As she stepped out into the dim corridor, the worn carpet swallowed her footsteps. A faint howling wind swept up the seaside cliffs outside, sending an unearthly whistle through the already foreboding atmosphere.

And yet, there was also a sense of stillness, as if time itself had stopped in this deserted mansion. The floorboards creaked beneath Rowan's weight, and the gloom seemed to swallow her up as she moved further down the hallway, suffocating her in its embrace. She shivered and cast a furtive glance into the windswept darkness beyond the windows, searching for hidden threats. Nowhere felt safe anymore. Even here, within the supposed refuge of Cole's opulent mansion, she couldn't shake the feeling of being watched. Every shadow stared back at her with unseen eyes that followed her every move, waiting to catch her unsuspecting. The hairs on the back of her neck prickled with fear and a shiver ripped through her body. She quickened her pace, desperate to reach the safety of the library before whatever lurked in the night could reach out and snatch her away.

She turned a corner and froze, her heart skidding on black ice. A dark figure stood in her way.

"Jesus." She breathed out in relief when she realized it was only Cole. "You scared me."

"Sorry," he said with a faint smile. "Just coming to check on you."

Rowan took a deep breath and tried to calm her racing pulse. "I'm fine. You find anything useful?"

A scowl flickered across Cole's face. "More than I wanted to. Come on…"

He motioned for her to follow him further down the corridor. Ahead, Rowan could see the firelight flickering within the library, casting eerie shadows along the walls. As they stepped through the doorway, the rich scent of old books and burning logs folded over her like a quilt stitched with memories. Her gaze swept the room, taking in the macabre curios and the towering shelves laden with leather-bound tomes. The fireplace danced and crackled, the wood-smoke mingling with the musty scent of old paper. It was a comforting smell in this dark and foreboding manor, one that reminded her of cozy nights by the fire with a family she had lost years ago.

Cole crossed the room to where the weathered parchments of the tablet rubbings lay spread across the heavy wooden desk. On the tabletop next to them sat a thick, leather-bound tome. Cole hunched and flipped through its pages with practiced ease. His steel-blue eyes darted back and forth, brow furrowed in concentration. The knife tattoos on his throat pulsed with each swallow as he muttered under his breath.

Rowan joined him at the desk and peered over his shoulder. She couldn't make sense of any of it—strange symbols, diagrams, and Latin phrases filled the pages. It all seemed like gibberish to her.

"We're running out of time," she said. "That thing won't stop until it gets what it wants."

"You think I don't know that?" Cole snapped, then sighed. "Sorry. This shit's getting to me, too."

Rowan's lips tightened as she turned her attention to the ancient book. "What is all this?"

"An old grimoire," Cole said without looking up from his reading. "This book of spells and rituals belonged to a French heretic who was burned at the stake."

Rowan raised a skeptical eyebrow while Cole turned a page and pointed to a series of strange glyphs accompanied by Latin words.

"See this? This is the key to deciphering the tablet."

Rowan nodded as she stared at the page. Her mind was spinning with questions, but before she could ask anything else, Cole turned the page again, his fingers tracing along the intricate illustrations as he continued to explain.

"These glyphs are part of an ancient language used by Sumerian practitioners of magic. It was used to communicate with the goddess Ereshkigal and invoke her demons in her name."

He pointed to a section of cryptic symbols scrawled across the parchment, steeling himself against the weight of his discovery. "From what I can make of this, it's guilt that's keeping the demon linked to us—*our* guilt."

A cold dread settled in Rowan's stomach as the implications sank in. Her hands clenched at her sides, knuckles whitening. "So you're saying…"

"We're both marked, Rowan." Cole's voice was tight with a grim certainty. "Our darkest regrets, our deepest shames— they're like a beacon, calling out to the demon. It's how it knows who to drag back to the underworld. And the more we torment ourselves, the stronger it becomes."

Rowan turned away, her mind reeling. *Guilt…* The very emotion that had driven her relentlessly for the past seven years. The constant, gnawing presence that whispered she could have saved Lily, could have protected her daughter.

"That's what this is about?" she choked out, anger flaring hot and bright within her. "So how am I supposed to escape it? What am I supposed to do? Just… let it go? Stop feeling guilty about my daughter's death? Stop beating myself up over the fact that I knew she was lying about watching a movie at friend's house that night and I let her go out anyway? That I just wanted her to leave so I could go back to drinking? The signs were all there, but I ignored them. I wasn't there for her. Not in the way she needed me to be. I was too caught up in my own grief, my own pain, to see what was happening right in front of me."

Rowan paused, taking a shuddering breath as the memories washed over her. The long nights spent alone, drowning her misery in whiskey. The missed piano recitals and parent-teacher conferences, the birthdays and holidays that passed by in a blur. The countless times she had pushed Lily away, too consumed by her own sorrow to be the mother her daughter deserved.

"I failed her," she whispered, the words tearing at her heart like claws. "What kind of mother doesn't notice her own child hurting?"

The question hung between them, unanswerable and damning.

Cole was silent for a long moment, his gaze fixed on the dancing flames. When he spoke, his voice was soft, almost gentle. "It's not your fault, Rowan. And it's not mine either. Those two boys are the ones who killed your daughter. You've got nothing to be guilty for."

"Try telling that to my nightmares," she retorted, her green eyes darkening with memories. "They're filled with her screams every damn night."

Silence settled over them, the only sound the crackle of the fire on the grate. Cole could deny it all he wanted, but deep down, Rowan knew the truth. The guilt was part of her now, as inseparable from her being as her own flesh and blood. How could she ever hope to banish it when it was the very thing that kept Lily's memory alive?

"So if Lily's murder isn't your fault, what *do* you feel guilty about, Cole?" Rowan demanded. Her words were sharp, accusatory, slicing through the tense silence of the library. "What deep, dark secrets are you hiding? Why is the demon after you?"

A muscle in Cole's cheek twitched and his gaze met hers, intense and unblinking.

"Answer me," she pressed, stepping closer. "If we're going to risk our lives together, I need to know the truth. What could the great Cole Abel possibly feel guilty about? If what you're saying is true, then this demon knows us better than we know ourselves. Why is it after you? And why did it say you would betray me?"

Cole's hard gaze flickered with a dark intensity as he leaned over the desk. His expression clouded, a storm of emotions brewing behind his eyes. He inhaled sharply, the sound cutting through the heavy silence like a knife.

"Devin," he said. "He was my oldest friend—my only *real* friend. Everyone else in my life was just a means to an end, but Devin and I shared a history no one else could understand. Still, when he started to lose himself, I didn't reach out to help him. I just turned my back and moved on. I left him. To the drugs. To the darkness. He wasn't… *useful* anymore. To the band. To me."

Cole's gaze drifted to one of the exquisite etchings hanging on the wall. "Do you know who the lowest circle of Hell is reserved for? Traitors to benefactors. That's what I did. I betrayed the one person who ever gave a shit about me… and that's why the demon has come for me."

The room seemed to close in around them, the shadows deepening as Cole's admission hung in the air. Rowan watched as his fingers traced the tattoos on his throat, the gesture unconscious and filled with a lifetime of pain. She remained silent, her eyes shadowed with wariness.

"You want to know how we met?" Cole went on. "Devin and I? We were in junior high. We didn't know each other, but we both used to ride the same city bus around the neighborhood for hours after school because we knew we'd get the shit kicked out of us once we got home. Devin's father was a drunk. And the things they did to me in those foster homes…"

Rowan felt her breath catch, a shudder climbing up her spine like frost creeping up a windowpane. Each word he uttered seemed to carve new scars into the air between them.

"Oh… you didn't know about that, did you?" Cole sneered, catching her reaction. There was a sharpness in his tone now, an anger awakening at being forced to throw open doors he struggled so hard to keep locked. "You didn't know about the foster homes? How I grew up? You know that song you sued me for? 'Defile the Innocent'? It's not about killing kids—it's about what they did to me in those places. My mother was sixteen when she was raped—at a Christian summer camp back in Iowa." He laughed, a bitter, broken sound. "Her parents were Bible-thumpers, and they blamed *her* for it. Abortion was out of the question, and when I was born, my mother… she couldn't bear to look at me, to see her violator's face staring back at her. Every breath I took was a reminder of her shame, so she gave me up for adoption. She killed herself out of guilt by the time she was nineteen.

"When no one wanted me, I bounced around from foster home to home, each worse than the last. I endured things you wouldn't care to imagine. *That's* what that song is about. I was raised in hell, Rowan—and that's why I write about it. But you don't give a shit about that, do you? You've never really cared about the truth until now. You just needed someone to blame for what happened to Lily. Well, tell me this: If my music was so fucking dangerous, why was your daughter allowed to listen to it? Where were *you*, Rowan?"

That was it. Rowan snapped. Without thinking, she swung at him with all the force within her slight frame.

Cole saw it coming and dodged out of the way. As he skipped back, his hand collided with a vase on the shelf behind him and sent it toppling over onto the floor, shattering into a million pieces.

Rowan trembled with the effort of holding back her rage. Her slender fingers tightened around the edge of the wooden table, knuckles pale as bone. His words had cut deep, reminding her of all the things she had tried to forget. But as much as she wanted to deny it, part of her knew he was right. She'd been too torn up by grief after her husband's death to pay attention to what her daughter had been up to. What else had she been oblivious to? What other secrets had Lily been keeping from her?

Tears burned Rowan's eyes, threatening to spill over. She closed them, willing herself to keep it together as she drew in a breath, as deep and vast as the chasm between them. She found herself at a crossroads, her mind racing with conflicting emotions. What if the demon was right about him? If Cole could abandon his bestfriend so callously, what might he do to her when she was no longer useful?

"I don't know if I can trust you," she admitted, her voice barely above a whisper. "How do I know you won't turn on me the moment it's convenient?"

"Is there really anything I can say to convince you?" he replied, his tone flat and even. "I need you as much as you need me. It's that simple. We're in this together, whether we like it or not."

Cole watched as Rowan's eyes flickered with indecision. She looked at him, searching his face for reasons to shake off the feeling of unease and mistrust that still lingered within her. And in that moment, she knew she had no choice but to trust him, to put her faith in a man she had once despised with every fiber of her being. After what seemed like an eternity, she let out a long sigh and nodded at the parchments on the table.

"Tell me you've found some way to stop it."

Chapter 14

The ancient oak door groaned open, revealing a spiral staircase that plunged into darkness. Rowan hesitated, eyeing the stairs warily while Cole's hand gripped the rusted iron railing.

"Watch your step," he warned, his voice echoing in the narrow passage as he began his descent.

Rowan followed, her fingers trailing along the damp stone walls. The flickering light from the candle Cole carried cast eerie shadows across his angular face. As they descended deeper into the mansion's mysterious depths, Rowan's chest tightened as if a storm gathered. The air grew colder the lower they went, thick with the dank smell of moisture.

At the bottom, another heavy door loomed before them, its surface carved with arcane symbols.

"Here," Cole turned to Rowan, his eyes piercing in the dimness. "What lies beyond this door may be our only hope of survival."

He produced an old iron key from his pocket. It scraped in the lock, and the door swung open with a mournful creak.

Within lay a sprawling vault lined with sagging wooden shelves. Arcane relics cluttered their surfaces—grotesque artifacts, ancient leather-bound tomes, and jars filled with murky liquids.

Rowan lingered at the threshold while Cole entered and lit the candles in the wall sconces.

"What you saw in my studio was just the showroom," he explained. "This is the warehouse. Some toys are just too dangerous to play with." He beckoned her forward with a wave of his hand. "Come on. Time's wasting."

Rowan steeled herself and followed him into the gloom. The air was heavy with the scent of aged paper and something metallic—blood? Her eyes adjusted slowly, the flickering candles casting an eerie light that illuminated cobwebs that draped from the ceiling like the veil of a ghostly bride. Each object seemed to hold a story, a history steeped in darkness.

"The house's original owner passed down this collection through generations," Cole said. "It's why I bought this place. They say he was a devil-worshipper, a member of a secret society of occultists known as the Crucible of Night. They were powerful. Dangerous. They made pacts with demons to amass power and bring about Armageddon."

Rowan crossed her arms, feeling the chill seep into her bones. Part of her still couldn't believe any of this was real. That demons and magic actually existed. But after everything she had seen, she knew better than to doubt it now.

"So, what does this have to do with the demon?" she asked. "What did you learn from the tablet?"

Cole's lips twisted into a humorless smile. "It says we can banish the demon by trapping it in a mirror and shattering it, sending the bastard back to the hellscape that spawned it."

A flicker of hope ignited in Rowan's chest. But doubt quickly doused it. "That's it? Just trap it and break the mirror?"

"Not quite that simple," Cole admitted. "We'll need a mirror with a history. One that has absorbed dark spiritual energies over the years. It will make the binding easier."

Rowan's mind raced. Could it really be that easy? No, nothing about this nightmarish ordeal had been easy. "Energy?" she repeated. "What kind of energy?"

"Pain," Cole replied, his gaze unwavering. "The more it witnessed, the easier it will be to bind the demon within. We need something powerful, something imbued with sorrow."

Cole moved to the far wall of the vault, his silhouette stark against the flickering candlelight. Rowan followed closely as he approached a large shape draped in a dusty black cloth.

"Here," Cole said. His tattooed arms flexed as he pulled the shroud away with a flourish, revealing an ornate mirror. Its surface shimmered like dark water, reflecting the ethereal glow of the candles.

Rowan stepped closer, drawn in by its haunting allure. The black frame was carved with twisted vines and grotesque faces that seemed to writhe under her gaze.

"It once belonged to the mansion's original owner," Cole said. "His descendants thought they could control the darkness. They were wrong."

"Does it hold his power?" Rowan asked, eyes fixated on the glass; a portal into the past. She could almost feel the weight of the dark energy emanating from the surface.

"Power, yes. But history too." Cole's tone darkened, his

eyes narrowing. "It's seen things… terrible things. And that makes it perfect for our needs. Centuries of occult rituals have left their mark on this glass." He ran a finger along the frame, and Rowan could have sworn she saw shadows ripple across its surface. She shivered. Was there a glimpse of movement in the glass—a flicker of something just beyond reach?

"But there's a catch," Cole continued. "In order to trap the demon in the mirror, we need to know its true name. And no demon will ever reveal that willingly."

"Then how are we supposed to find out?" Rowan asked, frustration edging into her voice. Every step forward seemed to come with a new obstacle.

Cole's gaze met hers, his voice taking on a grim edge. "We ask someone who's met the bastard face-to-face—one of the demon's victims. Someone like Troy Chapman."

The name hit Rowan like a physical blow. One of Lily's murderers. The monster who'd carved her baby while…

"Troy's dead," she spat. "The demon tore him apart in Bridgewater. I was there. I watched it happen."

Cole's lips curved into a humorless smile. "Death isn't always the end, Rowan. Not in our world. I know a seance ritual. One that can conjure Chapman's spirit."

Rowan's mind lurched like a ship caught in a rogue wave. "You want to… what? Talk to his ghost?"

"More than that. We need to bring his spirit here, give it a vessel to speak through. One of us."

The implication hung in the air between them, heavy and suffocating.

"You're talking about possession," Rowan said.

Cole nodded. "It's dangerous. But it's our only shot at getting the demon's name."

A shudder ran through Rowan. The thought of allowing one of Lily's murderers to inhabit her body, even for a moment, curdled in her stomach like soured milk.

"There has to be another way," she said, more to herself than to Cole. Her throat constricted as she fought back the bile rising within her.

The revulsion must have shown on her face because Cole quickly added, "I can do it. You don't have to—"

"No," Rowan cut him off, her voice hard as stone. As much as the idea repulsed her, she knew it had to be her. This was her fight, her chance to confront one of her daughter's killers, even from beyond the grave. "I'll do it. I'll be the vessel."

The vault suddenly felt smaller, like being locked inside a shrinking box. Rowan's pulse quickened. She closed her eyes for a moment, inhaling the scent of old wood and forgotten secrets. Something pressed against her thoughts, a creeping dread that whispered of failures yet to come.

Cole studied her for a long moment, as if searching for any hint of hesitation or doubt. Finally, he nodded. "We'll need to prepare the ritual space and gather the components." He paused, his gaze softening just a fraction. "Are you sure about this, Rowan? Channeling a spirit, especially one as dark as Chapman's… it won't be easy. It'll feel like—"

"Like violation," she finished, a bitter smile twisting her lips. "I'm familiar with the feeling."

Cole nodded again, a flicker of something—respect, perhaps—glinting in his eyes. "Okay. Let's get started then.

It's time to find out this demon's name, and end this once and for all."

Cole found an old leather satchel, and Rowan held it open for him while he gathered a variety of arcane items. He then located an ancient guitar and led her from the vault. Rowan cast one last glance at the collection surrounding them. Each item seemed to whisper of past horrors, of deals struck in blood and shadow. She shivered, wondering what dark bargain they were about to make themselves.

"We'll need silence," Cole explained as they ascended the stairs. "The great room should do."

Together, they made their way to a vast room lit by several ornate crystal chandeliers. Their shimmering lights cast intricate patterns on the high ceilings and walls adorned with expensive paintings and tapestries. A grand fireplace stood at one end, its mantle decorated with macabre curios. Plush damask curtains hung at the tall windows, shielding the room from the outside world. The opulent space spoke of a bygone era of wealth and luxury. But tonight, the room felt cold and hollow, as if the very walls were turning their backs on what they were about to do.

The heels of Rowan's shoes sank into the thick rug as Cole lit the fire and dimmed the chandeliers.

"Do you really think this will work?" The words slipped from Rowan's lips, coated in a brittle veneer of skepticism.

"We don't have any other choice," Cole replied. He took the satchel from her and handed her the strange guitar. "Careful with that. It's a martyr guitar from ancient Rome. The wood is from a crucifixion cross, the tuning pegs and frets are human bone, and the strings are made of the victim's hair wound around stretched intestine."

While Rowan studied the macabre instrument with disgust, Cole set himself to preparing the space. He began by using a vial of white bone dust to draw a sigil of summoning on the floor—a strange design comprising spirals and jagged lines that mimicked the chaotic energy of the undead, centered within a large circle. He then sprinkled consecrated graveyard dirt around the perimeter to form a protective barrier between the mortal world and the spirit realm. Finally, he lit a black candle at the edge of the circle. While it burned, he took a small silver knife and motioned for Rowan to offer her hand.

"What are you doing?" she asked suspiciously.

"Just a prick," he replied. "Spirits are drawn to the warmth of blood."

Rowan's stomach churned, and she winced at the bright flash of pain that sprung from her outstretched fingertip when Cole pierced her skin. He then drew his own blood, and together, they let the crimson drops fall to the center of the sigil.

Rowan's mind was a haunted house, every door creaking open to another unwelcome fear. What if it all went wrong? She was no longer a stranger to the occult, not after what she'd already witnessed with her own eyes. But this... this was something else. Summoning the spirit of a dead man, one of the very monsters who had taken her Lily from her...

Would she feel Troy's thoughts? His memories? The sick satisfaction he'd felt as he—

"Stop," she whispered to herself. "Focus."

Tendrils of dread slithered up her back like ivy climbing a

wall. Could she trust Cole to look out for her while she was possessed? Would he be able to bring her back if something went wrong? What if Troy Chapman wasn't the only spirit they conjured? What if the demon also lurked just beyond the veil, waiting for an opening to seep through?

The thought coiled tight in her stomach, but she pushed the fear aside, focusing instead on the desperation that simmered beneath her skin. She would do whatever it took to get the information they needed and finally end the nightmare that had become her life.

Cole took the martyr guitar from her and looked her in the face, his expression grim. "Last chance to back out, Rowan."

Rowan took a deep breath, squaring her shoulders. "I'm ready," she said, even though it felt like a lie, a mask she donned to hide the truth—the gnawing dread that thrummed beneath her skin. Yet, she still straightened her spine and willed her voice to sound steadier than she felt. "Let's do it."

They took their places on opposite sides of the circle, the black candle casting eerie shadows in the otherwise darkened room. Cole began to play a haunting melody on the cursed guitar, his fingers dancing across the ancient strings. The notes were sharp and icy, piercing through the stillness of the room like shards of glass.

When he chanted in a low, guttural tone, the words were unfamiliar to Rowan, a blend of ancient languages that seemed to vibrate in the air. She closed her eyes and felt the energy in the air shift and change. The words rolled from his lips like thunder rumbling in a storm, resonating against the darkened walls of the great room. Rowan let them wash over her like a warm tide, drawing her in deeper with its hypnotic melody and soothing undertow, despite the dark purpose it served. She felt a strange pull, as if something inside her was reaching out, yearning to connect with the unseen.

"Join me," Cole urged, his words cutting through her trance-like state. "Repeat after me: *From the salt of the earth and blood of my veins, I call thee forth to break thy chains. Spirit of shadow, heed my plea; Come forth and speak through me...*"

Rowan's eyes snapped open. Taking a breath, she summoned the strength buried beneath layers of anger and fear. The syllables felt heavy on her tongue, laden with power she didn't understand. But the tremor in her voice soon subsided as she spoke the ancient words, weaving them into the air like threads of a delicate web. She felt the energy in the room shift, as if the very fabric of reality thinned around them.

"Spirit wronged, bound in shadow and wrath; Hearken now to the winds of your despair. Rise through the storm, cry through the gale; And speak the name that binds your tormentor..."

As their voices intertwined, the air in the room shifted again. Rowan felt a shadow brush against her soul, leaving a trail of ice and raising goosebumps on her arms. The candle flickered, stirred by an otherworldly breath.

"Keep going," Cole urged, his eyes gleaming with an almost feverish intensity.

Rowan pressed on, her voice growing stronger with each repetition of the incantation. The words seemed to take on a life of their own, pouring from her lips with increasing urgency.

Suddenly, the temperature plummeted. Rowan's breath

came out in visible puffs, and she felt an overwhelming sense of dread wash over her. Something was here. Something dark and malevolent.

"Cole," she whispered, her voice tight with fear. "I think —"

"I know," he cut her off, his eyes darting around the room. "Don't stop. We're close."

Rowan nodded, forcing herself to stay anchored. But the chill was no longer just a sensation; it was alive, swirling around her like a predator stalking its prey. She gritted her teeth, willing the fear to recede even as her heart raced, pounding so loud she was sure it would drown out their chanting. Every shadow seemed to writhe and twist, reaching out with spectral fingers. The air thrummed with energy, a dark pulse synchronized with her racing heart. Rowan's fingers tingled, as if alive with electricity. Something was here, lurking just beyond sight, and the knowledge sent a surge of adrenaline coursing through her veins. She felt the unseen presence circling them, probing, searching for a way in.

The air crackled with an otherworldly energy, and Rowan felt a sudden, overwhelming pressure bearing down on her. Her vision blurred, the room spinning around her as if she were caught in a vortex. She gasped as the shadows thickened, swirling like ink in water. A cold grip encircled her throat, and she fought against it, clawing at the air as if to break free. But the darkness was insistent, a parasite burrowing beneath her skin. She tried to speak, to cry out to Cole, but her voice was trapped in her throat.

"It's happening," Cole's voice sounded distant, muffled.

"Don't fight it, Rowan. Let him in."

Rowan looked across the circle at him, the fear naked in her eyes. "Cole… I'm trusting you. Bring me back."

Cole's chanting only grew louder, more frenzied. The martyr guitar wailed, its unholy notes piercing through Rowan's skull.

And then, with a sudden, sickening lurch, she felt the presence of something else. Something dark and twisted clawed its way into her mind. Rowan felt herself unraveling, threads of her identity fraying as they swirled into the void. The world around her dissolved—a kaleidoscope of memories and nightmares intermingling, a cacophony of voices whispering her name.

A scream built inside her, clawing its way up from her core. Just as it was about to burst forth, everything went black.

Time fractured.

Chapter 15

The world tilted and spun, reality fragmenting like shattered glass. Rowan gasped, her consciousness lurching and plummeting through a vortex of disjointed memories and sensations. Her eyes—no, not her eyes—snapped open to a dark, claustrophobic room.

Disorientation crashed over her in nauseating waves as her unfamiliar surroundings came into focus. Moonlight streaming through a barred window. Sickly yellow cinderblock walls. A narrow cot with rumpled sheets. A squat stool positioned in front of a small desk, both bolted to the floor and wall. A heavy steel door standing between her and the dark and silent corridor beyond. The acrid stench of antiseptic disinfectant lingering in her sinuses, barely masking the more unpleasant odors that lurked underneath.

Recognition dawned, horror winding up her throat like smoke from a dying fire.

She knew this place. But never like this. Never from within.

Bridgewater State Hospital.

She was inside Troy Chapman's mind.

Rowan's thoughts ricocheted wildly, struggling to make sense of this impossible shift. Her consciousness collided with foreign sensations as she flexed unfamiliar fingers, feeling the coarse fabric of hospital-issue pants beneath them.

"No," Rowan growled, and Troy's lips moved in sync, the word strange and unfamiliar in his voice. "No!"

Her mind recoiled, struggling against the invasion.

This isn't me. I'm not him. I can't be him.

But she was.

She stumbled to her feet, legs trembling beneath her. The cell swam, nausea rising as she fought to orient herself in this stolen form. Troy's body felt wrong, alien. Longer limbs, broader shoulders. Even the air tasted different as it rasped through his lungs.

It was the deepest time of night, and the hospital for the criminally insane was locked in darkness. The only sounds were the faint hum of electricity, the soft trickle of water through the heating radiators, and the occasional creak of metal as the window contracted against the frosty night air.

Rowan's gaze fixed on the stainless steel mirror mounted on the wall. She approached it with a trepidation that clawed at her insides. As her reflection came into view, her heart constricted with a visceral loathing.

The face staring back was gaunt and haunted. Sallow skin. Sunken eyes ringed with bruise-like shadows. Lank, greasy hair hung in stringy clumps. A vacant stare that spoke of unimaginable horrors. It was the visage of a man hollowed out by guilt and fear.

It was the face of her daughter's murderer.

Rage exploded through her, white-hot and all-consuming. This was him. The monster who had stolen her Lily, ripped away her light and laughter forever. Disgust and hatred crashed over Rowan in relentless waves as she glared at the wretched figure in the mirror. Her fist—Troy's fist—slammed into the polished steel plate with a sickening crunch, as if she could somehow shatter the unbreakable mirror and obliterate the murderer before her. Blood welled from split knuckles that barely dented the reflective surface.

"You fucking monster," she snarled, voice trembling with fury and revulsion. "You took her from me. You destroyed everything."

Rowan's thoughts whirled in a maelstrom of hatred and grief. How dare he still draw breath after he had stolen Lily's life, had extinguished her bright existence? How dare he live while her little girl rotted in the ground? Her fingers twitched, longing to wrap around his throat and squeeze until the life drained from his wretched body. Instead, she raised her fist again, relishing the pain as she struck the unyielding mirror. Again. And again. Scarlet droplets spattered against the yellow walls.

"I'll make you suffer," Rowan hissed through Troy's clenched teeth. "I'll tear you apart from the inside out."

A distant part of her mind recognized the futility of this violence—she was trapped in Troy's body, after all. But logic didn't stand a chance against the tide of anguish that threatened to drown her.

Troy's voice seeped into Rowan's consciousness, a murky undercurrent beneath her rage.

"You already did, Rowan," he whispered bitterly. "You

already tore me apart. I am in Hell, and these are my memories."

Rowan stood back, struggling to make sense of the images assaulting her mind. Memories that were not hers but belonged to the disturbed man whose body she now inhabited. This wasn't just studying someone from a distance; this was being inside their head, experiencing their thoughts and emotions firsthand. It was overwhelming, suffocating. She remembered his childhood, a bleak and loveless existence with parents who viewed him as little more than a burden. She felt his rage at being overlooked and ridiculed by his peers, his twisted satisfaction in exerting control over those weaker than him. She experienced the solace he found in Cole's seething, rage-filled music.

And then there were the darker memories—the violent ones that made her shudder with revulsion and fear. Lily's eyes, wide and filled with terror. Her pitiful screams as she wailed and cried for her mother.

"I'm sorry," Troy croaked in her mind, "I didn't—I couldn't..." His voice cracked, the syllables shards of glass grinding in the silence. "God, I'm so sorry."

"Shut up!" Rowan hissed through clenched teeth, her fury barely contained. "You don't get to be sorry, you sick bastard!"

"Please," Troy's thoughts begged. "I was just a stupid kid. I didn't understand—"

"You understood enough to torture my daughter," Rowan snarled. Her nails—Troy's nails—dug crescents into her palms. She staggered back and sank onto the edge of the cot, head in her hands. This was too much to endure. How could she have made such a terrible mistake?

Rowan's panic rose like bile in Troy's throat. She needed to escape, to claw her way out of this stolen skin. But there was nowhere to go. She was here, trapped in this madman's body, depending on him for salvation.

A sudden noise jolted her back to reality.

A low scraping echoed from the corridor outside. It slithered across the floor, a grating sound that seemed to scratch along the very nerves of Troy's spine. It was a noise that belonged to no earthly creature, a rasping, desperate clawing that sent a cold tide sweeping through Troy's veins. Rowan felt his body stiffen, his breath catching in his throat. Something primal within them both recognized this sound: the harbinger of something dark and malevolent.

"No," Troy whimpered. "Not again. Please, God, not again."

The scratching grew louder, closer, a relentless, hungry sound that filled the cell with an overwhelming sense of menace. Goosebumps prickled across Troy's skin as the temperature in the room plummeted.

"What is that?" Rowan demanded, fear now threading through her anger.

The sound inched closer, a sinister presence that seemed to suck the warmth from the air. Rowan felt Troy's heart hammering in their shared chest, his palms slick with cold sweat.

"What's coming?" she pressed, fighting to keep her voice steady. "Tell me!"

The scratching morphed into a low, guttural growl that seeped through the cracks around the door like a noxious gas.

It was at the door now, a frenzied, inhuman scrabbling that froze Troy's marrow, as if winter had taken root inside his bones. His terror spiked, his thoughts a frantic whirlwind that threatened to sweep Rowan away. She felt his panic as if it were her own, her heart slamming against her ribs like the drums in one of Cole's songs.

"No, no, no…" Troy's inner voice whimpered as he scrambled backward on his cot, pressing against the hard concrete wall. Terror strangled the rest of his words before they could pass his lips. But he knew the thing outside heard him. It relished his fear and fed on terror as surely as maggots feast upon the dead.

"It's here," Troy whispered, his voice barely audible above the thundering of his pulse. "Oh God, it's here."

Rowan could feel his mind unraveling, his thoughts scattering like dead leaves in a bitter wind. She grappled with his rising panic, trying to anchor herself amidst the chaos.

"What's out there, Troy?" Rowan insisted. "Tell me what it is!"

Troy's consciousness trembled. "You know what it is," he rasped. "You're the one who sent it."

* * *

Cole stood transfixed in the mansion's great room, his steel-blue eyes locked on Rowan's levitating form. Her body hung suspended in the air, her toes inches above the circle of graveyard dirt on the wide floorboards. Her ginger hair was loose and wild, her eyes vacant and unfocused. She was nothing but a conduit to the spirit world now. Her limbs were splayed like a marionette held by invisible strings, and her back arched so far it seemed as though her spine would snap. Her mouth hung wide open like a broken hinge, and a cacophony of voices spilled out as if there was a speaker buried in her throat. Cole recognized Rowan's voice and another man's. Troy's? Cole could make out all the words, but they sounded desperate. Frightened.

"Fuck," he muttered, raking a hand through his black hair as he fought the urge to intervene. Every instinct screamed at him to reach out, to pull Rowan back from the brink of whatever abyss she teetered upon. But he knew, with a sinking certainty, that this was a battle she had to fight alone.

She was on her own now.

Cole threw an impatient glance at the clock on the wall. They were running out of precious time. He couldn't keep the portal open indefinitely; if he didn't close it soon, it could have disastrous consequences for both of them. The blades on his throat rippled in the flickering light as he swallowed nervously, eyeing the black candle burning at the head of the circle. If something went wrong, he would have to hurl it into the circle and extinguish the flame to prevent Troy's spirit from fleeing into their world. But if he closed the portal before Rowan's soul reunited with her body, it would strand her on the other side forever. One false step could mean her eternal damnation.

As he kept vigil in the candlelit room, Cole couldn't stop replaying the demon's words in his mind, its chilling promise that he was destined to betray Rowan, just as he had turned on countless others. He tried to push away the thought, but an icy fear gripped at his heart. What if it spoke the truth? If the moment came, would he turn his back on Rowan to save himself? He refused to even consider it, but a tiny voice inside whispered that maybe betrayal was simply in his nature, a primal survival tactic honed from years of abuse and trauma. The only person he had ever felt truly loyal to was himself.

He took a hesitant step forward, muscles coiled with tension, when Rowan's eyes snapped open, unseeing and milky white.

"Rowan?" Cole called, voice rough with concern. "Can you hear me?"

No response. Just the haunting echo of those two voices—Rowan's and Troy's—layered and discordant as they clashed on the other side of the veil.

I should never have let her do this, Cole thought, guilt gnawing at his insides. *I knew the risks, and I still let her walk into that monster's mind.*

That's when he heard the sudden sound reverberating through the mansion's silent halls. A heavy thud followed by the telltale scrape of a foot across the polished hardwood.

He wasn't alone.

Cole's eyes whipped toward the closed door, bracing himself for it to burst open at any moment.

* * *

The cell door groaned, its hinges protesting as an unseen force pressed against it. Rowan's determination surged, shattering her fear like a hammer striking glass.

"Troy," she hissed urgently. "I need its name. Tell me the

demon's name. Now."

The door creaked ominously, the sound stretching out like a death rattle. Troy's thoughts scattered like leaves in a storm and his body trembled violently, his eyes fixed on the slowly widening gap.

"I can't," he sobbed. "It'll kill me."

"Damn it, Troy! It's going to kill you anyway!" Rowan snarled, her desperation bleeding into her words. "It already did. These are just your memories, remember? Give me something, anything to fight it with. You owe me that much!"

"Owe you?" Troy sneered. "You're the reason it's coming. You did this to me. I was getting help in here. I was training to be a councilor. I was going to help others, maybe even save them… until you sent that thing after me."

The door let out another eerie creak, the thick steel flexing impossibly. A wave of terror washed over Troy, his heart pounding so hard Rowan thought it might burst from his chest. She delved deeper into his memories, plunging through the layers of his psyche in search of the answer. She sifted through the debris of his shattered life, the jagged shards of his past cutting into her as she rummaged through his darkest secrets.

But the demon's name still eluded her.

"Please," Rowan pleaded, her voice breaking. "For Lily. For all the lives you destroyed. Do one right thing."

Troy went silent and Rowan could feel the inner struggle playing out in his mind. He wanted to lash out at her for what she had done to him, but a small part of him yearned to make amends, to ease her sorrow and atone for the pain he had caused.

At last, his resistance crumbled like ash and he surrendered the one piece of power he possessed.

"Mal'akh," he whispered, the name slithering through Rowan's thoughts like a serpent. "Its name is Mal'akh."

The word hung in the air, vibrating with power, a talisman that held the key to salvation or damnation. For a heartbeat, everything was still.

Then the door exploded inward.

It smacked against the wall, a thunderclap that no one else would hear. In the morning, no one would recall anything unusual about this night, and the security cameras would reveal nothing. Because what stood in Troy's doorway didn't want to be seen. It wasn't after anyone else; it was after him and him alone.

Rowan's world tilted on its axis as she beheld the figure that entered. It wore Lily's face, but it wasn't her daughter. It was a nightmare come to life, a perversion of everything Lily had been. Its eyes burned with an unholy crimson fire, and its smile twisted into a rictus of malice, teeth too sharp, too numerous.

Troy's body shook uncontrollably, his throat working to form words that wouldn't come. The demon—Mal'akh— fixed its gaze upon him, and Rowan felt Troy's bladder release in abject terror. Trapped in his consciousness, she fought to maintain her sense of self.

This isn't real, she told herself, even as Lily's possessed form advanced into the room. *This isn't my Lily.*

The hellfire of Lily's eyes blazed, searing through Troy as if the demon within her was reaching for Rowan herself.

"Oh, but it is real, mommy," it purred, its voice a discordant mixture of Lily's girlish tones and something far older, far more malevolent. "I know you're in there. And you made all this possible."

It stepped into the cell and the shadows seemed to reach out for it, to glory in the majesty of its darkness.

Troy whimpered, shrinking back against the wall. "I'm sorry," he sobbed. "I didn't know… I didn't mean—"

"Didn't mean what?" Lily's face contorting into a mask of rage. "To rip the life from an innocent girl?"

Rowan struggled against the paralysis of Troy's fear, desperate to act, to fight, to do anything but watch as this abomination wearing her daughter's face approached. But she was trapped, a passenger in a doomed vessel, forced to confront the terrifying reality of what was about to happen.

Lily reached for Troy, her hand now tipped with razor-sharp claws, and Rowan felt a scream building in her throat. Her determination crystallized, her need to flee this place outweighing her terror.

"I won't let you drag me down with you," she snarled. Pushing against the boundaries of Troy's mind with all her might, she shouted the phrase Cole had taught her to break the chains binding her to Troy's accursed soul.

"By flame and salt, by blood and bone, I banish thee back to thy shadowed home."

Nothing happened. Troy's hold on her was too strong.

"I can't face this alone." His voice was a trembling whisper in their mind, and fear permeated every fiber of their shared being. "Please… Don't leave me."

The demon wearing Lily's face loomed closer, its putrid

breath filling the air.

Rowan's consciousness thrashed against Troy's, desperate to break free from this nightmare. "Let me go!" she screamed, her words ricocheting through their common mindscape.

Troy's grip tightened. "I can't," he whimpered. "I need you to understand, to forgive. It'll spare me if only you forgive…"

His psyche clung to Rowan like a drowning man to driftwood, unwilling to relinquish the life raft of their shared existence. His desire for understanding, for some twisted form of absolution, collided violently with Rowan's need to escape. Images flooded her mind—the strangling, the stabbing, Lily's screams, her body face-down in the dirt with her neck broken.

Rowan recoiled, fighting the onslaught of Troy's memories. "No!" she cried out, her anguish echoing in the confines of Troy's skull. "I don't want to see this!"

"Please," Troy begged, his mental voice cracking. "I never meant—"

"Liar!" Rowan's fury exploded, a searing heat that burned through the fear. "Let me go!"

The thing that was Lily took another step forward, its movements liquid and unnatural. Rowan felt Troy's body press against the cold wall, nowhere left to retreat.

"Such delicious despair," Mal'akh hissed, running a tongue too long and forked across Lily's lips.

Rowan's consciousness strained against Troy's iron grip, a tug-of-war between two tortured souls. The room around them blurred, reality and memory bleeding together in a nightmarish haze.

I can't be here, she thought. *I can't witness this…*

"You're not going anywhere," Troy's thoughts echoed, now tinged with bitter spite. His desperate grip on her tightened. "You wanted justice. Now you'll see. You'll understand. You're going to feel what I felt. Suffer as I suffered."

The demon wearing Lily's face inched closer, its eyes gleaming with unholy glee.

And in that moment, Rowan knew she was about to experience death itself.

Chapter 16

Cole ground his molars together as he listened to the panic in the otherworldly voices erupting like lava from Rowan's gaping mouth. "Damn it," he growled, his eyes darting anxiously between her and the closed door to the great room.

The sound of footsteps somewhere in the mansion had gone quiet.

But that didn't mean he was alone.

And then it hit him. Cole's heart suddenly tumbled like a stone into a dark well as he came to an awful realization—the goddamned mirror. They had left it hanging in the underground vault. It was a grave mistake.

With his thoughts crackling like a downed power line, he tried to devise a plan while listening intently for any hint of the intruder's presence. But it was as if the mansion was holding its breath, waiting to see what he would do next.

He took a halting step forward toward the door, then froze.

I'm trusting you. Bring me back.

Rowan's words echoed in his mind. If he left the great room, she would be defenseless against whatever was stalking through the house. And yet, the mirror was the only weapon they had against the demon that hunted them both.

I can't leave her like this, Cole thought. *But if I don't get that mirror...*

His tattooed hand clenched into a fist. "Rowan," he called, his voice low and urgent.

But Rowan's consciousness remained trapped in Troy's private hell, oblivious to his words. Cole cursed under his breath, torn with indecision. But he knew he had no choice. The cursed mirror was their only hope. He had to go back for it.

"I'll come back for you," he promised, hoping Rowan could hear him on some level. "Just hold on."

The distant, terrified cries issuing from her mouth chased him toward the door as he forced himself to move. With a final glance back at her levitating form, Cole steeled himself and stepped into the heavy gloom of the hallway. He moved cautiously, his muscles live wires humming with current. The mansion's deep silence pressed in on him, broken only by the soft creak of floorboards beneath his boots. Dust motes danced in the faint glow of the moonlight filtering through the windows, ghostly specters floating in the air.

Cole's heart thumped like the bass of a concert as he navigated the labyrinthine halls, his senses heightened to a razor's edge. His intuition screamed danger, urging him to turn back, to return to Rowan's side. Even as he tried to summon his usual bravado, he couldn't shake the feeling of being watched. The hairs on the back of his neck stood on end, and he found himself glancing over his shoulder every few seconds.

Whispers arose from the shadows, insidious and taunting.

You're a failure, Cole. You can't save her…

"Shut up," Cole hissed, his fists clenching at his sides. "Get out of my head."

You've abandoned her, just like you knew you would. She's going to die, and it will be all your fault…

A flicker of movement caught his eye, there and gone in an instant. Cole paused, senses on high alert, feeling an unsettling shift in the atmosphere. It was there—a glimpse at the periphery of his vision. A shadow, darker than the night itself, slipped away like smoke. Cole's pulse quickened, a feral instinct stirring within.

"Show yourself," he snarled, his voice echoing in the empty hallway.

Only silence answered him, but the shadows seemed to deepen, coiling at the edges of his vision. Cole's pulse raced like a freight train barreling down the tracks as he remembered what he had learned about the demon.

It's not enough for it to drag the souls of the guilty to Hell. It needs to punish its victims first, to torment them…

"Is this what you wanted?" he muttered. "To make me feel small again? Helpless?"

As if in response, a chill wind whispered through the corridor, carrying with it the faintest scent of decay. Cole's stomach churned, but he forced himself to keep moving, jaw clenched and eyes hard as flint. The mirror. He had to reach the mirror, or all was lost.

Each step seemed to take an eternity as Cole crept his way through the halls to the steep staircase that descended deep into the bowels of the mansion. He hesitated at the open door. The stairs spiraled down like a gaping chasm before him. Was that another flicker behind him? A deeper shade in the hallway's gloom? He spun, his ribs trembling under the relentless pounding of his heartbeat.

Nothing but the emptiness greeted him.

But he sensed it—something was there, waiting, watching. The very air seemed charged with malice, thickening around him like a living thing. He could almost hear it breathing, a low, guttural rasp that traced an icy finger down his spine. Filling his lungs with a breath, he plunged into the darkness.

The vault loomed as he neared the bottom of the steps. There was a faint tremor in Cole's hand as he reached for the lock. For a moment, he allowed himself a fleeting sense of relief. But that momentary respite evaporated instantly, replaced by a wave of creeping dread.

The door was already unlocked.

He never left it unlocked.

As he nudged it open, a fetid stench assaulted his nostrils, making his gorge rise. It was the unmistakable smell of decay, of flesh rotting from the inside out. Cole's breath turned brittle, that nauseating sense of dread roiling the pit of his stomach.

With a final push, the door swung wide, revealing the dimly lit interior of the vault. Cole's wary gaze swept over the cavernous space. It was still. Quiet. There was the mirror, hanging on the wall at the far end of the room where they had left it. Its surface gleamed with the reflected glow of the candles still burning low in their sconces. Their sickly flames threw deep shadows around the room.

Cole's nerves sizzled as he entered and rushed to the

mirror. He gripped the ornate frame, lifted… and froze with dawning horror.

There was someone else in the reflection. Someone who stood right behind him.

Cole whirled around…

…and came face-to-face with Devin's walking corpse.

Or what was left of it.

"Jesus Christ," Cole choked out, bile scorching his throat.

The thing that had once been Devin grinned, its flesh sloughing off in wet chunks that revealed the pulsing sinew beneath. Maggots writhed in empty eye sockets that still seemed to see everything, and the stench of putrefaction filled the air. The corpse's lips curled back in a grotesque mockery of a smile.

"Not quite," it rasped. The demon's voice was like gravel on glass as it spoke through the remnants of Devin's decaying flesh. "You're too late, Cole. The bitch is mine now… and you delivered her right to me."

The corpse lurched forward with inhuman speed, its putrid fingers clawing for Cole's throat. He barely managed to dodge, his back slamming against the cold stone wall.

"Come on, motherfucker," he snarled, summoning the aggression that had defined his life for so long. "You want a fight? I'll give you a fucking war."

The corpse lunged again. Cole ducked and drove his shoulder into its midsection. The impact was like hitting a wall of rotting meat, and he gagged at the sensation. They tumbled to the ground in a tangle of limbs, the corpse's strength far beyond what its decaying frame should allow.

Flat on his back, Cole's fist connected with the corpse's

head, sinking into the decaying flesh with a sickening squelch. He recoiled in disgust just as the corpse's hands flew out and found his throat, squeezing with terrifying force. Panic surged through him, primal and raw, as he gasped and struggled desperately.

"What's wrong, Cole?" the demon taunted, its fetid breath hot on his face. "Doesn't this feel familiar? Don't you feel like a little boy again?"

Cole's vision blurred, the vault's dim light fading as the corpse's putrid fingers dug deeper into his throat. The stench of death was overwhelming, filling his nostrils and making his head spin. He could feel the demon's malevolence seeping into his skin, a cold, oily sensation that made his stomach churn. As black spots danced at the edges of his vision, Cole's mind flashed to the countless foster homes, the abuse, the addiction, the rage that had fueled his music. He'd already survived hell. He wouldn't let this unholy creature drag him back.

With a burst of adrenaline, he drove his knee upward, feeling something crack in the reanimated body above him. The grip on his throat loosened—just enough for him to break free and roll out from beneath the corpse. Gulping air down his bruised throat, he scrambled to his feet and retreated until his back hit the wall. His gaze darted around the vault, searching desperately for a weapon, anything he could defend himself with.

That's when he saw it—there, on a nearby shelf. An ancient ceremonial blade, its silver tarnished but still sharp.

Cole lunged for it, his fingers closing around the cool metal just as the corpse descended on him once more. He lashed out blindly, feeling the blade sink into fetid flesh.

The demon howled in rage, its claws raking down Cole's arm in a white-hot blaze of pain. Cole grimaced, the silver blade falling from his nerveless grip. He grabbed a rusty candlestick from a nearby shelf, hefting it like a weapon, the metal cold and heavy in his grip. The demon screeched, a hideous sound that reverberated through the vault, rattling his bones. It lunged again, eyes blazing with fury, but Cole swung the candlestick hard, the metal connecting with the side of the corpse's head with a sickening crunch.

Cole maneuvered around, avoiding the thing's grasp, and dashed toward the mirror. With one desperate leap, he reached for it, fingers brushing the cool surface. The demon howled, rage exploding in a frenzy as it closed in on him. But Cole wasn't done. He turned, the candlestick raised high, and struck again, the iron meeting flesh with a resounding clang.

With a ferocious roar, the corpse seized him and sent him flying backward.

Right into the black mirror.

The impact shattered the glass, sending shards flying. Cole's eyes widened in horror as he watched the fragments scatter across the stone floor, each shard seeming to pulse with an otherworldly energy. The implications hit him like a freight train. Without the mirror, their plan to trap the demon was in ruins.

"No!" he snarled, his voice raw with despair.

He pushed himself to his feet, his body aching from the blow. He shook the blood from his arms, heart pounding, his gaze darting between the broken mirror and the walking corpse.

The demon's laughter filled the room, a sound that chilled Cole to the bone. The corpse surged at him, its rotting fingers clawing at his face. Cole ducked and weaved, delivering a brutal kick to the thing's midsection. The corpse stumbled back, but the demon's power kept it upright.

You're running out of time, a voice whispered in Cole's mind, a voice that sounded eerily like his own. *Rowan needs you. You can't fail her.*

He lurched for the vault door just as the corpse sprang at him again, a blur of rotted flesh and rage. Cole spun and gripped its putrid skull, fingers digging into its decaying flesh. In one fluid motion, he pivoted, slamming the corpse's skull against a nearby stone pedestal, once, twice, three times.

The sickening crack echoed through the vault. Rotting brain matter and congealed blood exploded outward, splattering across the stone. Cole staggered back, chest heaving, the adrenaline surging through his veins the only thing keeping him on his feet.

The corpse lay sprawled in a pool of gore, unmoving. But Cole knew this was just another hollow victory. The demon didn't need a body to hunt them—it could choose any form it wanted.

Cole slipped through the door and slammed it shut. He could almost feel the heat of the creature's breath still on his neck. His bloody hands trembled as he fumbled with the lock.

"Lock!" he shouted at the door, as if it would obey his command. His fingers found the mechanism and twisted it into place, sealing the corpse inside. He was free—at least for now.

Cole leaned against the hard timber. Blood trickled from cuts on his arms and hands, mixing with the putrid slime that clung to his skin. For a brief second, relief washed over him like ice water, even as he fought the urge to vomit, to spiral into despair. The mirror was lost, and with it, their one hope for survival.

Only one thing mattered now.

He had to get back to Rowan before it was too late.

* * *

The thing that was Lily, with her cracked skin and eyes that flickered with a malicious fire, towered over Troy as he cowered on his pitiful cot. He couldn't tear his eyes away from her, even as panic coursed through his veins and sent his heart racing. Rowan felt his wild urge to shrink away and hide, but he couldn't move. Couldn't do anything except stare up in horror at the teenage girl he had murdered.

Rowan's consciousness fought against Troy's grip on her, like a trapped animal desperately trying to escape its captor. But his hold on her mind was unbreakable, and she couldn't free herself from his control. She felt him pulling her down, down, down, like she was drowning in a sea of darkness, with only flickers of light shining through the surface.

All at once, her world shattered into a kaleidoscope of Troy's memories. She stumbled through the thick fog of one in particular that clawed at her with the ferocity of a wild animal. She saw herself in the woods, the night air heavy and suffocating, laced with the metallic scent of blood. She could feel Lily's fear rising like bile in her throat, raw and unyielding.

"*Mommy, help me! Please!*" echoed a voice that was both familiar and foreign. It belonged to her daughter, yet it seemed to belong to another time, another place. Rowan's heart raced as she grasped for clarity, but all she found were flashes—Troy's leering grin, the glint of a knife, and then the screams. Oh God, the screams.

"Lily!" Rowan's cry cracked, raw with anguish. But the voice wasn't hers. It belonged to Troy, the panic-stricken murderer whose mind she now inhabited. Blood-slick hands grasped at her ankles, dragging her down into a maelstrom of more fractured memories. Lily's screams pierced the darkness, a banshee wail that tore at Rowan's soul. She heard the boys' cruel laughter ring out as they stabbed and stabbed and stabbed.

Blood. So much blood.

"No, please! Not my baby!" Rowan struggled against the tide of alien sensations, her own identity slipping away like sand through an hourglass. The walls of her mind caved in, and she fought against the undertow, pushing back against Troy's memories with an intensity that left her breathless.

"This isn't real," she whispered, clinging to the mantra. "I'm not Troy. I'm Rowan. I'm…"

But the nightmare pulled her deeper, Lily's terrified eyes meeting hers across an impossible chasm of time and space. Rowan sobbed, lost in the echo of her daughter's final moments. Tears streamed down her face as she fought to surface from the depths of despair, to find the light beyond the blood-soaked darkness.

"Let me wake up. Please, let me wake up…"

And then she became aware of a heavy presence looming over her. Pain exploded through her as Mal'akh's claws pierced Troy's flesh, hot blood spilling, soaking his clothes. She screamed, trying desperately to wrench herself free from the horror as the demon inside her daughter flayed his flesh. But Troy's spirit wouldn't let go, not until she experienced every second of the agony he had felt when the demon she had summoned tore him to shreds.

Rowan gasped for air, her own voice hoarse and unfamiliar in her ears. The stench of blood was overwhelming, suffocating her with its metallic tang. She felt the demon's claws digging into Troy's skin, his screams echoing in her mind as the agony consumed him. His pain was her pain, and the hellish torment of Troy's death was a searing brand she couldn't escape.

"*Cole!*" she screamed. But no one answered. No one was coming to rescue her. Cole had betrayed her, just as the demon promised.

As Mal'akh stripped the flesh from Troy's bones, Rowan fought with all her might to free herself. She refused to let Troy's memories overpower her completely. With a surge of determination, she pulled back against his hold on her and reached deep within herself for any shred of power she still possessed. Her hand shot out and grasped her dead daughter's arm, feeling the cold, livid flesh beneath her fingertips. With all her strength, she willed herself to break free from Troy's grasp, and for the first time, she sensed a shift—a crack in his hold. Through the haze of pain and confusion, Rowan could feel Troy's grip on her mind beginning to weaken. It was as if somewhere, beyond the veil of this waking nightmare, someone was fighting for her, calling her back to the light.

And then, suddenly, she felt it—a spark deep within her core that ignited into an inferno. It burned through her veins like wildfire, filling her with a sense of power and purpose that she had never experienced before.

With a cry that came from somewhere deep within her soul, Rowan summoned all of this power, every ounce of her grief and fear and rage, and hurled it all against Troy's psyche like a battering ram.

The world tilted, fracturing at the edges. Rowan felt herself falling, or perhaps flying, suddenly untethered from Troy's mind. But as she slipped away, his final thought reached her:

"I'm sorry."

* * *

Cole burst into the great room, his bruised body screaming with every movement. The sight that greeted him sent a fresh wave of fear crashing through his already battered soul.

Rowan still hung suspended in the air, her eyes rolled back to the whites in her head. The air around her shimmered with an unnatural energy now, holding her captive in a prison of memories not her own. The agonized screams pouring from her gaping mouth turned Cole's veins to ice. Something had gone terribly wrong.

"Rowan!" he called out. "Rowan, can you hear me? Break the spell, damn it! Say the words!"

He limped toward her, reaching out to shake her shoulders. The moment his fingers made contact, a jolt of energy surged through him, forcing him back.

"Fuck!" he snarled. He reached for the black candle, ready to hurl it into the circle and seal the portal, but his hand wavered in the air, hesitant to touch it. He couldn't do this to her, couldn't strand her there in the underworld of the damned. The thought of failing her as he'd failed so many others was a rusted nail in his mind, impossible to endure.

"Fight it!" Cole's voice shook with raw emotion.

Rowan's eyelids fluttered, but she remained trapped in Troy's nightmare.

Cole gritted his teeth, frustration and fear warring within him. "Come on," he muttered, running a hand through his sweat-soaked hair.

A flicker crossed her face, an echo of life buried beneath layers of torment. He could see the struggle etched into her features, the way her fists clenched tightly, as if struggling against something intangible. Her will was there—beneath the surface—like a candle flickering against the encroaching dark.

"Come on!"

The air crackled with tension and Cole held his breath, waiting for a sign.

Then, suddenly, Rowan gasped, a sharp intake of air that shattered the spell binding her. She dropped from the air and hit the floor in a heap. Her eyes fluttered open, wide and luminous, as if she had emerged from the depths of a murky lake. Another gasp tore from her throat as she fought her way back to consciousness. She blinked rapidly, her gaze darting around the room in confusion before finally settling on Cole's face.

"Rowan!" Relief flooded him, but it was shot through with

uncertainty. Would she remain free? Had she truly shaken off the chains that bound her?

"Cole…" she whispered, a tremor weaving through her voice. Color flooded her cheeks, yet confusion still clouded her gaze. She looked around, as if awakening from a long, haunted sleep.

"I'm here," he said. "You're back, Rowan."

Rowan clung to him, her fingers digging into the fabric of his t-shirt as she buried her face in his neck. She could feel the steady thrum of his heartbeat against her cheek, a comforting reminder she was alive, that she had survived. Her breath came in shallow gasps, the remnants of Troy's awful memories clinging to her like cobwebs. The dim light of the room pressed down on her, and she blinked against the fragments of memories still flickering in her mind. She drew another deep breath, this one steadying her spirit, and with it came a sense of release—the tension in her frame dissipated, leaving behind only the weight of her trauma.

"Mal'akh," she whispered, the name slithering off her tongue like poison. "That's its name." The moment she uttered it, a chill swept through the room, as if the very essence of the creature recoiled at being named.

Cole nodded, feeling the significance of their victory settle in the pit of his stomach. "I know," he said. "I heard everything. You did it."

"It knows," Rowan breathed, her voice tinged with dread. "The demon knows we've discovered its true name. We need to end this. Now."

That's when her mind cleared enough to notice the blood streaking Cole's skin. Her brows knitted with confusion, and he answered her unspoken question.

"It's here, Rowan," he said. "Mal'akh. It shattered the mirror."

A stricken look crossed Rowan's face. "That's it, then. We're fucked, aren't we?"

Cole saw pain carved into every line of Rowan's face, the toll that this revelation had taken on her already tortured soul. "I'm sorry," he said. "I couldn't stop it. This was all for nothing. You suffered through that hell for nothing."

The weight of those words closed over them like a coffin lid. Rowan's eyes misted over, her grief as fresh as the day Lily was taken from her.

"What do we do now?" she whispered.

"We run," Cole replied with an edge of urgency. "We run like hell."

He helped her to her feet, and together, they made their way out of the room. As their footsteps echoed through the empty halls, the gothic mansion felt like a haunted tomb.

The moon hung low in the sky, casting an eerie silver glow across the grounds as they stepped out into the night. The sound of the waves crashing against the barren cliffs reverberated through the darkness like a booming cannon.

Cole led the way toward the Land Rover, eyes fixed on the long, dark stretch of driveway. The air was thick with foreboding as they approached the truck, both of them acutely aware of the danger that awaited them at every turn.

Cole fumbled with the keys, his hands shaking with adrenaline and fear. He finally managed to unlock the door, and they climbed inside, Rowan in the passenger seat and Cole in the driver's. Silence settled between them as Cole started the engine. Where would they go? Where would they possibly be safe from the unrelenting evil that hunted them?

"We need to get back to my house," Rowan suddenly blurted, breaking the silence. "There's something there that could help us."

Chapter 17

The porch boards groaned under Rowan and Cole's feet as they approached the front door of the house on Pennybrook Lane. The moon had climbed high in the sky, casting an eerie silver glow over the cold and silent street. At the far end, the gnarled trees of the Lynn Woods loomed like a nest of ancient predators, watching, waiting. Their hulking shadows cast a sense of foreboding over the darkened houses.

Rowan paused at her doorstep and threw a nervous glance over her shoulder. Her pulse jumped and stuttered like a skipping record, unable to find its rhythm, as she exhaled a cloud of frost into the chilly air. She couldn't shake the dreadful feeling that Mal'akh was lurking just beyond her vision, waiting for the perfect moment to strike. Every instinct told her to run, to escape the prying eyes that seemed to follow her every move.

"Cole," she whispered. "Do you feel that?"

Cole scanned the deserted street as he nodded grimly. "It's like it's watching us. Waiting."

Rowan's hand trembled slightly as she inserted the key into

the lock, the metallic scrape echoing through the still night air. They crossed the threshold into the darkened foyer, and Rowan paused, her eyes drifting to the staircase leading up to Lily's bedroom.

She took a shuddering breath. "It's up there."

Cole's eyes narrowed. "I'm still not sure about this, Rowan."

"You said we needed a mirror that had witnessed pain, one that was imbued with sorrow. Lily's mirror is saturated with it. It captured her reflection, an innocent child raped and brutalized. And then it witnessed my own grief and despair as I mourned my baby every night in that very room. That kind of spiritual energy... it could be enough to trap Mal'akh, couldn't it?"

Cole looked unconvinced as he shrugged out of his leather jacket and laid it across the back of the couch. Dried blood still streaked his arms as he frowned and shifted uncomfortably, his hands clenching and unclenching at his sides.

Rowan met his gaze, unflinching. Her lips thinned. "It has to be enough. We're out of options."

A heavy silence stretched between them until Cole gave a curt nod. "Alright, fuck it. You're right. We've got nothing to lose."

Rowan led the way up the stairs to where Lily's bedroom door stood closed at the end of the hallway. Her quivering hand rattled the doorknob. Steeling herself with a sharp intake of breath, she pushed it open.

The stale air of the room washed over them. Dust motes danced in the thin beam of light seeping through the drawn curtains from the streetlamp, illuminating the unmade bed and the stuffed animals at its foot. The posters of the heavy metal bands—a couple of Cole himself—stared back at them, faded and peeling at the edges. And there, above the desk, hung the antique mirror—its ornate frame tarnished, the glass dark and lifeless.

Rowan flicked on a lamp and approached the mirror, her reflection ghostly in the dim light. Cole stood back and watched silently, his expression unreadable as her fingertips grazed the photo of the family vacation that Lily had tucked into the corner. The image of her smiling daughter and husband, forever frozen in time, caused a lump to form in Rowan's throat. In her mind's eye, she could see Lily sitting here at her desk, brushing her hair and humming a tune, unaware of the horror that awaited her. For a moment, she swore she saw Lily's face staring back at her, pale and ethereal, before it dissolved into her own haggard visage.

A sob caught in Rowan's throat, tears blurring her vision as she snatched her hand back from the photo as if it burned, clenching it into a white-knuckled fist at her side. She closed her eyes and took a steadying breath, trying to push down the torrent of emotions. She knew what had to be done.

"Help me move the desk," she said, her voice rough and strained.

Cole stepped forward, his imposing frame dwarfing the delicate furniture. Together, they heaved the desk aside, spilling some of Lily's books and CDs to the floor.

"What do you need me to do?" Rowan asked.

Cole looked at her. "You sure about this, Rowan? There's no going back once we start."

She met his gaze, seeing her own desperation mirrored in his eyes. "I'm sure."

Cole nodded and retrieved his weathered leather satchel from the hallway, spilling its contents onto the floor—candles, bone dust, iron filings, and Cole's hastily written translation of the tablet passages.

As they arranged the candles and drew cryptic symbols and runes on the floor, the air grew thick with anticipation. Goosebumps prickled along Rowan's skin, and her heart raced with both fear and hope.

"We're almost ready," Cole said, his voice steadier than she felt. "Just one more thing." With a prick of his thumbnail, he opened the thin scab that had formed over the incision he had made in his fingertip earlier at the mansion. Fresh blood dripped from the wound. Rowan stood back as he went to the mirror and scrawled the demon's name on its surface.

Mal'akh...

Rowan stared at the mirror, seeing not her reflection, but the name of her tormentor written in blood. A sickening dread coiled in her gut and she closed her eyes, steadying herself for what was to come.

"It's time," Cole whispered, his voice a mere breath in the suffocating stillness. He handed Rowan what looked to be an ancient iron spike. "A crucifixion nail," he explained. "Once we trap the demon inside the mirror, you have to shatter it with iron. This spike is the only thing I could be sure of." He watched as she turned it in her palm, feeling its weight. "Remember the words I taught you. Be sure to say them."

He lit the candles, their wavering light casting grotesque shadows on the walls. The mirror loomed before them, a dark portal waiting to reveal Hell. The flickering candlelight distorted their reflections as they stood before it. Fear slithered down Rowan's spine like a drop of melting ice. The air crackled with an otherworldly energy, and for a moment, she could have sworn she heard Mal'akh's laughter echoing in the stillness.

Whatever happened next, there was no turning back.

Rowan's voice trembled as she began the incantation, her words mixing with Cole's deeper tones in an eerie harmony.

"Mal'akh, hear our call. We summon you from the depths of darkness."

Rowan's eyes darted nervously to Cole. "You feel that?" she muttered between phrases. "It's like the room's closing in."

Cole nodded, his jaw muscles flexing between the phrases of the incantation.

The ominous atmosphere intensified with each word that passed between them, as if the very air was being sucked out of the room. Rowan's chest felt like a cauldron, bubbling over with molten energy. She could feel the power building, gathering like a storm on the horizon. Her palms were slick with sweat as she struggled to maintain her focus. The ancient iron spike felt cold and heavy in her grip as she forced herself to continue, her survival instinct screaming at her to run, to hide, to protect herself from the horror they were inviting into the room.

"By blood and grief, we bind you. By innocence lost, we command you."

And within the depths of the mirror, something stirred—a malevolent presence uncoiling from the shadows, drawn by the siren song of their invocation. The mirror's surface began to ripple, like dark water disturbed by an invisible stone, distorting their reflections into disfigured caricatures.

Rowan's breath slammed to a stop, as if yanked back by an unseen hand. She felt a cold, creeping dread seep into her bones, a primal terror that threatened to overwhelm her and send her fleeing from the room. Her voice faltered, her face pale in the dim light. "Cole, I think—"

"Don't stop," he hissed, gripping her arm. "It's working. We can't stop now."

They pressed on, their voices growing hoarse as they chanted.

The mirror's surface writhed and twisted, a void of darkness that seemed to pulse with malevolent life. Rowan felt it then—an ancient, hungry presence that made her soul recoil.

"It's coming," she whispered. Icy tendrils of fear snaked beneath her skin, her body trembling uncontrollably.

The room plunged into darkness, the candles snuffed out like fragile lives extinguished. In the mirror's depths, a pair of crimson eyes flashed open.

Cole's breath snagged in his throat. "Jesus Christ," he muttered, his hands clenching into fists.

An image slowly took shape in the mirror. Staring back at them in the darkness was a ghastly mockery of her daughter. Lily's delicate features were twisted, her once-bright eyes now burning with unholy light. Limbs elongated into impossible angles, and where her skin should have been soft and warm, it rippled with a life of its own, pulsating with unholy energy.

Rowan felt a fragile hope spark within her. It was working, she could feel it. The mirror ensnared Mal'akh.

A low growl emanated from the demonic creature, its presence growing stronger. The air around them crackled with electricity, and Rowan could feel the hairs on her arms standing on end.

"Say the words," Cole urged. "Quickly, before it's too late."

The thing that was not Lily tilted its head, a sickening crack echoing through the room. Its mouth split into a grin far too wide, revealing rows of needle-sharp teeth.

"Mother," it hissed, the word dripping with malice.

"Don't listen to it!" Cole shouted. "Rowan, say the words and break the mirror! Now!"

Gripping the iron spike tightly, Rowan recited the last lines of the incantation with all of her voice.

"By bone and iron, by wrath and storm; Thy name is revealed, and thy power is torn. Depart, demon, and rest once more. Thy vengeance is served; thy torment is no more..."

The mirror shuddered, the glass cracking and spider-webbing as the demon fought to break free. Rowan felt a surge of power course through her, as if she was channeling every ounce of her grief and anger into this moment. She raised the spike, ready to strike, to finally end this nightmare.

And then, something very unexpected happened.

The mirror suddenly shattered with an ear-splitting crack.

A thousand glittering shards exploded outward in a cascading shower of breaking glass. Rowan and Cole reeled back, their arms raised to shield their faces from the razor-sharp fragments. A guttural roar filled the room, shaking the very walls. From the jagged remains of the mirror, Lily's figure emerged—twisted and monstrous, a nightmarish mingling of girl and demon.

Rowan stumbled backward, a shrill scream erupting from her lips. This wasn't supposed to happen. Their carefully planned trap had failed—and now Mal'akh was loose.

The creature before them was a grotesque synthesis of her daughter's sweet features and the very embodiment of all that was unholy. Eyes like burning coals glowed in Lily's sunken sockets. Bile rose in Rowan's throat as the creature's slick, black tongue slithered out from her daughter's mouth, obscenely long and forked.

Without warning, the demon lunged forward with blinding speed. Its form seemed to stretch and warp as it moved, claws materializing from its elongated fingers. It slammed into Cole, sending him crashing to the floor in a tangle of thrashing limbs. Rowan watched in horror as the thing inside her daughter tore into him, its razor-sharp talons ripping through his flesh with sickening ease. Blood sprayed across the room, painting the lilac walls in a crimson mist. Cole's agonized scream filled the air.

"Cole!" Rowan cried out, frozen with terror.

Lily's head whipped around, the demon's eyes finding Rowan. For a moment, she saw a flicker of her daughter in that monstrous face—an instant of recognition in those hellfire eyes. Then it was gone, replaced by a malice that chilled her to her core.

"This is what you wanted, isn't it, Mother?" the thing wearing Lily's face sneered. "To see the guilty suffer?"

Cole's tortured groans filled the room as the demon continued its assault. Rowan's mind raced, panic consuming her thoughts. *What have we done? How do I stop this?* Her heart felt like a sledgehammer pounding against her ribcage, her limbs paralyzed by terror. Lily's claws ripped into Cole again, eliciting another gut-wrenching cry. Rowan had to act, had to save him, but her body refused to obey. She couldn't move, couldn't breathe. The sight of Lily's face, twisted into a mask of sadistic glee as the demon tore into Cole, was too much to bear.

This can't be happening, she thought, her mind spiraling. *It was supposed to work. We were supposed to trap it, not unleash it.*

"Rowan, get out of here!" Cole choked out between gasps of pain.

His desperate plea jolted her from her paralysis. Rowan darted her eyes around the room, seeking something, anything, that could serve as a weapon. Her gaze fell upon a jagged shard of mirror, glinting in the darkness.

Without thinking, she lunged for it, her fingers closing around its sharp edges. Pain blossomed in her palm as the glass cut into her skin, but she barely noticed. Her focus narrowed to a single, deadly point.

Lily's head swiveled, the demon's baleful eyes boring into her soul. For a heartbeat, time seemed to stand still, the air crackling with unearthly energy. Then, with a howl of rage, the thing inside her daughter turned to face her, its features melting into a grotesque parody of a smile. It hissed, its eyes flickering with malice.

Rowan charged before it could make a move, the jagged mirror shard cutting a deadly path through the air. She plunged it into Lily's chest, driving it deep, choking on the nauseating feeling of stabbing her own daughter in the heart.

Mal'akh howled in agony, the sound equal parts Lily's voice and the grating of stone on bone. Rowan pressed her advantage, twisting the shard deeper into the demon's flesh, hoping against hope it would be enough. The creature's howls shook the room. Its form rippled and contorted, its features shifting between Lily's innocent face and something far more monstrous. For a precious instant, its grip on Cole slackened, and he crumpled to the floor in a heap. Blood pooled beneath him, a dark and spreading stain like a spilled glass of deep red wine.

Rowan's chest tightened like a noose pulling taut, a choked sob tearing from her throat. But there was no time for grief, no time for fear. If she didn't act soon, he would be dead, and she would be next. Even as she fought with all her strength, she could feel the demon's power surging beneath her hands, an unearthly force that threatened to consume everything in its path. Her grip tightened on the mirror shard, her palm sticky with blood now. Its surface began to crack under the strain of twisting. Rowan's mouth felt like it was packed with ashes, her heart pounding against her ribs like a caged bird. She could feel the dark energy emanating from the demon inside her daughter, the cold tendrils of its power reaching out to ensnare her.

The shard fractured in Rowan's hand, and she went stumbling away from the enraged thing inside her daughter. Her eyes landed on the fallen crucifixion nail, glinting dully in the dim light. It was her only hope. She lunged for it. Mal'akh's howl of fury tore through the room as it sensed her intent, its form surging towards her in a blur of infernal energy.

Rowan braced herself, channeling all her grief, anger, and determination into one final, desperate act. With a primal scream torn from the depths of her soul, she swung around and plunged the iron nail into one of those hellish orbs, driving it deep into her daughter's skull.

The explosion of energy that followed was blinding, a shockwave of otherworldly force that hurled both Rowan and the demon apart. She felt the air explode from her lungs as she slammed into the far wall with a bone-jarring impact, her vision swimming with stars and dark spots. Through the haze of pain and disorientation, she could make out Mal'akh clawing at the nail embedded in its eye. Cole's crumpled form lay across the room, a dark pool spreading beneath him. This was her chance, the only one she would get.

With the iron spike still gripped tight in her fist, Rowan scrambled across the room, glass crunching beneath her boots. The acrid stench of sulfur and blood filled her nostrils as she grasped Cole's tattooed arms. A strained groan escaped his lips. She hauled him upright, slinging his arm over her shoulder.

"Can you walk?" she demanded.

Cole's head lolled, his eyes unfocused. "Fuck... maybe," he mumbled.

"We don't have a choice," Rowan hissed, hauling Cole to his feet. "Move!"

As the demon's howls of fury echoed behind them, Rowan half-carried, half-dragged him through the doorway. They stumbled down the stairs, Cole's blood-soaked shirt clinging to his chest and leaving a glistening trail on the carpet.

"We have to keep moving," Rowan urged, her voice

strained with exertion and fear. "It's not over yet."

Cole nodded as he staggered alongside her, grinding his teeth tightly against the pain. "I'm trying," he managed, his free hand clutching at the deep gashes across his flesh.

They burst out of the house and the cool night air hit them like a physical force, a shock against their blood-soaked skin. Behind them, the house seemed to pulse with unholy energy, as if the very walls were alive with the demon's fury. Rowan didn't need to look back to know it was coming after them. Her eyes darted wildly, searching for a direction—any direction—away from the nightmare behind them.

Cole started for the truck, but Rowan dug her heels in and shook her head as a terrible realization struck her. "The keys," she gasped. "They're in your jacket. Inside."

Cole's face, already pale from blood loss, drained of what little color remained. "Fuck," he spat, his eyes darting back towards the house's depths.

Before either could speak again, a bone-chilling shriek tore through the air. The very foundations of the house shook, picture frames crashing to the floor and cracks spider-webbing across the walls.

Rowan's mind raced as she scanned the surroundings, desperately seeking a path to safety. She couldn't risk going to any of the neighbors. What if Mal'akh followed them? And what could the police possibly do? How could anybody possibly save them? They had failed, and they were going to die.

The woods, she thought, her gaze settling on the dense tangle of trees at the end of the street. *We can lose it in there. It's our only chance.*

"Come on," she muttered, her voice a hoarse croak. "We can't stay here." She tightened her grip on Cole, urging him forward as she propelled them toward the tree-line. Her thoughts were a jumbled mess of fear and desperation as they fled, their feet pounding the pavement. The trees closed in around them, swallowing them into the shadows, and the undergrowth seemed to reach out to them, its thorny tendrils snagging at their clothes and skin as they plunged into the pitch-black maze of the Lynn Woods.

Chapter 18

The gnarled branches clawed at Rowan's face, and her lungs burned with each ragged breath. Her muscles screamed in protest as she half-dragged Cole's blood-soaked body through the dense undergrowth. The musty scent of damp earth and decaying leaves mixed with sharp, metallic whiffs of fresh blood. The weight of Cole's muscular frame slumped against her was like an anchor pulling Rowan down into the earth. She could feel her strength waning with each step, the adrenaline that had fueled their escape slowly ebbing away.

We can't keep this up forever, she realized, a cold dread seeping into her bones.

Still, she pushed forward, determined to put as much distance between themselves and Mal'akh as she could manage before it was too late. She navigated the darkness by instinct, her pulse pounding in her ears as she wove through the maze-like trails. The branches scraped against each other like rusted swords, creaking and groaning with every breeze.

Just keep moving, she repeated to herself, a mantra to stave off the rising panic. *Don't look back. Don't think about what's behind us.*

She glanced at Cole's face, his features full of shadows in the faint moonlight. The gashes across his chest still seeped and his skin had taken on a ghostly pallor. He looked like a broken marionette, strings cut, awaiting one last dance.

"Stay with me, Cole," she grunted through gritted teeth. "We're going to find a way out of this. We're going to—"

She stumbled, nearly falling, and felt a surge of frustration rise in her chest. The fear and desperation that fueled her for so long was now a shadow growing long enough to eclipse her. She tightened her grip on Cole's shirt, leaving crimson handprints on the fabric.

A twig snapped in the distance. Rowan froze, her muscles coiled tight. Was it Mal'akh stalking them through the shadows? The sinister presence seemed to seep from the very trees around them, an unseen predator circling its wounded prey.

"It's coming," Cole whispered. "We can't outrun it."

Rowan's jaw clenched. "Watch me," she spat, but the words rang hollow in her own ears. Time was slipping away, and she knew deep in her bones they were losing this race.

"Move," she commanded, her voice cracking with the strain of holding back her fear. "One foot in front of the other. We're not finished yet."

Cole let out a wet, gurgling cough. Blood leaked from the corner of his mouth. "Yeah… I'm trying…"

His words were fading like a candle flame guttering in the wind. Rowan tightened her grip on his shoulders, ignoring the warm stickiness of his blood seeping through her fingers. She couldn't let him slip away. Not now, not like this. Her thoughts spun, grasping for a solution. The old Rowan, the one who existed before Lily's death, would have broken down in tears. But that Rowan was long gone, replaced by a harder, colder version forged in the crucible of grief.

"We need... to stop," Cole wheezed, his voice barely audible over the crunch of leaves and snapping twigs.

Rowan shook her head. "Can't. It'll find us."

"Rowan," Cole murmured. "Look."

She followed his gaze to the forest floor. A trail of dark liquid glistened in the moonlight like a macabre breadcrumb trail marking their passage through the woods. *Cole's blood*, she realized with a sickening lurch in her stomach. They were leaving a path for the demon to follow.

"Shit," Rowan hissed, her eyes darting around the shadowy woods. "We need to throw it off our trail. Can you walk on your own? Just for a bit?"

Cole nodded grimly, straightening up with a grunt of pain. Rowan tore a strip from his shirt to bind his worst wound.

"I'll go east," she said, pointing. "You head west. It can't follow both of us." She prayed Mal'akh would choose to follow her instead of Cole, despite the trail of blood he was leaving behind. The thought should have terrified her, but she felt a grim sense of purpose. If this was to be her last stand, she'd make damn sure it counted.

But Cole only frowned and shook his head. "It doesn't need to follow us, Rowan. It'll find us wherever we go."

She stared at him, his words crashing through her. He was right. It didn't matter how far they ran. The demon would always find them. They could never escape it—because it *was* them.

Rowan felt black tendrils of despair creeping into her heart, the realization that they were utterly alone against an adversary they couldn't possibly defeat. The ritual had failed, the mirror shattered, and now they were alone in the woods, with no plan and no hope of escape.

Is this what Lily felt while she lay dying? she wondered, a pang of grief piercing her heart. *This overwhelming sense of hopelessness? The knowledge that no matter how much she wanted to live, she would not leave these woods alive?*

She inhaled, refusing to entertain such thoughts. Instead, she followed her own command to Cole and started moving, one foot in front of the other. She didn't know why she did it, other than as one last stubborn act of defiance. She refused to surrender to her fate and simply wait there to be slaughtered.

With a shuffling of leaves and snapping twigs, Cole trailed after her. Together, they ventured deeper into the heart of the woods. Twisted branches blotted out the sky, making them feel trapped in an endless, suffocating void. The sense of isolation was overwhelming, the silence broken only by the rasp of their labored breathing and the muffled crunch of their footsteps.

"Why?" Cole's voice was a hoarse whisper. "Why risk everything for me?"

Rowan's step faltered. She looked back at the man she had dragged through the forest, his face a mask of pain and his body a bloody mess.

"Because," she said, her voice thick with emotion she rarely allowed herself to feel, "no one deserves to die like this. Not you. Not... not Lily."

The name hung in the air between them, fragile and raw. But there was no time for grief or guilt now. Not with Mal'akh's presence growing stronger with each passing moment. The woods seemed endless, a labyrinth of shadow and despair. But Rowan wouldn't give up—she couldn't.

As they stumbled forward, Rowan felt the weight of every decision that had led them here. The path of grief and vengeance she had walked for seven long years. The unlikely alliance with the man whose music had sparked the tragedy that shattered her world.

"Rowan," Cole's voice cut through her thoughts. "If we don't make it—"

"Don't," she snapped, her tone sharp with fear and desperation. "We're going to make it out of here. Both of us."

But even as the words left her lips, Rowan wondered if they were hollow; a false comfort offered to a dying man.

The trees suddenly parted and moonlight spilled over them, revealing a towering structure silhouetted like a monolith against the night sky—the Stone Tower of Lynn Woods.

Originally built as a fire observation tower for the town of Lynn, it resembled a medieval turret rising from the crest of Burrill Hill. It loomed high above the trees, the tower's stones and mortar weathered and worn with age and covered in lichen. Ivy clung to its sides like creeping fingers, reaching toward the crescent moon as if seeking to escape the darkness that shrouded the woods.

Cole's labored breathing grew fainter as he collapsed at the base of the tower, too exhausted to stand. He rolled onto his back, his bloody shirt steaming in the cool night air as he stared up at the stars. His blood soaked the ground, black in the moonlight.

"I'm sorry, Rowan," he rasped. "I never meant for any of this to happen."

Tears streamed down Rowan's face, hot and stinging. She clutched his hand, her heart breaking. "I know, Cole. I know."

As she watched the life slowly ebbing from him, a cruel irony struck her like a punch to the gut. After years of hating him, she'd found an unlikely reflection in Cole. Someone who understood her pain, her darkness. And now she was about to lose him, too.

"Just go," Cole murmured. "Leave me."

But Rowan wasn't going anywhere. She wasn't about to let him die alone, not like Lily had. As she kneeled there in the dirt next to him, she wondered how everything had gone so terribly wrong. Was the energy in Lily's mirror not strong enough to contain Mal'akh? Had she waited too long to shatter it? Had they somehow made a mistake in the incantation?

Cole's breathing grew more labored, each breath a battle. Rowan's thoughts tumbled like a landslide, desperate for a solution. There had to be a way to save him, to stop Mal'akh. She couldn't let it end like this.

And then, as her thoughts continued to spiral deeper into despair, a sudden clarity pierced the darkness like a bolt of lightning.

An unlikely reflection...

The ancient tablet's inscription flashed through her mind, its true meaning finally revealing itself, hidden in plain sight all along. She gasped and jolted upright; the pieces falling into place with terrifying precision.

"The mirror," she whispered, her eyes widening. "It's not a physical object. It's… It's *me*."

Cole's eyes fluttered open, his gaze hazy with pain. "What are you talking about?"

Rowan's voice trembled as she spoke, the gravity of her revelation settling in her bones. "We got it wrong. The mirror isn't a thing, it's a *person*. To banish Mal'akh, the demon needs to be made flesh. It needs a living reflection on Earth, a vessel to trap it." She swallowed hard. "I have to let it possess me, just like it did the night we conjured it. And then…"

"No," Cole interjected, grasping at her arm.

"It's the only way," she said, raising her voice to be heard above the wind whispering over the hilltop. "To end this. To save you. Cole, I have to let Mal'akh in, then end it. A last act of atonement for the guilt that gave the demon life."

"No…" Cole coughed and struggled to push himself up. "I won't let…"

Rowan shook her head. "You don't have a choice. Neither of us do." A sad smile played at the corners of her mouth. "This is my fate, Cole. My chance to make things right."

As the words left her lips, the air around them thickened, the stench of sulfur and decay rolling over them in nauseating waves. Mal'akh was close, drawn by the scent of their desperation. Rowan's pulse thundered in her ears, fear and resolve warring inside her.

In the end, there was no choice at all, not if she wanted to stop Mal'akh from dragging her soul to Hell. This was it. Her last stand. She would embrace the demon, let it take her, then drag it screaming into oblivion.

She pushed herself to her feet, swaying as her gaze traveled from the top of the Stone Tower down to the jagged boulders strewn around its base. Yes, the fifty-foot fall would be enough to kill her. All she needed was the strength to fling herself from the pinnacle once Mal'akh was inside her. She closed her eyes, steeling herself for what was to come. In the darkness behind her eyelids, she saw Lily's face, smiling and radiant, untouched by the horrors that claimed her life.

"I'm coming, baby," Rowan whispered. "Mommy's coming home."

With a deep breath, she opened her eyes and stepped toward the tower's arched entrance, ready to face her destiny. The shadows within seemed to beckon, eager to claim their prize. But Rowan no longer feared them. She had nothing left to lose, and everything to gain. In death, maybe she would find the solace that eluded her in life.

Cole's hand shot out and wrapped around her ankle before she could take another step, his grip weak but insistent. "No," he rasped. "I'll do it. I'm the one who needs to atone."

A bitter laugh escaped Rowan's lips. "Atone? What are you talking about?"

Cole's gaze dropped, shame etching deep lines around his eyes. "My music... my fucking existence... It's what led those kids to Lily." His voice cracked. "I filled them with darkness, and I've been drowning in that guilt ever since."

Rowan felt her heart shudder, torn between disbelief and a terrible understanding. "No, I was wrong. About all of it. You can't blame yourself for—"

"Can't I?" Cole's eyes met hers. "If it wasn't for me, your

daughter would still be alive, wouldn't she? This is my chance, Rowan. My only shot at redemption. Look at me… I'm already dying." A wry smile twisted his lips, a ghost of his former sardonic grin.

Rowan stared at him. "But it can't be you, Cole. You said it yourself. It had to be *me* who conjured Mal'akh. *I'm* its vessel."

Cole's lips pressed into a thin line and he shook his head. "It wasn't you I needed for the ritual… it was *this*." He pointed to the necklace hanging around Rowan's throat.

The one Lily wore the night she was murdered.

The one by which Rowan had identified her daughter's remains.

"*This* drew Lily's avenging demon to us… and whoever wears it is its vessel." Cole coughed and grimaced at the pain. "I've never been a very good person, Rowan. I can't bring your daughter back, but if there's still a chance I can save you, let me finally do the right thing. I owe you that much."

Rowan opened her mouth to argue, but the words died on her tongue. In the depths of Cole's eyes, she saw the truth of his words. The pain, the remorse, the desperate need for redemption. The same emotions that had driven her for so long.

"You don't have to do this," she whispered. "It's suicide."

Cole's hand gripped hers, his skin slick with blood and sweat. His lips quirked into a bitter smile. "Maybe. But it's a hell of a way to go out."

With a shaking hand, Rowan reached out and cupped Cole's face, feeling the warmth of his skin beneath her palm. His eyes widened in surprise, a flicker of vulnerability crossing his hardened features. Without thinking, she pressed her lips to his. It wasn't a kiss of passion or romance, but one of absolution. When she pulled away, tears glistened in her eyes.

"I forgive you," she murmured, the words she had never thought she would say.

A flicker of peace crossed Cole's face. "I don't deserve—"

"You do," Rowan interrupted. "We both do."

She leaned forward, pressing her forehead against Cole's. For a moment, they simply breathed together, two broken souls united by grief and the promise of redemption. Then, with a last squeeze of her hand, Cole pulled away and struggled to his feet, his movements sluggish and unsteady. He swayed, and Rowan reached out to support him, her hands gripping his arms as she helped him find his balance. His blood-soaked shirt clung to his skin, a gruesome reminder of the terrible price he'd paid for their vendetta.

The air grew thick, a suffocating blanket of malevolence pressing down upon them. Rowan's skin prickled with the sensation of unseen eyes, Mal'akh's presence intensifying with each passing second. She could feel the demon's hunger, the insatiable desire to claim their souls and drag them into the abyss. They had to act fast while they still had the chance.

Cole's gaze met hers, and a silent understanding passing between them. With blood-stained fingers, he reached for the delicate chain around Rowan's neck and lifted it over her head. The metal was warm from her skin, the silver pendant glinting in the moonlight as he fixed it around his own neck. Rowan's heart clenched. She felt naked without it, as if a piece of her soul had been stripped away. Her mind swam, a maelstrom of emotions threatening to overwhelm her. She wanted to scream, to beg Cole to reconsider, but the words lodged in her throat. Deep down, she knew this was the only way. Cole's guilt had haunted him for years, a festering wound that refused to heal.

As he straightened, squaring his shoulders, Rowan saw a strange sense of serenity settle over him. This was his purpose, his calling. To be the light that banished the shadows. To be the mirror that trapped the demon. To be the sacrifice that saved her life.

The air thickened, Mal'akh's presence growing stronger by the second. Rowan's skin crawled, a miasma of evil seeping into every pore. She could feel the demon's malevolent gaze upon them, could sense its black-hearted malice.

"It's here," she hissed, her light green eyes darting wildly. "We're out of time."

With a last, lingering look at Rowan, Cole turned to the tower and the spiral steps that would lead him high up to its peak. "Come and get me, you motherfucker," he growled, his voice a low, menacing rumble. "I'm ready for you."

Chapter 19

A gust of wind tore through the hilltop, whipping Rowan's hair across her face. She squinted against the stinging sensation, her heart drumming a frantic rhythm as she and Cole waited by the parapet high atop the Stone Tower. Neither spoke as they stood together, perched like two ravens overlooking the moonlit woods below. There was no need for more words. They both knew what had to be done.

Rowan's gaze swept over the gloomy landscape, her sharp eyes searching the swaying branches below. And then, all at once, an ominous feeling descended on them, a miasma of dread and doom that seeped into their very marrow. It was as if the air itself had turned rancid, heavy with an unearthly taint that sought to crush their spirits. The sensation slithered through Rowan's bones like a whispering wind, every nerve alight with the certainty that they were no longer alone. Mal'akh's insidious presence permeated the air, an unseen but undeniable force stalking them with sadistic glee. She could feel its hunger, its ravenous anticipation of the bloodshed to come.

"You feel it too, don't you?" she whispered, her voice low and taut.

Cole's gaze tightened. "It's here. In the tower."

In that moment, the full weight of the danger they faced crashed over Rowan, threatening to buckle her knees. She nodded, unable to speak past the lump of fear in her throat. Only one would survive this night, and she knew the survivor would carry this moment like a scar for the rest of their days.

A bone-chilling shriek pierced the silence, reverberating through the tower's ancient stones and freezing Rowan's blood in her veins. The rotting wooden door burst inward, splinters flying like shrapnel as Mal'akh tore through, its form a grotesque fusion of Lily's once-beautiful features and demonic flesh. The eye Rowan had impaled was a bloody ruin, but the other glittered with malice, set in a face that was at once achingly familiar and utterly alien. A forked tongue flicked out to taste the air as its gaze locked onto them. Its mouth stretched into a rictus grin, revealing rows of needle-sharp teeth.

Rowan felt the pull of the demon's power, a seductive whisper in her mind urging her to surrender, to embrace the darkness that had consumed her for so long. It would be so easy to give in, to let the rage and despair take hold and drown in the hell of her own grief.

Cole stepped forward, putting himself between Rowan and the abomination that looked like her daughter. His voice shook as he began the binding incantation, the ancient words spilling from his lips like blood.

"Mal'akh, hear my call. I summon you from the depths of darkness…"

The air crackled with otherworldly energy. Each syllable seemed to ignite the very air, leaving trails of shimmering heat that danced and coiled around them. Rowan saw the determined set of Cole's jaw, the way his knuckles whitened as he gripped Lily's necklace.

"By blood and grief, I bind you. By innocence lost, I command you..."

The demon recoiled, its shriek rising in pitch. Cole's eyes squeezed shut in concentration, sweat beading on his forehead. His voice rose, the incantation growing louder, more insistent. The air shimmered around him, a tangible force building with each word. Mal'akh faltered, a flicker of uncertainty crossing its ghastly features. But Rowan could also see the strain etched on Cole's face, the way his body shook with the effort of projecting such power. Would he have the strength to finish the incantation?

Cole pressed on, the words flowing faster now, blurring together into a continuous stream of power. Mal'akh howled, its form beginning to waver and distort.

But even as the incantation built in power, Mal'akh closed the distance between them with terrifying speed. The demon's claws extended, eager to rend and tear. Cole stood his ground, the last words of the binding hanging in the air between them like a fragile shield.

And then Mal'akh was upon him.

Those razor-tipped claws sank into Cole's flesh just as the demon's essence poured into him like a torrent of liquid darkness. Cole's body contorted, his spine arching at an impossible angle as he fought for control over the invading presence. His eyes rolled back, the steel blue of his irises consumed by an oily black that seemed to churn with ravenous hunger. A scream tore itself from his throat, equal parts agony and defiance.

Rowan watched, transfixed, as the binding took hold. Cole's body jerked violently, his muscles constricted beneath his tattooed skin, veins bulging as if they might burst.

"Cole!" Rowan cried out, her voice raw with fear.

Cole's features flickered, morphing between his own and the demon's grotesque visage. One moment, she saw the man she'd come to trust—his blue eyes wide and sightless. The next, a hellish creature snarled back at her, all razor teeth and burning eyes.

Rowan clenched her fists so tight her nails dug into her palms. She clung to the hope that somewhere, beneath the demon's vile presence, Cole's spirit still fought on, that there was enough of him left to see this through to the end. But doubt gnawed at her. She'd seen what Mal'akh could do, the devastation it had wrought. How could any man, even one as hardened as Cole, hope to contain such evil?

For a moment, just a heartbeat, something shifted in those obsidian eyes—a glimmer of recognition, a fleeting glimpse of the man trapped within. Cole's body jerked, his face contorting in a rictus of agony as he struggled against Mal'akh's control.

Hope, fragile and desperate, bloomed in Rowan's chest. She took a step forward, hand outstretched, willing Cole to keep fighting. "That's it, Cole!"

Summoning all of his remaining will, he lurched toward the tower's edge, his movements jerky and uncoordinated as he charged headlong for the precipice.

All he had to do was jump and this would all be over.

Just a few more feet and Rowan would be safe.

But then the demon surged forward. Its presence engulfed Cole completely, and he halted dead in his tracks, just inches away from the parapet.

Rowan's heart shattered, and with it, any hope of survival.

The demon had won.

She stumbled back as Cole's body contorted, his features twisting into a nightmarish mask. The air around him shimmered with an infernal heat, the stench of brimstone and decay filling the air.

"Cole, fight it!" she cried, reaching out instinctively.

But her words died in her throat as a triumphant roar shook the very stones beneath her feet. Cole's body went rigid. And then, with a final, shuddering gasp, he was gone, consumed by the demon. An inhuman growl rumbled up from his chest, and when he turned to face her, Rowan's heart became a stone in a frozen river.

The thing before her was no longer the man she knew. In his place stood a creature of pure evil, a vessel for Mal'akh's unholy power.

"Cole?" she whispered, her voice fragile and trembling as she backed away, her hand raised in a futile gesture of defense.

The thing wearing Cole's face grinned, a rictus of cruelty stretching from ear to ear. Its eyes blazed with a hellish light, its claws flexing with deadly intent.

"Cole, if you're in there, fight it," Rowan pleaded. "We can still—"

"He can't hear you," the demon-Cole hissed. "Cole is

gone. Just like your daughter. Just like your husband. Everyone leaves you in the end, don't they, Rowan?"

Rowan flinched as if struck, the demon's words ripping open the barely healed wounds of her grief.

The demon lunged with unearthly speed, its claws slashing through the air in a blur. Rowan dodged to the side, feeling the rush of air as the razor-sharp talons narrowly missed her face.

"Always the fighter, aren't you, Rowan?" it taunted. "Just like your precious Lily. She fought too, right until the end."

White-hot rage surged through Rowan, eclipsing her fear. "Don't you dare speak her name," she snarled.

The demon's laughter echoed off the ancient stones, a guttural sound that made Rowan's bones go numb. It reveled in its victory, savoring the despair that emanated from her in palpable waves. "Oh, but I know her so well now. I tasted her fear, her pain… her disappointment at the bitch of a mother who failed to save her."

Rowan's breath slammed to a halt, the old guilt threatening to paralyze her. But she forced it down. She may have failed Lily, but she wouldn't fail again. Not here. Not now.

"I'm going to send you back to Hell," she growled, her voice low and dangerous.

The demon's grin widened. "My dear," it said, flexing Cole's muscles in anticipation, "I'm not leaving here without you."

Rowan's heart pounded as she circled warily, each step bringing her closer to the tower's precipitous edge. The wind howled, carrying the metallic scent of blood—her blood, she realized, feeling the sting of the cuts across her body and face.

"Come now," the demon-Cole purred, "don't make this difficult. Lily's waiting for you on the other side."

The words cut deeper than any claw. Rowan stumbled, the backs of her thighs pressed against the cold stone of the parapet. The tower's edge loomed behind her, a yawning void that promised a swift and merciless end. The demon lunged again, its claws raking across her shoulder. She cried out in pain, her vision blurring.

That one moment of vulnerability was all it took. In a blur of motion, demon-Cole's fist connected with Rowan's jaw. A sickening crack echoed through the night. The world spun as she staggered sideways, her feet catching on the edge of the spiral staircase. Then, with a sickening lurch, the ground vanished beneath her feet.

Time slowed. Rowan felt herself falling, tumbling down the stone steps. Each impact sent shockwaves of agony through her body. Ribs cracked. Skin tore. Her head smashed against an unforgiving edge, and darkness threatened to swallow her whole. Stars exploded behind her eyes as she struggled to maintain consciousness.

Finally, she came to a merciful stop at the base of the staircase. Rowan lay there in a crumpled heap on the cold stone floor. The metallic taste of blood filled her mouth, and she could feel a warm, sticky sensation trickling down her face. Every breath was torture, each inhalation a battle against the searing pain in her ribs. She became aware of something sharp spearing her side just above her pelvic bone. Her hand shook as she fumbled for whatever was causing the lancing pain.

The iron crucifixion nail. Rowan had jammed it into her pocket in her mad scramble to rescue Cole and flee her house. Now, its sharp tip had pierced her flesh during her tumble down the steps. Blood seeped in a rivulet from the wound.

The searing pain was almost unbearable, yet Rowan couldn't afford to dwell on it. Not now. She grit her teeth, tasting the blood in her mouth as she gripped the spike and wrenched it free. A sickening squelch echoed in the dimly lit space and the metal scraped against her bone, sending waves of fiery agony through her body. Blood welled from the wound like a crimson blossom, dark against the pale moonlight filtering through the arched stone windows. Gasping for breath, she pressed her filthy sweater against the gash, the blood staining it a deeper shade of black.

Get up, she commanded herself, her mind still swimming.

Rowan's fingers clawed at the ground, seeking purchase. With a shaking hand, she pushed herself up, gritting her teeth against the white-hot agony that shot through her limbs. Her vision swam, the chamber blurring in and out of focus as she struggled to rise. She used the wall for support, leaving bloody handprints as she hauled herself upright. Her legs trembled, threatening to give way at any moment.

From above, she heard the demon's laughter. It was coming for her.

Rowan knew she had to move, had to find a way to survive this nightmare and regroup. She took a shaky step forward, then another.

The demon's laughter echoed down the staircase, its inhuman cackle twisting her guts with icy fingers. She pressed herself against the cold stone wall, her breaths coming in short, ragged gasps.

"Where are you, Rowan?" Cole's voice, distorted and grotesque, reverberated through the tower. "Don't you want to see your precious Lily again?"

Rowan's heart clenched. She could hear the slow, deliberate footsteps descending the stairs, each one bringing the possessed Cole closer. Her body was a constellation of pain, every movement threatening to topple her. With a grimace, Rowan forced herself to move. She stumbled towards the tower's exit, her steps unsteady but driven by sheer will.

The dark woods loomed before her as she burst through the tower door. The shadows reached out to embrace her, and all she could do was keep moving, keep putting one foot in front of the other until she found a place to rest and heal. But even as she stumbled toward the trees, Rowan knew Mal'akh would never stop hunting her, not until it had claimed her soul as its own. And with Cole lost to the demon's control, she was more alone than ever before.

Chapter 20

Rowan's shoes crunched across the forest floor, her desperate strides sending jolts of pain through her battered body. Blood oozed from her wounds, the coppery scent mingling with the musty odor of decaying leaves. Her ragged breaths came in sharp gasps as she crashed through the shadowy maze of trees.

She could feel it behind her, the crunch of heavy footfalls and the snarling breaths. Cole, or the demonic thing that now possessed him, was relentless in its hunt. Its malevolent energy permeated the forest, turning each shadow into a leering specter, each rustling leaf into a sinister whisper.

Rowan's grip tightened on the ancient nail in her hand, the metal cool against her palm. Fear and adrenaline coursed through her veins. She had to keep moving, even if there was no way of escaping this nightmare.

The trees loomed overhead, their canopy blocking out what little moonlight filtered through the passing clouds. The forest seemed to conspire against her, the gnarled branches clawing at her clothes, the thorny vines lashing at her skin. Roots lifted from the ground, threatening to snare her ankles and send her sprawling. She stumbled more than once as her exhaustion took its toll. Her legs burned, her lungs screaming for air. How long had she been running? Minutes? Hours? Time blurred in this dreadful forest.

A branch whipped across her face, leaving a stinging cut on her cheek. But it was just one more for her collection, and Rowan barely noticed, too focused on the pounding of her heart and the shallow sound of her own breathing. Ducking under a low-hanging bough, she veered to the right. Her foot caught on a tangle of roots, sending her crashing to the ground. Pain exploded through her body and the crucifixion nail flew from her grip as she rolled down a small incline, coming to rest at the base of a massive oak.

For a moment, Rowan lay there, struggling to catch her breath. Every instinct screamed at her to keep moving, but her limbs felt too heavy, her strength ebbing away with each beat of her thundering heart. How easy it would be to just stay there. To just close her eyes and wait…

Move, she commanded herself. *You can't die here. Not like this.*

With a groan of effort, Rowan pushed herself to her feet, leaning heavily against the oak's rough bark. The forest seemed to pulse around her, alive with malicious intent. Branches creaked and swayed in the wind, roots curled beneath her heels like serpents poised to strike.

She spun, searching for any sign of the demon-Cole. The shadows seemed to conceal threats from every angle. Her blood thundered in her ear as she pushed away from the tree and dashed deeper into the woods. Shadows danced at the edge of her vision, taunting her with glimpses of her unholy stalker that vanished when she tried to focus on them. For an instant, she wondered if she was losing her mind.

Oh, Rowan, a taunting voice purred in her head. *You lost your mind long ago. The moment you let your daughter die.*

Rowan stumbled again, this time falling to her knees. Tears stung her eyes as she struggled to rise, her body trembling with exhaustion and fear.

"That's not true," she whispered, more to herself than to the demon. "It wasn't my fault."

But even as she said the words, remorse gnawed at her. The guilt she'd carried for seven long years threatened to crush her, right here in this godforsaken forest.

Get up. You have to get up.

With a groan of pain, Rowan forced herself back to her feet. She could hear the demon-Cole crashing through the underbrush behind her, no longer bothering with stealth. It was toying with her now, enjoying her fear.

The sound of pursuit grew closer, branches snapping and leaves rustling as Mal'akh closed in. Rowan's world narrowed to the drumbeat of her heart and the burning in her lungs. She knew she couldn't outrun him forever, but she'd be damned if she'd make it easy for that monster wearing Cole's face.

The trees suddenly parted, revealing the jagged silhouette of a massive outcrop of rock looming before her. Rowan's breath crashed to a stop in her throat, the air punched from her lungs. She stumbled to a halt, her heart constricting like a clenched fist.

Dungeon Rock.

"No," Rowan whispered, her voice cracking. "Not here.

Anywhere but here." Her knees buckled beneath her, the sight dredging up images she'd spent seven years trying to bury.

This is where her daughter took her last breath, a frightened girl crying out for her mother before those two boys brutally ended her life.

Agony lanced through Rowan, body and soul. The very air seemed to vibrate with the echoes of her daughter's screams, forever etched into the fabric of this cursed place. The images in her mind were too much to bear, and her carefully constructed walls crumbled under their weight. She unleashed tears she had held back for far too long.

The massive rock loomed over her like a monument to her darkest nightmares. Dungeon Rock was the mouth of a cave carved deep into the stone ledge by a man named Hiram Marble in the mid-1800s. Marble was a spiritualist who believed the cave contained pirate treasure, left behind by a buccaneer named Thomas Veale. According to legend, Veale hid treasure there in the 1600s, and during an earthquake, the cave collapsed, entombing him and his loot.

Hiram Marble, along with his son, spent years tunneling into the rock using pickaxes, chisels, and dynamite, guided by spiritualist visions of Veale's ghost. Despite their tireless efforts, they found no treasure. An iron door had been installed to keep intruders out of the subterranean labyrinth, but the lock was constantly being cut, the door pried open by curious visitors. Visitors like Daley Banks and Troy Chapman, who were drawn to the dark energy of this place where ghosts were said to wander. That's why they chose this place for their bloody sacrifice.

And Lily chose to come here with them, Rowan thought. *Those boys didn't force her to come. She came here because she wanted to—because she needed to get away from you and your misery.*

Now, Rowan's gaze darted to the dark maw of the underground tunnels that snaked beneath the rock. She could hide in there, couldn't she? Maybe even take Mal'akh by surprise in that labyrinth of darkness? For a moment, she wavered, her instincts screaming at her to flee and hide while there was still time.

But even as the thought crossed her mind, Rowan knew she couldn't hide forever.

"No," she muttered, her voice hoarse. "No more running. Not anymore."

The time had come to face her demons. To confront the guilt that had haunted her for so long, the nagging voice that whispered she could have done more, should have been there to save her precious child.

She turned to face the forest, her back pressed against the cold stone. Years of guilt and fear crystallized into a sharp, painful resolve. As she scanned the tree-line, she glimpsed something from the corner of her eye—a dull glint of metal protruding from the rock face. She looked closer and found an ancient spike leftover from the treasure hunters' excavation efforts, its surface pitted and worn by time. Rowan's heart leaped. Was it iron? Could she use it against Mal'akh?

She grasped the big nail, tugging with all her might. It refused to budge, stubbornly embedded in the unyielding stone.

"Damn it!" she hissed, frustration mounting as she heard

the demon's approach growing ever closer. She pulled again, harder this time, feeling the skin of her palms tear against the rough metal. Tears of rage and helplessness stung her eyes, blurring her vision as she redoubled her efforts.

I can't do this, she thought, panic rising. *I'm not strong enough.*

A guttural growl echoed through the clearing, freezing Rowan's blood. She whirled, her fingers still wrapped around the stubborn spike.

There, in the shadows between the trees, she glimpsed Cole's imposing figure.

Except it wasn't Cole anymore. Not really.

A chill slithered down Rowan's spine as he emerged into the moonlight and she got a good look at him. Malevolence twisted Cole's features into a grotesque mask. Mal'akh's influence oozed from every pore, distorting the man she'd come to know into something monstrous. His muscular frame was distorted, limbs elongated unnaturally. His tattooed skin seemed to ripple and writhe, the ink-etched knives at his throat pulsing with a sickening rhythm. The thing wearing Cole's face grinned at her, revealing rows of needle-sharp teeth. Its eyes gleamed with an unearthly hunger that sent ice through her veins.

Rowan's mind raced, her grip tightening on the spike. "Cole," she said, her voice steady despite the fear coursing through her. "I know you're still in there."

The creature threw back its head and laughed, a sound like breaking glass. "Cole is mine now. There's no saving him."

No time for hesitation, Rowan thought.

With a desperate cry, she launched herself at the demon-

Cole. Her fist connected with its jaw, the satisfying crunch doing little to slow the monster down. She barely managed to duck, feeling the air whistle past her ear as it lunged at her, claws extended. She rolled, coming up in a crouch, her back to the rock face.

"I don't believe that," Rowan spat, her eyes darting around for any advantage. "I've lived through too much to believe anyone's beyond saving."

The demon-Cole cocked its head, a mockery of curiosity on its ghastly face. "Even the monsters who took your precious Lily?"

White-hot fury flooded Rowan's system. With a cry of rage, she charged, catching the creature off-guard. Her shoulder connected with its midsection, driving it back a few steps.

The demon-Cole's claws wrapped around Rowan's throat, slamming her against the cold, unforgiving rock face. Her lungs burned, desperate for air as she struggled to draw a breath. Darkness crept at the edges of her vision as she stared into those hellish eyes.

Cole's once-handsome features twisted into a monstrous mask of malice. "Time to join your daughter," the creature snarled.

No! Rowan thought desperately. *This can't be the end!*

As Mal'akh's grip on her throat tightened, a shimmering form materialized between them, its ethereal glow casting an eerie light across the rock face. The figure, translucent and delicate, slowly took shape, and Rowan's heart seized as she recognized the achingly familiar features. She gasped, gulping in precious air.

"Lily?" she croaked.

Mom…

Lily's voice echoed, a whisper that struggled to be heard through the very fabric of reality.

The demon-Cole recoiled, its grip on Rowan loosening.

The ghost smiled, a bittersweet expression that spoke of love and sorrow. With a delicate motion, Lily's spirit reached for the iron nail embedded in the rock, her ghostly fingers passing through the stone as if it were water. The nail shuddered and then slid free, hovering in the air between them.

Rowan's eyes widened as she realized what her daughter's spirit was offering her. A chance to strike, to banish the demon once and for all. She reached for the nail, stretching her fingers, brushing the cold metal until she was able to grasp it.

But as she whirled to face her attacker, she froze.

The demon's hideous face was gone. There was only Cole —vulnerable, confused, and terrified.

"Rowan?" Cole's voice broke through, thick with pain. "What's happening to me?"

Rowan's hand trembled, the spike suddenly feeling impossibly heavy in her palm. "Cole?" she whispered, torn between hope and suspicion. She faltered, the spike poised to plunge into his heart. She couldn't do it. Not if he was still fighting in there, trapped beneath the demon's control.

You have to do it, Lily's voice urged. *It's the only way to set him free.*

Mal'akh seized upon Rowan's hesitation with savage glee. Cole's face twisted back into a grotesque mockery of itself, a snarling grin splitting its cheeks. The demon inside him lashed out with blinding speed and raked its claws across Rowan's abdomen.

White-hot pain exploded through her body as she staggered back, her hand instinctively pressing against the warm, sticky wetness that seeped through her shredded clothing. A scream of agony tore from her throat as she crumpled against the rock face. Warm blood seeped between her fingers as she clutched at the gaping wounds. God, how deep had she been slashed? Deep enough to spill her insides?

The iron spike slipped from Rowan's grasp, clattering at her feet as she sank to the ground, her blood painting the stone a glistening crimson as she slid down it. Her vision swam, darkness creeping at the edges. Through the haze of agony, she stared up at the creature wearing Cole's face, its steel-blue eyes now pools of inky malevolence.

So this is how it ends, she thought bitterly. *Bleeding out in these godforsaken woods, just like Lily.*

"Your daughter begged for her life here, too," Mal'akh taunted, its voice a grotesque parody of Cole's gravelly baritone. It raised its claws, poised to deliver the final, fatal strike, and Rowan knew that this was the end. She had failed, and now she would pay the ultimate price.

But as the darkness closed in, threatening to engulf her, Rowan felt a sudden warmth enveloping her, a gentle light pushing back against the encroaching shadows. A shimmering figure materialized beside her, bathing the hollow in an ethereal, silver glow. Lily's gossamer spirit knelt at her mother's side, her translucent hand reaching out to touch Rowan's tear-stained cheek.

You're not alone, Mom... Lily murmured, her voice soothing Rowan's battered soul. *And neither was I. You were with me.*

As their spirits merged, the union hit Rowan like a thunderbolt. A torrent of emotions flooded through her—grief, love, rage, hope—all magnified a thousandfold. She gasped, feeling as if her heart might burst from the intensity. Tears streamed down her face as she felt her daughter's presence, so heart-breakingly familiar.

Mom... Lily's voice echoed in her mind. *We can end this. Together.*

A surge of power coursed through Rowan's veins. The pain of her wounds faded, replaced by a newfound strength that filled every fiber of her being. She reached for the iron nail, the metal thrumming with an ancient, holy power. As her fingers closed around it, Rowan felt Lily's presence guiding her, their shared purpose driving her forward.

She rose to her feet and met Mal'akh's gaze, her eyes blazing with an inner fire as she faced the demon once more. This time, she was not alone. She carried the love of her daughter, the weight of their shared grief and the unbreakable power of their connection, and with that, she knew she could face anything, even the darkest depths of Hell itself.

"You're right," Rowan said, her voice a blend of her own and Lily's. "All I need is you."

With a fearsome cry that echoed through the dense woods, Rowan lunged forward. In one fluid motion, she drove the spike deep into Cole's chest, right where the demon's blackened heart should have been. The impact sent shockwaves through her arms, but she held firm, twisting the makeshift weapon.

A deafening shriek split the night, a sound that was both Cole's agonized scream and the unearthly wail of the demon within. Cole's body convulsed violently, his back arching at an impossible angle as the demon fought to maintain its hold. Rowan stood firm, her hand still wrapped around the nail embedded in his chest.

"Leave him," she commanded, her voice ringing with a power she had never known she possessed. Dark energy erupted from the wound, tendrils of inky blackness writhing in the air.

The rest was lost in an explosion of darkness as Mal'akh was forcibly expelled from Cole's body. The blast knocked Rowan back, sending her tumbling across the forest floor.

As she struggled to her feet, she saw it—a writhing mass of darkness and malice that coalesced into a formless shape above her. It surged toward her, desperate to possess her, to drag her down into the abyss with it.

Mom, the words! Lily's voice rang in her mind.

Rowan's lips moved of their own accord, her voice harmonizing with Lily's in a haunting duet. The ancient words screamed from her mouth with a throat-scorching intensity that rivaled any song Cole had ever written.

"By iron and blood, by wrath and storm, Thy name is revealed, and thy power is torn. Depart, Mal'akh, and rest once more. Thy vengeance is served; thy torment is no more!"

The demon recoiled, shrieking in fury and pain as each word struck it like the blow of an ax. Its howl of rage turned to one of distress as its form began to dissolve, unraveling like smoke in the wind. And then, with a final, unholy shriek,

Mal'akh was ripped from the mortal plane, leaving behind only the echo of its screams and the acrid stench of brimstone.

The sudden silence was deafening. Rowan sagged and her legs buckled, her body finally giving in to the exhaustion and pain. She collapsed beside Cole's still and silent form, her breath coming in ragged gasps.

"Cole?" she whispered, reaching out with trembling fingers to touch his pale face. His skin was cold, his chest breathless. For a moment, the woods were silent, as if the land itself was holding its breath, waiting to see what would happen next.

But Cole remained unresponsive, his eyes closed, his body limp. Rowan's vision blurred, tears of exhaustion and fear welling up in her eyes. She blinked rapidly, trying to clear her sight, but the world seemed to be fading around her.

A soft metallic tinkle drew Rowan's attention. The iron nail, still protruding from Cole's chest, began to crumble. Rowan watched, mesmerized, as it disintegrated into rust—colored dust, carried away by an unfelt breeze.

"Lily?" Rowan's voice was barely audible, even to herself. "Are you still…?"

But the connection had faded. The comforting presence of her daughter's spirit had vanished, leaving her feeling hollow and alone once more.

Rowan's gaze drifted to Cole's face, peaceful now in the moonlight, the lines of pain and anger smoothed away for the first time she had ever seen. "I'm sorry," she murmured, as a heavy darkness pressed in on her. Part of her was unsure if she was apologizing to him or to the memory of her daughter. "I tried… I tried to save you."

As her fingers brushed Cole's cold skin, the strangest thing happened. She felt his flesh soften and dissolve beneath her touch, disintegrating into nothingness like the ashes of a dying fire. A shudder ran through her.

"It's over," she whispered, her voice sounding hollow in the vast expanse of the forest. The trees seemed to close in around them, shadows deepening despite the approaching dawn. Rowan's hand fell away from Cole's face and she slumped to the ground beside him, her breath shallow and uneven.

In the depths of her mind, Rowan saw Lily's face, a bittersweet memory that brought both joy and pain. "I miss you," she murmured, her words slurring as unconsciousness beckoned. "Every day, every moment. I'm so tired, Lily. So tired of fighting."

As her eyes fluttered closed, a faint whisper of wind stirred Cole's remains and scattered them away like black snowflakes, carrying with them the ghost of a familiar melody. But before Rowan could grasp it, her consciousness slipped away.

This is a good place to die, she thought, her mind drifting. *Here, where my daughter's blood soaked the earth...*

From the Boston Herald - Nov. 17, 1997

Jogger Discovers Critically Injured Woman at Dungeon Rock

By Staff Writer, Lynn Daily Item

LYNN — An early morning jog at the Lynn Woods Reservation took a harrowing turn Thursday when a local woman discovered a gravely injured victim near the historic Dungeon Rock site. The victim, identified as 45-year-old Rowan Pierce of Lynn, is in critical condition at BayRidge Hospital after suffering multiple life-threatening lacerations.

The jogger, Karen Delaney, 34, of Lynn, said she was running her usual route through the wooded trails just before dawn when she spotted what she thought was a bundle of clothing near the entrance to Dungeon Rock. Upon closer inspection, Delaney realized it was a woman, barely conscious and covered in blood.

"At first, I thought it was someone camping or maybe hurt from a fall," Delaney recounted. "When I got closer, I saw the blood and realized how bad it was. She was trying to say something, but I couldn't make it out. It was terrifying."

Delaney immediately ran to the nearest house and called 911, before returning to stay with Pierce until emergency responders arrived.

"I just kept talking to her, telling her to hold on," Delaney said. "It felt like forever before help came, but I'm praying she makes it."

Lynn Police have launched an investigation into the

attack, describing the scene as "suspicious" but declining to provide further details pending the ongoing investigation. Pierce's injuries include deep lacerations that authorities believe were inflicted by a sharp object.

Detectives are also examining potential connections between this incident and the mysterious deaths of Daly Banks and Troy Chapman, the two men convicted of murdering Rowan Pierce's teenage daughter, Lily Pierce, at Dungeon Rock seven years ago. According to police, Chapman was found dead in his cell at Bridgewater State Hospital late Saturday night, while Banks' body was discovered in a Dorchester apartment early Sunday morning. Their deaths are being treated as suspicious.

"At this time, we are exploring all angles, including any links between the recent deaths and the assault on Ms. Pierce," said Lynn Police Detective Michael Yates in a statement. "We urge anyone with information to come forward."

Lily Pierce's murder in 1989 shocked the nation. The 14-year-old was lured to Dungeon Rock by her classmates, Banks and Chapman, where she was brutally beaten and left to die in a ritual sacrifice inspired by heavy metal music group Haruspex. Chapman was convicted of first-degree intentional homicide in 1990 and sentenced to life in prison without parole, but was transferred to the psychiatric institute at Bridgewater due to mental illness in 1992. Banks was given a reduced sentence in exchange for his testimony against Chapman and served three years of his sentence at the Plymouth Juvenile Secure Unit before being transferred as an adult. He was recently granted parole and released from the

Massachusetts Correctional Institution in Shirley.

The deaths of Banks and Chapman have only deepened the mystery surrounding the presumed attack on Rowan Pierce. Corrections officials have not released details about the circumstances of Chapman's death but confirmed that both men died within hours of each other. Autopsies are pending.

"This is an incredibly complex case with many moving parts," Detective Yates added. "We are working diligently to piece together what happened and ensure the safety of the community."

In the meantime, Rowan Pierce remains in the intensive care unit, fighting for her life. Doctors have not yet issued a public statement, but community members have expressed their support and concern.

"This is just unimaginable," said Lynn resident Patricia Greene. "First losing her daughter in such a horrific way, and now this. We're all praying for Rowan to pull through."

Anyone with information about the incident is urged to contact the Lynn Police Department's tip line.

Epilogue

Rowan stood at the precipice, the cliffs dropping away to the roiling sea far below. The wind whipped her ginger hair, pulling strands loose from her ponytail. Her silhouette cut a lonely figure against the bruised sky. Beneath her boots, the chalky cliff crumbled, sending pebbles tumbling into the churning gray water. Waves crashed against the jagged rocks as she inhaled deeply, tasting salt on her tongue. Seven months since that hellish night, and still the memories roiled inside her like the tempest-tossed waves. Her mind drifted back, as it so often did, to the aftermath at Dungeon Rock.

She remembered the pain, the searing agony that had ripped through her body as Mal'akh's claws shredded her flesh. She remembered the cold stone beneath her cheek, slick with her own blood, as consciousness slipped away like water through desperately grasping fingers. And she remembered waking, the world a blur of muted colors and muffled sounds, to see a stranger's face hovering over her, haloed by sunlight.

"Can you hear me? Oh God, just hold on, I'm calling for help." The woman's voice had seemed to come from a great distance, echoing strangely in Rowan's ringing ears.

She had tried to speak, but her tongue was thick and heavy, the words sticking in her throat. Darkness beckoned, an alluring void promising respite from the pain. It would be so easy to let go, to sink into that welcoming oblivion and leave the agony behind…

But Lily's face swam before her, urging her to keep breathing.

"Don't move," the woman's voice said. She sounded distant and distorted, as if she were underwater. "Help is on the way."

Rowan parted cracked lips, tasting blood. The words scraped her throat. "Lily… Lily. Where…?"

But darkness claimed her once more, dragging her down into oblivion.

A week later, the media descended upon Rowan like a murder of crows as she emerged from the hospital, their cawing questions pecking at the raw wounds of her soul. Cameras flashed, disorienting in their intensity. Microphones thrust into her battered face, demanding answers she didn't have.

"Ms. Pierce! Can you tell us what happened at Dungeon Rock?"

"How did you survive the attack?"

"Are the murders of Daley Banks and Troy Chapman connected to your case?"

Rowan flinched, her green eyes wide and haunted. The world swayed around her, the cacophony of voices blurring into a dull roar. She lurched forward, desperate to escape the suffocating press of bodies, her jaw clenched so tight it ached.

She longed to scream her grief, to make them understand the unrelenting hell she'd endured. But she knew better. The vultures would only pick her bones clean, leaving nothing but a hollowed-out husk.

A vulture-eyed reporter blocked her path and thrust a microphone at her face. "The public has a right to know, Ms. Pierce. Your daughter's killers, the attack on your life—it's all connected, isn't it?"

Something snapped inside Rowan. She whirled on the reporter. "My daughter," she hissed, "is not your fucking story."

The crowd fell silent, shocked by the raw pain in her words. Rowan seized the moment, shoving past them toward her waiting taxi. As she slammed the door shut, she caught a glimpse of her reflection—a haunted woman, trapped in a nightmare she couldn't escape.

The police proved just as merciless in their questioning. Detective Hanson had loomed over her hospital bed, his gaze sharp and probing. "Walk me through it again, Ms. Pierce. Every detail, no matter how small."

Rowan's throat constricted. How could she explain the inexplicable? The demonic force that had invaded her mind, the ghostly visage of her daughter? They'd lock her in a padded room, another raving lunatic spewing nonsense.

"I don't remember," she whispered, the lie bitter on her tongue. "It's all a blur."

Hanson's frown deepened. "And you have no idea how Banks and Chapman ended up dead? No clue who or what attacked you?"

Rowan shook her head, wincing as pain lanced through her

skull. The detective sighed, frustration clear in the tense set of his shoulders.

"If you're hiding something..."

"I'm not." Rowan met his gaze. "I want answers just as much as you do."

But of course, the answers never came. Weeks turned to months, and the investigation stalled, mired in dead ends and unanswerable questions. The media frenzy died down, the vultures seeking fresher carrion.

And Rowan? She was left adrift, haunted by visions of that terrible night, of the man who sacrificed himself for her. In her sleepless hours in the house on Pennybrook, she could still feel the demon's insidious presence. It felt like a shadow poised to strike, until one morning, a sharp rap at the door jolted her from her brooding thoughts. She tensed, her hand instinctively reaching for a weapon that wasn't there—old habits dying hard.

Cautiously, she approached the door, peering through the peephole. A man in a crisp suit stood outside, briefcase in hand. Not a reporter, then. Curiosity piqued, Rowan opened the door a crack.

"Ms. Pierce?" The man's smile was polite, professional. "I'm Jonathan Blackwood, Cole Abel's attorney."

Rowan's heart stuttered. Cole. The name hung heavy in the air, a phantom of the past. She'd tried to bury the memories, but they refused to stay dead.

"What do you want?" Rowan's voice was rough, guarded, a flicker of dread coiling in her gut. No one had seen or heard from Cole Abel in months. As far as the world was concerned, he had simply vanished. But had someone finally connected the dots? Traced his disappearance back to her?

"May I come in?" Blackwood asked. "There's something we need to discuss."

Rowan gave him another wary look before stepping aside, allowing him entry. He settled himself on the couch, all business, as he opened his briefcase. As he explained the purpose of his visit, Rowan's world tilted on its axis once more.

"He left… everything to me?" she asked, disbelief coloring her words.

Blackwood nodded. "You are now the owner of his considerable assets, including his mansion, his music rights, and his rather… extensive collection of occult artifacts."

The revelation hit Rowan like a physical blow. She stared at Crane, uncomprehending. "I don't… why would he…?"

"Mr. Abel was very specific in his wishes," Blackwood replied, his words measured and precise as he handed her a thick manilla envelope. "If he did not contact me by a certain date, legal ownership of his entire estate and assets were to be assigned to you. That date has now come and gone and, well… here I am."

Rowan sank into a chair, mind reeling. Had Cole known this might happen? Had this been his plan all along?

"Why?" she whispered, more to herself than to Blackwood. "Cole and I barely knew each other. Why would he give me anything?"

"Mr. Abel was a complicated man, Ms. Pierce. His reasons were his own. His exact words were, 'She's the only one who understands the weight of it all.'"

Whatever Blackwood said next was swallowed by the

sudden, deafening silence of Rowan's racing thoughts. A hysterical laugh bubbled up in her throat. It was too much, too fast, the implications staggering. Cole's music now belonged to her, to do what she pleased with it. She could erase it if she wanted to; have it pulled from the shelves before it inspired more young minds to commit violence.

But none of that seemed important now, not after everything she had experienced. Evil didn't need music in which to hide. It was ancient and eternal, lurking in the human heart and waiting with undying patience for a moment of weakness—for our angels to look away.

Beneath Rowan's shock and confusion, a tiny spark of something else flickered to life, a glimmer of light in the suffocating darkness. There were some people who needed the aggression of Cole's music—people like Lily, who knew it was better to let the pain out than let it devour her. Rowan thought of the royalties, the wealth that now lay at her fingertips. It was blood money, tainted by the suffering that had inspired Cole, but perhaps she could transform it into something good.

A flicker of purpose kindled in Rowan's heart, a flame to ward off the chill of her losses. With Cole's royalties, she could make a difference. Turn tragedy into something meaningful.

"I want to start a non-profit," she heard herself say. "For troubled teens. Give them a safe haven, a chance at a better life before it's too late."

Blackwood nodded, unperturbed. "A noble endeavor. I can put you in touch with the right people to make it happen."

Now, a bitter gust tore Rowan from the memory and

rocked her on her heels. She stood back from the edge of the cliff, stones skittering beneath her feet. What an irony it would be to have survived so much only to fall to her death on the very day she signed the final papers to fund Forever Fourteen, the organization founded in Lily's memory. Its goal was to ensure no other child suffered as Cole did. To give hope to lost and broken kids like Daley Banks and Troy Chapman before it was too late.

With a last glance at the turbulent sea, Rowan turned from the precipice. Her steps were light as she walked the path back to the mansion—her new home. She had found a flicker of purpose now, a reason to press on, even as the shadows of the past nipped at her heels.

Her footsteps echoed on the marble floor as she crossed the cavernous foyer, alone with the promise of an uncertain future. She wandered through the halls, her fingers trailing over the ornate furnishings, but it was the locked room at the bottom of the stairs that drew her like a moth to a flame.

The occult collection.

With trembling hands, Rowan unlocked the door, the key cold and heavy in her palm. As she stepped inside, the air appeared to thicken, the shadows pressing in around her. Shelves lined the walls, crammed with ancient tomes and artifacts that seemed to pulse with a malevolent energy.

She ran her fingers along the spines of the books, their leather bindings cool to the touch. Her thoughts drifted back to that fateful night at Dungeon Rock once more, the memories jagged shards in her mind. The acrid stench of brimstone, the bone-deep chill of Mal'akh's presence, the searing pain of its claws raking her flesh—it all swirled together in a nightmarish kaleidoscope.

But amidst the chaos, one moment stood out with crystalline clarity: Lily's ghost, luminous and ethereal, standing between Rowan and certain death.

Had it been real? Or just a desperate hallucination, a trick of her fractured psyche?

The rational part of her mind insisted it couldn't have happened, that the ghost of her daughter was nothing more than a pain-induced fantasy, a desperate conjuring of her mind creating what she needed to survive.

And yet…

Rowan couldn't shake the feeling that Lily's presence had been more than a figment of her imagination. The warmth of her touch, the love in her eyes—it had felt so real, so tangible.

You saved me, she thought. I felt you. I swear I did.

In the days that Rowan had spent lying in her hospital bed, drifting in and out of consciousness, she had clung to that memory like a lifeline. The thought that Lily was still with her, watching over her, had given her the strength to keep fighting, to claw her way back from the brink of oblivion.

But in the months that passed, doubt crept in. Had it truly been Lily's spirit that saved her that night? Or was it nothing more than a beautiful lie, a comforting delusion born of desperation and despair?

Rowan's gaze drifted to the occult tomes lining the shelves, their ancient spines whispering secrets of power and forbidden knowledge.

If Lily's ghost was real, if she really had reached out from beyond the veil to save her mother… could Rowan reach back?

The temptation sang to her, a seductive melody that called to the aching void in her heart.

Rowan's breath quickened as she stood in the silent vault, her gaze roaming over the artifacts of untold power, imagining the possibilities. Cole had opened her eyes to a world she had never believed could exist, a world of dark magic and demons from other realms… and maybe even ghosts.

Rowan's fingers trembled as she reached for one of the books, its leather spine cool beneath her touch.

"What if I could see you again?" she whispered, her voice echoing in the silent vault. "What if I could talk to you just one more time?"

The words tasted like ashes on her tongue, bitter and acrid.

She knew the dangers, the risks of delving into such dark magic. She had seen firsthand the destruction it could wreak, the lives it could shatter.

But the allure was too strong, the promise of Lily's presence too sweet to resist.

With a shaking hand, Rowan opened the book, its pages rustling like the wings of a thousand moths.

And as she began to read, the world fell away, the shadows deepening around her until there was nothing left but the drumbeat of her own heart and the whisper of forbidden incantations on her lips.

The ancient words danced before her eyes, their meaning both obscure and tantalizingly clear. Rowan's breath caught in her throat as she traced the intricate diagrams, the symbols seeming to writhe and twist beneath her fingertips.

"I could do it," she murmured, her voice barely audible

over the pounding of her heart. "I could bring you back."

But even as the words left her lips, the memory of Mal'akh's cruel laughter echoed in her mind, a reminder of the darkness that lurked out there in the dark unknown.

In that moment, a flicker of clarity pierced the haze of her grief. The dead were meant to rest, their memories cherished but their spirits unbound by the desires of the living. To disturb their peace would be an act of selfishness. A betrayal.

With a shuddering breath, Rowan closed the book, the sound echoing like a gunshot in the silent room. Lily was gone, but she was at peace. And Rowan knew, with a certainty that settled deep in her bones, that she had to live with that truth.

No matter how much it hurt.

She stepped back from the shelves and turned away. As she locked the door behind her and ascended the steps, a fragile peace settled over her, a whisper of acceptance she hadn't known in a very long time.

Not for the first time since she had moved in, Rowan found herself drawn to Cole's recording studio high in the upper reaches of the mansion. She always hesitated at the threshold, memories rushing over her like a tidal wave, before easing the door open with a creak.

She stepped in, her feet quiet on the carpeted floor. Her eyes swept over the mixing board, the soundproofed walls, and Cole's prized instruments.

How many hours had he spent here, pouring his pain into the music that both defined and consumed him? The studio was his sanctuary, a place where he exorcised the demons of his through the raw power of his lyrics.

Rowan crossed the room to where the guitars lined the walls, their polished surfaces reflecting the dim light. In the center hung Cole's favorite. Rowan had been teaching herself how to play, making her way up here to practice on the long nights when she'd been unable to sleep in the new and unfamiliar environment of the mansion. But not with the guitars they had used to summon Mal'akh—never those. Instead, she had claimed a sleek, jet-black model with pointed ends that resembled a deadly weapon as much as a musical instrument.

Slowly, almost reverently, Rowan settled the guitar in her lap. Her fingers found their place on the strings, the countless night of practice guiding her movements. She drew a shaky breath, clearing her thoughts. And then, with a hesitant strum, she let the music come out.

The chords were clumsy at first, her fingers stiff and uncooperative. The sound reverberated through the studio, raw and imperfect, yet hauntingly beautiful. As she played, the music took shape, a melody that spoke of grief and longing, of hope and redemption. It was a song without words, a primal cry torn from the depths of her sorrow.

Rowan's eyes drifted closed, her body swaying to the rhythm of her own creation. She lost herself in the music, the world falling away until there was nothing but the guitar and the sound it made. She played with a desperate intensity, each note a tiny offering of herself. And in that moment, she felt a flicker of connection, a gossamer strand that linked her to something greater than herself. The music was a bridge, spanning the chasm between the living and the dead, between the woman she had been and the one she could become.

God, she thought. *It's like… It's like they're all here with me.*

Memories flooded her mind as she played—Lily's laughter, her husband's embrace, Cole's fierce determination. The melody shifted, taking on a haunting, ethereal quality. In her mind's eye, Rowan saw Lily's face, not twisted in terror as it had been in her nightmares, but smiling, radiant.

Is this what you felt, Cole? This… connection?

Her fingers moved faster, the melody growing more complex. Rowan leaned into the music, letting it guide her, surrendering to its ebb and flow. For the first time in years, she felt a shift within herself. The weight of her grief, the suffocating burden of her guilt, lifted, carried away on the wings of her song.

And then, with a final, shimmering note, it was over. Rowan's eyes fluttered open, her gaze unfocused as she emerged from the trance-like state. The studio was silent, but the air hummed with the aftershocks of her performance.

Rowan realized she was trembling. The music had scoured her clean, burning away the layers of guilt and despair that had shrouded her for so long. And beneath the intensity of her emotions, she felt something unfamiliar stirring in her chest.

It wasn't happiness—not yet—but perhaps the first fragile seeds of healing.

Author's Note

Thank you, dear reader, for the generous gift of your time and attention. If you enjoyed this book and would like to see more, please consider taking a moment to leave a quick review on Amazon and/or Goodreads. A kind word from a reader like you is one of the best ways you can support independent authors and is very much appreciated.

Until next time, look under the bed, close the closet door, and whatever you do, don't turn around…

BOOKS BY MICHAEL PENNING

Book of Shadows Series

Novels:
All Hallows Eve
The Suicide Lake
The Wolf Society
The Black Testament

Companion Stories:
The Damnation Chronicles

Other Novels
Solitude
Devil Music

Michael Penning is a best-selling author and award-winning screenwriter of horror and dark fiction, crafting stories so chilling they could make a ghost shiver. He has been weaving nightmares since before he could finish his own sack of trick-or-treat candy. When he's not conjuring new ways to make readers sleep with one eye open, he enjoys traveling, photography, and brewing beer. He lives in Montreal with his wife and daughter, who have yet to flee in terror. For updates and free giveaways, visit www.michaelpenning.com and follow Michael on social media @michaelpenningauthor.